TURNING FOR TROUBLE

Familiar Legacy #7

SUSAN Y. TANNER

KaliOka Press

Copyright © 2018 by Susan Y. Tanner

All rights reserved. Published by KaliOka Press.

No part of this book may be reproduced in any form or by any electronic or mechanical means, including information storage and retrieval systems, without written permission from the author, except for the use of brief quotations in a book review.

Cover design by Cissy Hartley

For Brayden, my second-born grandchild. His smile lights up any room and my whole heart. Love him always.

CHAPTER ONE

I will own up - if I must - to being a bit of a romantic at heart. Perhaps more than a bit. Even so, never think that small flaw in any way undermines my inherent ability to solve any mystery placed in my path. I am, after all, my father's son. My sire, the wondrous Familiar, passed on to me his ability to discern between fact and fiction, to detect truths however skillfully buried amongst untruths. These are no small traits and are essential to my stock-in-trade of master detective.

June has long been touted as the premier wedding month but no one could find fault in this flawless October day. And I don't believe I've ever seen a bride more lovely than our Ms. Gorgeous, the intrepid Avery Wilson, momentarily to become Avery Hanna. The name has a nice ring to it and I will accept some accolades as to having ensured the likelihood of a happy outcome for the bride and groom. But that was another day and another story for my memoirs.

It's good to be at Summer Valley Ranch once more and without ominous clouds of danger hanging overhead. Good, too, that the sweltering humidity of summer in Alabama has been swept away on the dry, crisp breezes of earliest autumn. Now, with the afternoon fading to evening, the fairy lights twinkle to life in the soft twilight.

And there! The deed is done. The knot is tied. Let the party commence!

I shall celebrate in my own way. As the humans twirl around a dance floor constructed for that purpose, I will indulge in the fact that Ms. Gorgeous has instructed the waiters at every food station to ensure I'm given a sampling – and more if I desire! – of each of their savory offerings.

Cade Delaney watched the wedding couple as they danced. The bride was radiant, looking half her age and spinning in the arms of her handsome groom as if she were a teenager. The throng around him ebbed and surged trying to get a better glimpse of the two and Cade stepped back. His height gave him an advantage some didn't have.

Smiling at the wedding couple's happiness, he turned just as another guest stepped forward. Instinctively, he caught slender shoulders in a light grip. He registered a swift impression of silken skin and the light scent of fragrance mixed with pure femininity. But when he looked into wide brown eyes flecked with gold, his heart stopped in his chest. He had no doubt he'd remember those eyes until his dying breath and had long ago accepted that fact.

For a brief moment, he saw not the woman she'd become but the girl she had been. He held forever in his mind an image of Malone astride a powerful horse as they arced around then pushed away from a barrel. Of her leaning low, urging the horse for more and more speed, hair and mane tangling against her face.

"Excuse me," she murmured, stepping back and out of his light grasp as if she hadn't recognized him even though he knew she had. And he let her go, once again, because that was what she wanted.

He wished – just for a moment - sincerely wished that he hadn't come to Avery's wedding. Or that Malone had not come. She was a complication he didn't need. Hell, he hadn't even known that Avery and Malone knew each other. His world was peaceful. Orderly. His memories of Malone Summers were anything but that.

Cade stared after her, noting legs that looked damned good in the kind of heels he'd never seen on any rodeo grounds. A slim-fitting dress hugged her slender back and waist then swirled into frothy layers just below her hips. He couldn't have said what the material was called but he sure as hell could've described the way it flirted with the flesh just above the back of her knees. He watched her walk away and she left him smoldering now, just as she'd done countless years ago.

With a physical reaction he wouldn't acknowledge, he turned to search the dance floor for a partner who wouldn't remind him of Malone. Two hours later, he acknowledged failure. Not a single woman reminded him of Malone but every one of them reminded him that she was not Malone. With a sincere word of congratulations to the bride and groom, Cade sought the sanctuary of the bungalow that had been assigned to him.

He'd get up early, he thought as he stretched out in the dark, even earlier than he'd planned, and be out of here and on the road by first light. His Australian Shepherd padded around the room before settling quietly on the rug beside his bed. Within moments, Townsend's breathing evened into sleep. Cade's, unfortunately, did not.

DAY WAS BARELY BREAKING as Malone, already feeling a sense of loss, looked into the trusting eyes of the big silver gelding she was leaving with Avery's resident vet. If anyone could accurately diagnose the reason for Mylo's sudden lameness, it would be Tucker. Mylo had already been seen by some of the nation's best veterinarians with no real diagnosis or prognosis made. But, in Malone's estimation and that of Avery, who was unstinting in the care of her horses, Tucker was 'the best'.

She crossed to the next stall to put a halter on Jaz and led the big sorrel mare out of the barn and into the morning toward the truck and trailer. It was still early, still chilly, that peaceful time of day she enjoyed most when the sun was just peeping over the horizon.

Normally, she would have lingered, at least for a little while. Avery's ranch, filled with talented rescue horses who provided equine therapy for patients in need, was one of her favorite places to visit. Today, however, she wanted to be gone before any of the other wedding guests roused themselves. Not even to herself would she admit there was only one person she hoped to avoid. With any luck at all, Cade Delaney was sleeping off a good time.

Malone smiled at the sight of Avery propped against the hood of her truck, two steaming mugs in her hands and a black cat twining around her dusty boots. Though she didn't see the other woman often enough, they had become good friends through their shared love of horses. At her approach, Avery pushed away from the truck and handed her one of the mugs.

"What in the world is the bride doing up at this hour?" Malone eyed Avery over an appreciative sip of coffee that tasted every bit as heavenly as it smelled.

Avery chuckled. "I couldn't keep my eyes from opening. I'll nap on the plane."

"I can't believe you're taking time for a honeymoon."

"I can't either, to tell you the truth. I've always wanted to see Wales but never dreamed I would. Dirks smooth talked me into it."

"Good for Dirks. And good for you for finding a way to trust again." Malone was more than happy for the bride and groom. Heaven knew Avery deserved this second opportunity at a happy marriage. Malone didn't much believe in second chances where love was concerned but she wished the best for Avery.

Avery nodded. She would know where Malone's thoughts had gone. "It wasn't easy, but if I can, you can."

"I'd have to want to," Malone said lightly, "and I don't." To take any sting out of her response, she added with real honesty, "I'm too happy with my life now – finally – to risk changing anything."

As if on cue, the door to the guest cabin closest to them opened and Malone caught a glimpse of Cade in her peripheral vision as he stepped through with a small tote in hand. Damn. And he naturally turned toward his hostess and Malone. Double damn.

A beautiful dog, Australian Shepherd from the coat and color, walked beside him. She glanced at the black cat but Trouble showed no sign of interest, much less alarm. Of course, the cat was considered to be something of a hero, credited with abilities that wouldn't lend themselves to his cowering in fright at a mere dog.

"Avery. Malone." Cade greeted them both in the same pleasant tone.

Avery's eyes widened. "You two know each other ... but, of course, I forget. You both make your living in rodeo."

Before Malone could speak, before she could casually agree as she intended, Cade said, "We knew each other before that." His gaze caught on Malone's. "Long before."

Mercifully that silver gaze moved on to Jaz standing quietly on her lead line. "Nice mare. Yours?"

Malone let a little of the tension ease from her shoulders. "Yes. I got her here last summer. She's been pulling some nice checks at the pay window since January when I started hauling her in earnest. She's been at the top of my string the last couple of months. I'm grateful to Avery and her team for allowing me to have her."

"We were glad to match her with you." Avery said.

The expression on Avery's face telegraphed her curiosity at the earlier nuances of her exchange with Cade but, to Malone's relief, Avery asked no questions. Instead, she said, "We've watched your success, the videos you've posted, with a lot of pride at her accomplishments. It's clear your first assessment was right. She loves her job."

Feeling antsy under Cade's steady regard, Malone handed Avery the empty mug. "I appreciate the coffee and the wedding was lovely. I'm going to get my girl loaded and head out. I've got a full week ahead of me."

"Both Dirks and I were happy that you could be here. I put a thermos of coffee in the front of your truck when I saw you throw your bag in the truck and head for the barn but we'd love for you to have brunch before you leave. Dirks was already poking around in the kitchen when I stepped out. He's planning to feed anyone who is awake enough to eat."

No way was Malone spending the next couple of hours with Cade watching her. She declined with a smile and a word of thanks and led Jaz around to the side of the trailer. To her consternation, Cade and his dog followed. Without asking, Cade lowered the loading ramp with quiet efficiency.

Not wanting to sound as ungrateful as she felt, she murmured thanks she didn't feel. She'd been taking care of herself for a long time.

"Where are you headed?"

Cade's question surprised her, not the words, but the fact that he'd asked. She didn't want to tell him but he'd find out anyway if he really wanted to know.

"LaGrange."

His brows lifted at that. "Opposite direction of Oklahoma." She knew the comment wasn't as casual as it seemed. LaGrange had once been home to both of them, but he'd most likely know her mother had died and her father had remarried, sold their property there, and moved out of state. She wasn't about to ask how he knew she was entered in a competition in Oklahoma City in little more than a week. Cade might be the new Director of Operations for Twin Circuit Rodeos but exactly what competitor was entered where wasn't something anyone would expect him to be aware of. In the end, she simply answered his question as if there were no unhappy history between them.

"Granddad left me his place. I suspect there are some things of his I'll want to keep so I need a day or two to sort through them before I list it with a realtor."

"I heard you'd lost him, not long after your grandmother." All of the edge had left his expression and his voice. "I know that hurt."

"It did." She didn't need to ask how he'd known. Her granddad's place bordered the Delaney property and Cade and his family had probably remained close, talking often and sharing life's moments big and small. He hadn't disappointed his family, hadn't shamed his parents as she had hers.

For the next few minutes she focused on loading Jaz but she knew Cade was there, watching, and wasn't the least surprised when he helped her raise the ramp and secure the doors.

She turned to face him, feeling unexpectedly awkward. "Thanks for the help. I'll see you down the road, I guess."

"Yes." That was all he said and she couldn't read a thing in his expression. Or maybe she just didn't want to.

He stepped back as she climbed up into the cab of her truck and closed the door.

INTERESTING THING ABOUT HUMANS, they don't always say in words what's communicated in their eyes and their expressions. While these two friends of my Ms. Gorgeous dance around their emotions, I shall stroll about the rather large truck and equally massive trailer to ensure all is in good repair and safe for the long haul. That's western speak for the lengthy trip ahead.

I've learned through my cases that the female of the human species is as capable and competent as any male. There is, however, a point of chivalry in any real male that simply requires this extra vigilance on her behalf. Indeed, I noticed Mr. Silver Eyes surreptitiously eyeing the tires of her rig to ensure they were up to the trip.

All of the various side compartments that, as I learned during my previous sojourn at Summer Valley Ranch, contain various grains and supplements as well as buckets and fans and extension cords and other equipment, seem securely closed.

But wait. What's this? As I turn the corner to peruse the opposite side, an inch or two of faded denim along with worn leather boots disappear beneath a long, narrow access that is slowly lowered. The trailer is about to have a stowaway and I can see little but a pair of eyes staring back at me! Those eyes are dulled by some emotion, at best despair, at worst something more ominous. I can't tell if this is friend or foe and cannot leave Ms. Rodeo to be taken unaware somewhere down the road, perhaps at an isolated rest stop. I'd better warn her.

Oh, my! The truck engine has started with a bit of a roar and there's no time. I leap forward praying that the opening of the compartment is wide enough for me to slip through and that the somber-eyed human does not discern my intent in time to lower the metal hatch even more.

There, I'm in! And just in the nick of time, as the truck and trailer move forward. I hear a gasp as the hatch slams shut and deduce that may present a problem for both of us.

Well, this was certainly not my plan for the day. As soon as possible, I'll need to let my precious Tammy Lynn, the human who claims me as her very own moggy, know my whereabouts.

For now, my excellent night vision shifts into gear and I study the human who stares back at me with no small measure of consternation.

CHAPTER TWO

Malone pulled into the drive, cut the engine, and simply sat at the wheel of her truck, drinking in the remembered beauty of the place with its weathered but stout fencing and sturdy outbuildings. The house itself was by no means grand, but the wrap around porch was homey and welcoming. It invited her in as it always had.

The two-hour drive to the property her grandparents had left her had been uneventful, giving her plenty of time to think, to wonder if she were making the right choice in even considering calling a realtor.

This had once been more home to her than the house and property where her parents had raised her. She knew she'd disappointed her folks, even embarrassed them. She wondered if they ever realized they'd done the same to her. Her father's distant reserve, never speaking or smiling when her friends came around. Her mother's relentless fault-finding, regardless of who was within hearing. The years and miles had taught her that only they were to blame for their discontent, but there'd been a time she'd blamed first herself, then each of them for the other's miserable outlook. She knew better now, but it had been a lesson only time and experience could teach.

As a child, she'd fled their unhappiness every chance she could. She'd been seven the first year she'd been allowed to stay with her grandparents for the three blissful months of school vacation. Twelve-year-old Cade had taught her to ride fearlessly. Summer after summer, her granddad had permitted her to tag along with Cade's family, who were friends as well as neighbors, to local rodeos. Cade had shared his rope horse with her, helped her train him for barrels, paid her entry fee from time to time with cash hard-earned at summer jobs. If she closed her eyes, she could see him now, stepping into the alleyway, catching her rein, his face beaming with pride. And if she looked toward the rolling hills just to the north, she had no doubt she'd see a younger Cade letting his horse pick his way carefully across the uneven ground toward her with the summer sun beating down.

But that had been a lifetime ago and time moved on.

Sighing, she released her seatbelt and stepped down into the sunlit morning. The first order of business was to get Jaz someplace she could move about in safety, someplace she could roll and stretch with a playful buck or two.

Her phone was ringing as she stepped to the ground but stopped before she could fish it from the back pocket of her jeans. Not recognizing the number, she turned toward the rear of the trailer only to have the same number ringing in again. It could be a new client with a horse rodeo-ready but in need of someone to do the hard part of hauling and seasoning until the animal was rock-solid. The fact that she was currently booked never made her ignore courtesy. And she had never become so complacent as to lose sight of the truth that her success was as much on her reputation and interaction with her clients as on her riding skills and tireless work.

She answered as she always did, "This is Malone."

"Put Cowboy on the phone."

The voice was unfamiliar and rude, so rude that she tempered her own tone to cool restraint.

"You have the wrong number."

"No, you have the wrong answer. We know where LaMonte goes to ground."

The use of the word *We* rather than *I* sent a small prickle through her veins. She leaned against the side of the truck wondering what trouble Tyge had gotten himself into this time. "I haven't seen Tyge in over a year. I don't know where you got my number but I'd like for you to lose it."

"You tell Cowboy he can't hide behind a woman's skirts forever. It might take us a while, but we'll catch up with you. And him."

Again, us not me. Without answering, Malone disconnected the call, feeling that old flare of tension. She pushed it aside, gratified to realize that it took far less effort these days. Tyge, the rough stock rider she'd left home with at seventeen, had lived and loved with, but never married, had been in some kind of trouble off and on for years. He always found a way to finagle himself out of the repercussions of his actions.

Resolutely, she turned her mind to making Jaz comfortable before going inside to see what kind of mess might await her. The house had remained vacant since her grandfather's death. Malone paid a local service to walk through it once a week to open windows and air it out for a few hours, to make certain appliances were running, doors remained locked, and windows unbroken. Mostly Malone needed to ensure no vagrants had taken up residence until she felt herself capable of making a decision about the house, the property. She didn't know for sure if she'd reached that point, but it was past time to do something.

For a moment, she leaned against the fence rail, watching as Jaz explored the grassy paddock. She sent a check each month to her grandfather's closest neighbor and best friend. He'd engaged a local handyman to bush hog the fenced areas around the barn and house on a regular basis. Her gaze lifted to the empty slope of the hills. The cows had been sold at her request. Those hills would soon be overtaken by scrub trees. Or housing projects. The thought depressed her and she turned resolutely to get Jaz fresh water.

As she neared the truck and trailer, the sound of a cat yowling startled her. Glancing around, she saw nothing, but the closer she came to the trailer the louder the sound.

Well, this is a bit of a predicament. These side compartments open easily enough from the outside but - not being designed for occupancy, human, or feline! - have no handles on the inside. I feel the sense of desperation growing in the young girl beside me as she runs her hands along the crevices. I better understand the chock of wood she held in her hand when I first saw her. I suppose my precipitous entrance thwarted her plan to use it to prevent the hatch from closing securely.

I've at least had time to ascertain that this young miss, desperate though she may be at the moment, poses no threat. Although strong fright can make the actions of any human unpredictable, I detect no meanness in the girl. I allowed her to pull me onto her lap for the ride. It gave her comfort to hold another living creature I think. It also gave me a warmer, softer ride than the unyielding metal of the compartment floor.

She's not a talkative thing for certain. Other than a whispered, "Oh no!" she hasn't spoken since I leapt into the hatch with her.

I must alert Ms. Rodeo to our presence. I'm not certain she'll discover us soon enough for my comfort. I have no idea how the girl will react for she most clearly didn't want her existence known.

Malone stopped at the trailer and listened, but the cat had stopped yowling. She reached into the trailer compartment for a water bucket and the sound came again, louder and closer, with an echoing quality. She had no idea how a cat came to be trapped in her trailer but it was there somewhere, and close. Malone reached cautiously for the handle on the next compartment and lifted the door, stepping to one side as she did. She didn't want a frightened cat to take a flying leap toward her face.

But, no, a sleek, black cat sat quietly watching as she raised the door. And, there, pressed into the shadows of a corner, a young woman – no, certainly not more than a school girl – stared back at her.

"You'll need to climb out now." She made her voice no nonsense.

"Don't tell them where I am." The voice held both fear and defiance.

"Climb out," Malone repeated, more calmly than she felt, not ready to admit she was alone on the property. She couldn't be certain the girl was unaccompanied. She had a concealed carry in the truck but it wasn't much use to her from here.

The cat leapt out first and Malone gave a groan as she caught full sight of him. "Good grief! You're Tammy Lynn's Trouble. What in the world were you doing in there?"

The girl emerged more slowly and Malone took in the faded jeans and nondescript tee shirt. Green-gold eyes with heavy lashes brushed fair skin as she blinked at the bright sunshine. Her hair was pulled up under a plain red ball cap. The wisps that escaped were dark, almost black, even in the daylight. Any lingering uneasiness at discovering a stowaway yielded to dismay when the morning rays revealed the ugly bruise on one cheek.

Malone caught her breath audibly. She said nothing for a moment, then, softly, "You're hurt."

The girl shrugged without responding. Her gaze was steady and guarded.

Malone's sweeping glance caught a glimpse of another bruise just below the sleeve of her tee shirt. Keeping her tone even, she asked, "Do you need medical attention?"

At the suggestion, something flashed deep within those green eyes. "No." She shifted a tiny step back. "I just needed a ride, just needed to get away."

Realizing the girl was on the point of flight, Malone gestured around her at the empty property with its aura of abandonment. "You're very much *away* here. Who are you running from?"

"It doesn't matter. We've got to be far enough away from Louisiana that surely it doesn't matter. What state is this?"

"Georgia." Then the girl's words caught up with Malone. "What? Wait! Are you saying you got on this trailer in Louisiana? At the rodeo in Lake Charles?" That had been Malone's last stop, her last run, before arriving at the Hanna's.

At the girl's nod, Malone blew out a breath. She had questions. Too many. And most weren't going to be answered any time soon if that closed expression was any indication. "Okay, this can wait. I've got to get my mare some water, then we'll go inside and talk."

"No, ma'am, I'll just be on my way."

Trouble growled low in his throat at the girl's words.

Malone studied her in consternation. The girl was a stranger with a past that could hold anything, any amount of trouble that Malone didn't need. But, to just let her wander away to an uncertain fate was beyond Malone. "Where are you headed?"

"Anywhere." The girl reached back and pulled a duffle bag from the trailer compartment. "Someplace I can find work."

She didn't look old enough, Malone thought and almost asked, then realized the girl would only lie if she were as young as Malone suspected. Clearly, she had no one to help her, at least no one she trusted. Malone had stopped acting on impulse long ago. At least she thought she'd stopped until she opened her mouth and said, "I could use a hand here, at least for a couple of days."

"Here?" The girl looked suspicious. "Doing what?"

Exasperated with herself at making the offer and at the girl's suspicions, Malone asked with a trace of asperity, "Does it really matter? Work is work. Money is money. Food and a roof over your head are just that."

For the first time, a glimmer of a smile touched the girl's face. "No, ma'am, I don't suppose it does matter."

Malone took a deep breath, wondering what the hell she thought she was doing. This girl was more than likely underage – Malone would get around to asking – and she was most likely a runaway. And it was equally likely that she was running away from something very mean and ugly. Malone would get around to asking that as well. For now, she had to keep the girl from running into worse danger than she'd left. The world was full of predators.

"I've got to get water to my mare. You first job is to go in and make sure things are on and working ... lights, water heater, refrigerator, which is probably empty but we'll worry about that later." Malone pulled out the key chain she'd slipped into her pocket earlier and held it out to her stowaway.

With clear reluctance, the girl took it and started toward the house. Halfway there, she stopped to look back at Malone. "How much are you paying?"

Malone matched her look for look. "We'll negotiate later. Get moving."

As she'd expected, the girl responded immediately to that tone of authority. She wasn't a renegade or a rebel, then, just a little girl lost. Malone watched her walk away, Trouble at her heels, and realized she didn't even know her name.

I AM doubtful there's much in the way of true cuisine, but like myself, the young human's first thoughts turn to food. First stop, the kitchen, painfully clean. No one has cooked here in a while. Not even that menu of British sustenance, fish and chips. While she rummages through the cabinets, I shall make a tour of the other rooms. I sense no other human presence, but far better to be safe than be taken by surprise. Besides, there is little that can be found in a cupboard that tempts my gastronomic interest. Boxes and tins of food hold no appeal for me.

Room by empty room. At least empty of recent human inhabitance. Furnishings, to be sure, clean and bare of any clutter. Someone took the time to clear away any mementos. No photographs in frames. No magazines or books lying about. Even with that clearing away, there's a story to be read in the polished wood furnishings and chenille bedspreads with filmy curtains over windows that overlook the hills beyond. Whoever passed their years here did so with more of an eye to need and comfort than any fashion of the moment.

Upon my return to the kitchen, I find the girl leaning against a counter, staring out a window unframed by curtains. She remains a mystery, but one I will solve, given time. I leap lightly to the counter, careful to land some distance away so as not to startle her. I peer through the window as well and together we watch as Ms. Rodeo walks purposefully toward the house.

CHAPTER THREE

Cade accepted Avery's offer of the last cup of coffee in the carafe and she returned to the kitchen for a refill. With Malone on her way to Georgia, he no longer needed a hasty departure and had joined Dirks' impromptu breakfast party with several other lingering wedding guests. He wondered when he'd gotten to be such a coward, that a woman could make him bolt. But she wasn't just any woman. Malone was ... Malone.

He wished again that he hadn't seen her up close and personal, hadn't felt the warmth of her skin beneath his hands when she'd turned and stepped into him. Her shoulders had been silky smooth and it would be a long time before he forgot the fragrance she'd been wearing. Hell, who was he kidding? He wouldn't forget. He would simply store the encounter along with all of his other memories of her.

Avery returned to the dining room with the carafe in one hand, her cell phone in the other, and an odd look on her face. She handed the phone to Tammy Lynn who sat opposite of Cade. "This is for you. It's Malone."

Avery's expression and tone, as well as the mere mention of Malone's name, had Cade on alert as Tammy Lynn put the phone to her ear. To his chagrin, Tammy Lynn spent the next few minutes simply listening to whatever Malone had to say. When she finally spoke, Cade found nothing reassuring in her words. "Trouble doesn't act on whim or chance. If he chose to go with you, there's a reason. I promise you have a problem whether you know it or not. Are you certain everything is alright? You didn't see anything odd around your truck or trailer before you pulled out?"

Cade would have given a small fortune to hear Malone's response. A glance around told him that Avery and Dirks felt the same. The atmosphere in the room had turned from festive to concerned.

Tammy Lynn frowned. "No, he'd best stay right where he is until you figure out why he's there. Keep your guard up. I'm going to have Avery text you my cell number and your number to me. If you need help, you call me. And, Malone, keep in touch. Please?"

She broke the connection and looked at Avery with faint lines of disquiet creasing her forehead. "Trouble hitched a ride in Malone's trailer. She found him when she got to her grandfather's property."

"She didn't see any signs of a problem either with her truck or when she arrived?" Dirks asked.

"Well ..." Tammy Lynn's tone was hesitant. "She said she didn't, but I sensed something in her voice, that perhaps she wasn't telling me everything."

"Do you seriously think the cat ended up in Malone's trailer for some reason other than getting trapped in there?" Cade asked.

Tammy gave a rueful smile. "Well, yes. Maybe. He does seem to place himself in the mix of things when there's trouble brewing."

"I have no doubt that Trouble knew I was in danger," Avery said.

That was all Cade needed. He'd heard the tales of the cat's brilliance and had taken them with a grain of salt. Still, Dirks swore the cat had saved Avery from the young woman determined to kill her. That, coupled with Tammy Lynn's suspicions that Malone was withholding something of concern, was more than he could ignore.

Cade stood decisively and looked at Dirks. "You two have a plane to catch. Make sure you're on it. I'm going to see what's going on with Malone." It was what he wanted to do deep down at his core and the fact made it easier for him to act on the premise that a black cat had somehow deduced Malone was in danger of some kind.

Avery gave an audible sigh of relief. "That would ease my mind, Cade. Thank you so much."

Cade took his leave in short order. He didn't bother admitting to Avery that his purpose in making the trip was far less for Avery's peace of mind than for his own.

It's interesting to watch these two females dance – conversationally speaking – around each other in Ms. Rodeo's quest for the truth. I'm listening hard because I remain convinced there is misfortune following the younger of the two. It's as clear to me as the heartache that follows the older woman. I remain hopeful that I'll be able catch some nuance that will enlighten me as to what hazards are in the offing. The more information I have, the better prepared I can be.

MALONE PLACED a glass of tea in front of her stowaway. So far, the girl had volunteered nothing except the fact that the refrigerator was running but bare of food as were the pantry and cabinets. Malone, who'd expected as much, had retrieved a few items from the tiny kitchen space in the living quarters of her trailer.

"Let's start with you telling me your name."

"Joss."

Malone didn't know whether to believe her or not. "Just Joss?"

"Yes."

"Last name," Malone prodded.

The girl hesitated. "Anything I tell you will be a lie."

Malone gave a short burst of laughter that faded quickly. "Well, that's honest. What or who are you afraid of?"

"What I was running from."

Ignoring her stubbornness, Malone propped her elbow on the table, chin in hand, studying the dark bruising along the girl's cheekbone. "Who hit you?"

"My husband."

"You aren't old enough to be married."

"My folks didn't think so either. That's why we ran off together."

That struck a strong cord in Malone though she hadn't gotten married and Tyge had never laid a hand on her in violence. But there was something too steady, too detached in the girl's words and Malone suspected they were no more than that. Just words. A story invented and memorized for exactly a moment such as this. She tested the waters. "So, you got married too young and he couldn't take the pressure and took it out on you with his fists."

Joss shrugged. "It happens."

"But not to you," Malone said softly.

It took only a heartbeat for the girl to realize that Malone was calling her on the made-up story. As she tensed to rise, Malone placed a hand on hers. "I'm not going to do anything to put you in harm's way, but I'm not going to pretend I believe that tale of yours. Your first words to me were 'don't tell them where I am.' *Them* not *him*, not some made up husband."

The girl leaned back in her chair but didn't bother to argue the point. Malone could see the weariness and creeping despair in the rich hazel eyes.

"Whoever they are, I won't give you away. You're safer here with me and Trouble than anywhere outside these walls."

At her words, Joss glanced at the cat. "He's hungry, I think."

Malone interpreted that to mean the girl was hungry ... and that she didn't plan to bolt, at least not for the time being. Pushing aside the questions that clamored in her mind, she rose to her feet. "I turned the water heater on so we'll be able to shower soon. After we eat, I'll dig out some clothes that should come close to fitting you. You're as tall as I am but they may be a bit loose on you."

"Why would you help me?"

For a moment, Malone just looked at her then she sighed. "Because I can. Because you need it." It wasn't a complete answer but it was all she could offer. "After we clean up, we'll make a trip into town for a few things. Maybe I can talk to the county sheriff while we're there, see what he can get started to make sure you have legal protection."

WELL, we learned nothing there except the fact that young Joss is not an accomplished liar which, all things considered, is at least a good thing to know. Panic can make the mildest of souls a hazard to themselves and others, but I don't believe – at this point – that I need to keep an eye on her for anything except risk of flight. I am, however, confident that menace follows her.

It would take a particularly nasty person to strike a young lady in the face and young is the appropriate descriptor. Young and vulnerable though she bears a quiet dignity that others, far greater than her in age, would do well to emulate.

So now I must put my mind to the task of defense from some unknown threat that could come from any direction. While I await the pleasure of lunch, I shall reconnoiter the house once more with an eye to protecting the two females that fate has entrusted to my care.

I find the rooms in this house an interesting design but not the most defensible. Most are unexpectedly connecting so that – although there is a central hallway as well – it is almost possible to make a full circle of the house room to room.

Hmmm, a curtain is lifted ever so slightly by a breeze in the far bedroom. The open window is low enough to the ground that an intruder could easily gain silent access. Fortunately, I haven't sensed anything sinister here. It's plain the house, though vacant, has had caretakers. One was careless, no doubt. However, should some nefarious person seek entry, far better they be compelled to break a glass or force a lock, either of which would be sufficiently noisy to give warning of the act.

As I step into the room, I freeze. Our stow-away stands at one side of the window. The disreputable looking bag, which doubtless contains all she can now claim as her own, sits on the bed behind her. It's not difficult to deduce that she contemplates flight.

When Trouble came to get her – and there was no doubt in Malone's mind that that was exactly his intent – Malone followed much more promptly than she might have prior to this morning's disconcerting cell phone call and the unexpected arrival of Joss into her orderly though fast-paced existence.

As Trouble led her down the hall it occurred to her, that as satisfying as her career was to her and as exciting the world of rodeo might seem to others, she'd gotten comfortable with being alone, responsible only for the horses – her own and those entrusted to her by others – and herself. It was work, hard work, but it was gratifying labor. Sure, there was heartache but also quiet pleasures and breathtaking successes.

Suddenly, unexpectedly, she'd had thrust upon her a girl patently too young to be on her own and a black cat with a reputation for turning up where danger lurked. As convinced as Avery was of Trouble's abilities, Malone retained a certain skepticism but wasn't foolish enough to discount the possibilities. She'd lived close to horses for too many years not to realize there were depths to animals that some people never discerned.

When Trouble led her straight to the farthest bedroom, she

took in the scene at a glance. Joss had one leg swung over the window sill, the duffle bag balanced in front of her.

"Wait!"

Joss glanced at Malone then flung the bag out the window. She ducked her head and pulled her other leg through the opening. Malone hesitated long enough to wonder if she could run down the hall and out of the house faster than she could dive through the window after the girl. She dove.

Scrambling to her feet, she sprinted after Joss, knowing she'd have aches and pains come morning from her landing. Joss was fast, even hampered by the duffle bag which banged against her with every stride. They neared the end of the long dirt drive. Out of breath and desperate to stop the girl, Malone lunged and caught the shoulder strap of the duffle bag.

Joss stumbled and turned toward her, eyes frantic. "Let me go! They'll send me back! If you go to the law, here or anywhere, they'll send me back."

Jerking free, Joss staggered backward. Tears slipped from her eyes and Malone's heart broke for her. "I won't," Malone whispered, stricken by the girl's fear. "I promise. I won't. Not a word."

Joss sank to her knees there in the grass and Malone went with her, wrapping her arms around too thin shoulders. The girl wept and Malone asked no more questions. She simply held her through the storm.

When Malone finally coaxed Joss back inside, Trouble followed Malone through the house to her room. He leaped upon the bed, watching her with a steady emerald green gaze.

Malone looked back at him. "Thank you." She felt foolish for saying it but …

Trouble stretched and circled slowly before he lay down. He swished his tail just a bit then curled it around him and closed his eyes.

And I am dismissed, Malone thought.

. . .

Lunch was adequate, I suppose, but a trip into town will be just the thing as I'm hopeful we'll return with fare that is more than just adequate! But, of course, Ms. Rodeo must first ensure that her Jaz continues safe and happy in her surroundings as appears to be the case. I wonder if she noticed that Joss appears at ease in the presence of the very large equine. I deduce this wasn't our runaway's first close-up encounter with that species.

As I settle upon the rather comfortable back seat of the truck, I debate if the time required for the drive will allow for a bit of a nap. But, no, I hear from the front seat that we need only the local feed store and small grocer in a nearby community. Jaz must have fresh hay and stall bedding for a night or two and we, of course, must have an adequate supply of provisions.

I do feel vindicated that Ms. Rodeo recognized my superior capacities so quickly. Rarely do humans respond to my commands within the first day of our acquaintance. I do sense, however, that she may not be crediting my abilities with the significance they deserve. Hopefully, there will be no need for her to learn the true and far-reaching extent of my talents. But we shall see. Here I am and here I shall stay until convinced there's no danger to this extremely independent barrel racer.

I hear her comment to Joss upon the girl's apparent comfort with equine and I settle into my nap, pleased at such an observant nature. My job is always much easier when the human in my care is aware and perceptive.

"Have you broken any laws?" Despite Joss' reticence, Malone was working on a need-to-know basis. Some questions had to be asked and answered. Non-negotiable.

"No, ma'am." The lack of hesitation and calm in Joss' response was reassuring.

"Where is your family?"

"I don't have any." Before Malone could challenge her on that, Joss added softly, "Not anymore." And Malone left that heartache alone.

"Is anyone going to be looking for you?"

For a while, Malone thought she wouldn't answer, but she finally admitted, "Maybe. I don't know. I don't think so but, if they do, I'll kill or be killed but I won't go with them."

Malone felt a chill down her spine. Them, again. Plural. That had an ugly sound to it. She sighed, not happy with the complicated turn her life had taken. Nothing to do about it now, because she wouldn't put the girl out on the street.

Time to turn the subject. "You've spent time around horses?"

"Once upon a time. Not so much this past year."

"How well do you ride?"

"Better than most, not as well as some."

"Barrels?"

Joss shook her head. "Brush track racing. I jockeyed for trainers. But not on race day."

Malone heard the slightest edge of resentment in the last part. There remained a lot of discrimination against female athletes in every sport and racing was no exception. Barriers were being broken but slowly.

"Well, here's what I can offer you for now. Food in your stomach, but you'll be expected to help cook and clean up after. A roof over your head, most often in the living quarters of my horse trailer as I'm on the road a lot. A little cash in your pocket." She named a by-the-day figure she could afford and seemed fair when coupled with room and board.

"In return for?"

Malone glanced over to find herself being watched with more than a trace of suspicion.

"Maybe exercising horses since you've got the skill but I'll have to watch you first," she cautioned. "Grooming, cleaning stalls, all the things I have to do each and every day. I'm only in LaGrange for a day or two then I'm headed back to Oklahoma City for a last run before the circuit finals in Montgomery. I've got horses to pick up along the way – more than I usually try to take on in the same trip – but I've ridden them to success this year and I'm being paid well to run them in the finals. I can use the help. It's up to you."

"I feel safer here. Maybe I could just stay in the house until you get back. Take care of it and all. You wouldn't have to pay me anything. I could get a job in town."

"Well, my plan right now is to put that property on the market." But even as Malone said the words, she felt something deep inside tugging her in a different direction. Regardless, she wasn't about to leave a young teen there alone. "You don't have a way to get to and from town. Besides it wouldn't be long until someone figured out you were there and called the authorities."

Joss huffed and the sound of teen frustration brought a smile to Malone's lips though this certainly wasn't a matter for much levity.

Malone pulled into a parking place in front of the feed store and turned to look at Joss. "I'll keep you as safe as I can, as safe as I keep the horses in my care, but the more information I have about who or what might come looking for you, the better I can do at that."

Joss met her look steadily and said, "I don't know. I'll think about it."

Malone wasn't sure if Joss meant she'd think about the job or owning up to what she faced but Malone held her peace. She had a strong-willed girl on her hands. She ought to know. It felt a bit like looking into a mirror from her own distant past. Except she'd been running *to*, not running *from*.

They made a quick trip into the feed store and Joss proved she was no stranger to ranch work. Without hesitation, she jumped lightly into the back of the truck to catch and land a couple bags of feed followed by bags of stall shavings and bales of hay. All were tossed to her by a young man who looked like he wanted to flirt. Though Joss kept as much of her hair stuffed under that well-worn ball cap as she could, Malone noted it did nothing to hide the fact that she was very much a girl and a pretty one at that. Regardless, the young man's efforts to catch her attention got no encouragement from Joss.

After gathering horse supplies, they shifted gears and walked into a rather quaint market which had all they needed and then some.

Not until they were settled into the truck with their few bags of food did Malone check the phone she tended to keep on silent and see she had a missed call. Reluctantly, she hit play to listen to the message. Tyge's voice, his tone of despair, caught her like a throat punch. "Malone? Babe?" There was a long pause and for a moment she thought he'd broken the connection with just that. "I'm so damned sorry about this mess. Let me hear from you. Please, Malone."

The sound of weariness at the end affected her even more than the initial desperation. Good God in heaven, what had Tyge done this time? And what did it have to do with her?

With Joss' curious gaze fixed on her, Malone hit redial but the call went straight to voice mail. She didn't leave a message. What could she say?

With a shrug at Joss as if the call were of no consequence, Malone turned the key in the ignition. But inside, she was trembling with all too familiar anxiety. And she had never, ever wanted to feel this way again. Vowed she never would.

CHAPTER FOUR

𝓜alone turned into her grandparents' drive and wondered if she would ever consider this place anything but theirs. She saw and recognized Cade's truck pulled to one side and stifled whatever feeling stirred somewhere deep within her. She sensed Joss' quick tension and said, "Friend, not foe," before she stepped out of the truck and started pulling bags out of the back seat. The friend part wasn't quite accurate, but whatever Cade was to her, he was not her enemy.

Anything Joss might be thinking, feeling, she hid it well as she helped Malone with the bags. And, with her own nerves on edge from Joss' precipitous entrance to her life and Tyge's ominous phone message and now Cade's unexpected appearance, all Malone wanted to do was get a grip so she didn't fall apart. Not here and not now. Not in front of Cade.

ALL THINGS CONSIDERED, *the trip into town was productive as well as enlightening as to the character of the woman I am here to protect. Nosing through the market bags during our return trip, I found not one package of dry cat food nor a single tin filled with typically smelly ingredients while* carrying the inappropriate labeling of feast or cuisine in regard to feline nourishment. It is clear she understands that my tastes are far more sophisticated than that.

As we descend from the heights of this rather massive truck, I hear the tiny hum of dismay as she casts another glance at the truck I recognize as belonging to Mr. Silver Eyes. I agree with her that he is not foe so I'm not alarmed at his presence. I am, however, curious that he isn't waiting in the truck. I feel confident he wouldn't be the type to enter her home uninvited even should he find the front door unsecured which it was not. I turn from watching her unlock the aforementioned door and saunter in the direction of the barn and paddock.

Saunter. Rather a nice word. It conveys my supreme confidence in my assessment of the situation as well as my absolute certainty that I can manage any troublesome circumstance that might arise. At the other end of the spectrum, I am equally capable of lethal speed and use of force when and if I find either a necessity.

I spy the object of my search with both arms propped against a fence rail watching Jaz graze. I'd gotten attuned to equine nuances during my sojourn at Summer Valley Ranch. This rather large specimen is comfortable with the human's presence though attentive to the canine sitting quietly at his side. I can tell this primarily by the periodic twitching of the ears in that direction as if to gauge any untoward movement.

Those ears prick forward and, though the noble steed's head does not lift, the grazing ceases as the dog stands at my approach.

Without turning, the man murmurs a quiet, "Whoa, Townsend."

And, what, I ask myself, is a name like Townsend to bestow on a canine? Gleaming – though oddly patterned – black and white fur and a fit physique aside, this is a dog. And, generally speaking, I do not much care for dogs. They bark at inopportune moments and oft times must be put in their place with a quick swipe of an extended claw - or two.

This one, I am pleased to note, heeds the softly spoken command of his master but my final judgement of character remains on hold.

. . .

CADE WAITED for Malone to come to him. He'd heard her truck pull in, truck doors opening and closing. She couldn't have missed the presence of his own pick-up parked at one side of the drive.

He sensed the black cat before he saw him, watched as the lithesome feline leapt to a fat, corner post. Large green eyes stared back at him without blinking. The highly-vaunted Trouble, no doubt. That green stare shifted from his only when Townsend's tail began to whip in greeting as Malone walked up.

"Hi."

One husky word from her and years blinked out of existence. He saw them squared off as they'd been so long ago, experienced once again his frustration, saw the mix of anger and hurt on her face. He couldn't count the times he'd regretted those moments, the heated, cutting words that had sent them spinning in opposite directions.

"I was wrong." It wasn't exactly what he'd intended to say but once the words were spoken, he wasn't sorry.

"Yes." For a moment, he thought she would stop there, with that single acknowledgement of his fault, his failure. Then she added, softly, "And I wasn't old enough or wise enough to know what I didn't know." She broke their eye contact and turned to look out across the paddock. "But I suspect you didn't drive all this way to tell me that."

"No, but I should have. I'm proud of you, Malone. Of who you are and what you've made of yourself. Your success." He wasn't just talking about the fact that she'd managed to make a truly good living in an industry that was as demanding, as competitive, and as heartbreaking as any athletic sport on national television. She'd done it with grace and style. And she'd done it alone, succeeding despite her ex-boyfriend.

"Thank you."

Her profile was to him, her attention fixed on the horse in the paddock. He couldn't tell if his words mattered to her at all.

Wasn't sure how he felt about saying them but didn't regret that he had. It was past time they made peace with each other.

A brisk wind sent a scrap of paper toward the mare. She snorted and shied away from it in play, prancing halfway around the pen for good measure before settling again to graze on the last grass of summer.

Malone's lips curved in a faint smile that faded when she turned back to Cade. "So why *are* you here, Cade?"

He tilted his head toward the black cat sitting motionless and watchful on the corner post. "To find out what that cat knows and make sure you're in no danger."

"As you can see, I'm fine. You can head back out with a clear conscience."

He ignored the suggestion. "How long are you staying in LaGrange?"

Her glare held pure exasperation. "I don't need taking care of, Cade. I never did." It was a deliberate jab.

Cade wanted to tangle with her over his motives on that long-ago and ill-fated day, but now wasn't the time or place. "I promised Dirks and Avery I'd check things out here. If I hadn't, they would be standing here themselves instead of relaxing in a first-class cabin on a jet headed to Wales." It wasn't his only motive by a long shot. Regardless, it was a true statement and succeeded in taking the starch out of her shoulders. He didn't see much need to go any deeper into his reasons, not now and maybe not ever.

He waited - patiently for him - until she turned her attention from the red mare he suspected she wasn't actually seeing at this point back to him. "So, why don't you tell me why the cat, which I'm assured has amazing detective skills, decided you needed his company?"

Malone hesitated for a long, long moment before admitting, "I had a stowaway in my horse trailer. Trouble must have been prowling around the hatches and saw something because he somehow ended up coming along for the ride as well."

The skin tightened on the back of Cade's neck. Only the fact that Malone was beside him unscathed by any encounter along with the fact that the black cat had nonchalantly lifted one paw to begin grooming himself kept Cade from a sharp rejoinder. At least verbally. Internally, was a different matter. The hell she didn't need taking care of.

"And just where is that *stowaway* now?"

"She's inside. At least I hope she is. She's a flight risk and I won't put it past her to slip out a back window and run if she thinks you're a threat. She tried that once already. She barely trusts me."

She. Some of Cade's tension eased, but only some. "Is she running from the law?"

"I don't think so. She's got a few bruises, blamed them on an ex-husband but she's lying about that."

"Husband? How old is she?"

"If she's sixteen, I'll be surprised."

"So, she's run away from home."

"I'm not sure about that part. She's hiding but I don't have a clue from who or what. I'm planning on looking up some recent Amber Alerts to see if I can find anyone who looks or sounds like her. She got on board in Lake Charles but I don't know if that's where she's from."

"Have you called the authorities?" Somehow, knowing Malone, he'd already surmised the answer to that.

"No, and I'm not going to."

"You could be putting yourself into some real legal difficulties here, Malone."

"And I could do worse than that if I do call them. They'll contact some state department who'll come after that girl. They'd never get her into a vehicle with them, not without force, which means I'd be arrested for fighting them off her."

Cade rubbed the back of his neck battling every wrong word he wanted to say.

Unexpectedly, Malone smiled though her gaze retained just a bit of poignancy. "You always did that when you were getting ready to lecture me."

"I'm not going to lecture you, Malone."

"What *are* you going to do?"

"Damned if I know." And damned if he did. "Maybe a better question is, what are you going to do?"

He wasn't surprised when Malone pushed away from the fence rail and said, "Right now I'm going to unload feed and make sure Jaz has a comfortable place for the next two nights."

Malone tried not to think about spiders as she checked out a stall close to the barn door, but then again, thinking about spiders was almost preferable to thinking about Cade. She'd made herself *not* think about him for so many years that his presence was unnerving and every single memory, every moment of teen angst came flooding back. And it did no good to tell herself she was a different person now. She wasn't that seventeen-year-old half in love with, but furiously battling, a guy who hadn't the slightest idea what she needed or wanted from him. And she'd driven him away with bitter, angry words.

Somehow, somewhere inside of her, that younger self had expected Cade to realize his mistake and come after her, wrest her away from Tyge because he'd know, surely he'd know, Malone didn't really love Tyge, didn't really plan to tie her life to his. She'd just desperately wanted out of a small-town future, out of her parent's plans for college, and into the world of rodeo. She'd packed her bags in the dead of that summer night and loaded her barrel horse beside Tyge's in his old two horse trailer with stars glittering in a midnight sky. Even as she reminded herself that Tyge believed in her, believed she could make it on the circuit, a part of her heart had hoped and watched and waited, looking back at the empty highway miles for those familiar headlights to come racing after her. But Cade, who'd strode away in fury, appeared to have taken her words to heart and he never came and life went on.

Halfway through Tennessee, in a roadside motel, she gave her virginity to Tyge but she never quite gave him her heart.

And, now, when she didn't want him, didn't need him, Cade had reappeared, hefting feed bags and hay bales with ease, seeming not to notice the dust they left on crisp jeans and navy-blue polo with their rodeo association logo on the front. She tried not to notice *him*. After all these years, he was just someone she used to know.

But when their hands brushed as they both reached for the same water bucket, she pulled hers back as if she'd touched fire. And Malone had quit playing with fire years ago. Somehow, she had to get Cade on the road, on his way back out of her life. She had enough on her hands with whatever problem her stowaway had brought and whatever trouble Tyge had stirred up and seemed to fear might spill over onto her. At least Tyge had enough decency left to care about the possibility.

Cade had fallen silent as they worked together after asking only if she didn't want to put the feed and the hay in the barn. He'd nodded at her quiet statement that she didn't plan to stay for long and was used to working between her trailer and whatever barn her horses were in. He, of course, understood living on the road.

For years Cade and his cousin had been top earners in team roping in their circuit, but he'd gradually transitioned from competition to management of a rival association. Recently, he'd stepped up to become a director for the association where she competed and paid her dues. She'd realized she would no doubt encounter him at some point. But, she'd expected to be better prepared for the moment.

Malone found herself sending frequent glances toward the house, wondering each time if Joss was sliding out some window, knowing there was nothing she could do about it if she were. The girl would stay and allow Malone to help her or she would go. Malone wouldn't take her choices from her but she couldn't help the nagging worry and knew she'd carry it with her down the road if the girl left.

As they finished, Malone looked around the barn. The aged wood was solid, undoubtedly far stronger than what passed for lumber in more modern barns. Jaz's stall for the next day or two was large and safe.

She turned to look at Cade. "I appreciate the help."

"But you didn't need it."

"No, I didn't. And, as you can see, I'm fine and safely settled in now."

"Malone, I'm not leaving."

Hmmm, such tension in the air. I will say I'm rather amazed that Ms. Rodeo does not deign to argue but simply turns on her heel and strides toward the house, leaving him to follow if he will. And, of course, he does with the devoted Townsend at his heels. Oh, and I cannot continue to call that canine by such a ridiculously refined name, not with his tongue lolling happily out of his mouth as he prances at his master's side. Townsend, it cannot be. Townie, perhaps? As in one of those poor suburbanites who have no inkling about serious outdoor living? Hmmm. Apropos, perhaps. I'll try that for a bit to see if it fits, although, I'm not sure how long the duo will be staying. We shall see who has the stronger motivation, she to send him on his way or he to remain in the event recent happenings are not as benign as they seem.

I am amazed further to find Joss standing in the kitchen with her back to the counter. I rather thought she would be hiding in a back room, waiting for the man to leave and hoping he'd go away without coming inside. Regardless of her youth, she has courage, as I suspected she must by virtue of having fought and run rather than choosing to succumb to whatever fate had been planned for her. Too often humans fear the unknown much more than the known, regardless of however unpleasant, even treacherous, their circumstances may be. Felines never choose to remain in unwelcoming environments.

Ms. Rodeo performs the briefest of introductions, saying, "Joss, this is Cade."

He extends a hand to her but Joss' arms remain crossed in front of her. She watches him carefully, rather similar to the manner in which I might regard a snake that has slithered too close, not certain it is a threat, but neither certain it is not, until it has passed me by without incident.

To his credit, he ignores the slight as he accepts a glass of tea and an offer of a seat at the well-used kitchen table.

To keep the overly friendly Townie from flouncing down on top of me, I leap to a corner of the counter beside Joss who chooses not to join them at the table. I think she takes a bit of comfort from my presence though her shoulders stiffen as our visitor fixes his gaze on her. "I'm not here to hurt you nor will I allow you to be hurt, but I do need to know who will come after you." *Oops, Ms. Rodeo is looking daggers at him.* "We need to know." *Heh, heh, fast – and wise – reaction to that pointed look cast his way.*

MALONE WAITED, smug in her certainty that Cade would have no better luck getting information from Joss than she had.

With the unerring accuracy of every teen ever, Joss deflected his question by looking straight at her and asking, "Instead of focusing on me, why don't you tell him about the phone message? The one that made your hands shake."

CHAPTER FIVE

Cade held his temper, by a thread, but he managed. He might *not* have managed if he'd known where to unleash it. A part of him acknowledged that whatever was happening with Malone – whatever troubled her – was hers to resolve. Another part of him said, "hell no" to that. Maybe it was because of their past, their shared memories of good times and bad. Maybe it was because of feelings that had resurfaced at seeing her again, after years of keeping those feelings tightly contained. Maybe it was because he *was* the 'tyrannical despot' she'd once called him. Even at seventeen, Malone, who'd divided her time between horses and books, had owned an extensive and imaginative vocabulary.

Regardless, Cade wasn't just going to drive back the way he'd come and leave Malone to whatever fate someone wanted to dish out to her. Nor did he trust one black cat to protect her, despite Dirks' faith in that cat's abilities, despite even the fact that Cade himself had been unpredictably and intrinsically reassured by Trouble's calm response to Malone's pronouncement that she'd found a stowaway on board her trailer.

To that end, he was patient through a meal a reluctant Malone invited him to share because she was too polite to ask him point-blank to leave. Patient as they talked about which ropers and rough stock riders and barrel races were moving into which circuit finals, who might move on to the association finals the first week of December, what contestants had been successful the previous year but less so this year and the whys and wherefores. Idle chit-chat he could accomplish while his mind wrestled with how to keep Malone from harm when she didn't want his help. And the truth of the matter was that he couldn't. Couldn't when he was twenty-two, couldn't through the years since, couldn't now. Not unless she allowed him to and he didn't think that likely.

He noted that Joss listened to their conversation but didn't offer a single word, answering only if asked a direct question. He'd never seen a person that young that quiet. But he'd also never seen a young girl with bruises across her face that may well have been from someone's fist. It clenched the muscles in his gut every time he glanced her way. Deep down he knew he'd sometimes feared that was Malone's fate after she'd run off with Tyge LaMonte. Cade had kept tabs, though and - despite Tyge's reputed propensity for using his fists instead of his wits in any dispute - Cade had never heard one word that he'd used them on Malone. LaMonte wouldn't be in one piece today if he had.

Dusk lit the skies with purple and put the hills in shadows when he stepped out of the house, watching from the porch as Malone headed back out to feed Jaz. She hesitated halfway along the path to the barn and glanced back as if she'd sensed his stare. She wore one of her grandpa's plaid flannel shirt-jackets and her hair spilled to her shoulders in a silken sheen of rich caramel. She'd never looked more vulnerable – or more beautiful – than she did in that moment.

Knowing it was a mistake before he ever made a move, Cade stepped off the porch to follow.

The years fell away as Cade watched Malone measure feed and supplements for her mare and he automatically reached for the pail when she closed the top of the feed bag. With an unfathomable glance, she yielded it to him and separated a section of hay to take with her. They fell in step together as they walked the short distance from her trailer to the barn.

The mare greeted them with a nicker, butting Cade's arm as he emptied the pail into her larger feed bucket. Malone talked softly to the mare as she refilled Jaz's water bucket and used a manure fork to clean her stall. She had yet to speak a word to Cade and – for the moment – he didn't mind the fact. If they weren't talking, they weren't arguing.

Malone latched the stall door behind her and turned to face Cade. Her eyes searched his face as if looking for a hint as to his thoughts. "What now?" she asked at last.

Cade didn't bother with words. He leaned in and brushed her mouth with his, not daring to pull her in close and hard against him, though he longed to do just that. For too brief a moment, he felt her lips soften and yield before she stepped back and away.

"No." That one soft word was all she said before she turned and walked back to the house.

No was right. Cade knew it, even agreed with it on some level. But there were other, more visceral levels where he did not. There was a lifetime of experiences between who they were now and who they had been. Instead of giving way to the temptation to touch her, taste her, he should have taken the moment to ask whose phone call had the ability to make her hands shake. She wasn't likely to give him that opportunity now, much less give him an answer.

Townsend bumped his leg and he looked down at the ball the dog carried in his mouth and Cade spent the next half hour burning his pent-up frustration and making his dog ecstatic.

The house was dark and quiet when he went back inside with Trouble and Townsend trailing after him. He bolted the door and found a spare bedroom by the simple act of walking past two doors which were solidly closed and into the first one that stood open. There'd be hell to pay if his folks knew he'd come back this way after the wedding and not come by but he'd had a good few days with them beforehand and there just wasn't time for another visit now.

DISCARDING her plan to stay at least one more day, Malone had the trailer loaded and what now seemed like an entourage on the road well before noon. She gave a last glance around the old farmstead and knew she wasn't ready to make a decision on what to do with the place. It was home to her in a way no other place had ever been. She had enough regrets in her past. She wouldn't add to that by acting in haste – not when she could help it. There was time for her to be sure of her own mind. She would give herself that time.

Cade didn't press her for any more information, didn't give her any advice, but she knew in her heart she hadn't seen the last of him and not just because they belonged to the same rodeo association now. Whatever they were or weren't, they had a past. Although she didn't intend for them to have a future, they had a past.

To her relief, Cade didn't try to hang with her as she headed back west though he'd followed her onto the interstate because they were headed in the same direction. When she made her first exit to stop for fuel, she saw his truck hold steady on the interstate. She took a deep breath and squared her shoulders. Time for her to focus on the competition ahead, on giving one hundred percent to each horse and each run.

As they traveled, with Joss riding shotgun and Trouble stretched out on the back seat, Malone gave Joss control of the radio and found they liked the same station, same songs. The girl had a soft contralto voice, unusual enough in itself, but also one that was far above average. "You could be the next Reba McEntire or Jennifer Nettles." Malone was only half kidding.

Joss flashed her a half-smile. "I'd aim for Miley Cyrus. Or maybe Bonnie Tyler."

"So, you understand your voice and music." That seemed odd to Malone. Most teens were more into the lyrics than an understanding of vocal range and which singers were what.

Joss' smile disappeared. "My mom taught me. She named me after Joss Stone. She called her Britain's version of a soul singer."

"I'm familiar with her." But Malone was more interested in Joss' mention of her mother and the sadness that accompanied her comments.

"Where is your mother now, Joss?"

"St. Luke's Cemetery."

Malone felt the weight of Joss' sadness but also the absence of any faith. Not heaven. Not hell. St. Luke's Cemetery.

"I'm sorry for that. You miss her."

"I miss a lot of things. But life goes on and I will too."

Malone could agree with that and she didn't press further, didn't have the inclination and didn't really have time when her phone rang. She glanced at the truck display, saw Tyge's name flash and hesitated. She wasn't sure what was up with him. With Joss' presence in mind, she hit *accept*, hoping he'd at least mind his language. "You're on speaker, Tyge. I'm on the road with a friend."

"Are you okay?" He sounded edgy.

"I'm fine." She kept her tone relaxed despite a rush of anxiety. "What's going on with you? I got your voice mail and tried to call you back."

"Yeah, I turned it off for a while when I couldn't get you. I just need to know you're okay."

"I'm fine. Who are you hiding from?" And what had he done now?

"Don't tell them where I am. Don't tell them anything."

"Tyge, I don't *know* where you are. And who is 'them'?"

"Just be careful, babe."

Malone sighed as Tyge cut the connection. He hadn't answered her questions and she hadn't expected him to.

She felt Joss staring at her and wasn't surprised when the girl said, "Seems like I'm not the only one with a problem."

"No," Malone agreed, "seems like you're not."

She thought of her empty search through recent, and some not so recent, Amber Alerts. Her laptop, brought in from the living quarters of the trailer, had yielded nothing. No one was looking for a girl matching Joss' description, at least not openly. Malone took comfort from the thought that no one who wished Joss harm could possibly know where she was now or who she was with. They had traveled miles and cities and states away from where she had first slipped aboard Malone's trailer and they were headed even further away.

An unexpected thought caused a frisson of alarm. "Do you have a cell phone?"

"Had one. Threw it away so they couldn't use it to find me."

"Smart girl."

"No way to pay for the service at the end of the month anyway."

Malone glanced at her and then away, dismayed. Malone had run away from home, it was true, but she'd never had to run away from danger.

*H*MMM, *what manner of man is this Tyge? And what manner of name is that? Short for Tiger, an animal known to be lithe and graceful and deadly? Surely not, for I detected from his comments that this Tyge is more fearful for himself than for Ms. Rodeo, despite the fact that he did ask after her well-being. Regardless, he appears a harbinger for danger, and I shall be wary and watchful for its approach.*

CHAPTER SIX

Cade parked behind the show office, a long building with plenty of windows. He stepped out, waiting as Townsend leapt down behind him before closing and locking the door of the cab of his truck. Though it was days early for most of the contestants to arrive, there were several trucks and trailers scattered around the parking areas marked for big rigs. He studied the acres of asphalt and security lighting that fronted both the office building and the coliseum. Beyond were barns and paddock areas.

Cade felt more anxious than he'd anticipated he might in this moment. He'd moved the venue for the southeast circuit finals, initially amid protests from every other member of the board. It was a business decision and he'd convinced most of them he was right, especially when he'd shown them the math. Plain and simple, Montgomery, Alabama had more to offer in terms of convenience for the competitors as well as for their followers. The newly built coliseum could house twice the number of fans. Last year they'd lost significant revenue from having to turn away potential ticket-buyers which meant fewer customers for the vendors who were, in large part, their sponsors.

The city and surrounding area had things to offer as well.

While there was little in the way of real tourist attractions, there were decent hotels and plenty of restaurants, even one or two that could boast fine dining. Despite his own good intentions, he pictured himself escorting Malone, dressed as she'd been the evening of the Hannas' wedding, into one of the nicer establishments. He had a quick, unexpected vision of her as he'd last seen her, in jeans and boots, loading her mare onto the trailer and he smiled. He'd take Malone Summers anywhere in any attire.

For a moment, he wondered if thoughts of Malone had conjured an image of the black cat sitting at the door of the show office. But no, at his approach, the image stood and stretched and gave him a look that would have been withering under any circumstances. Cade felt a touch of humor as he realized the crushing look was directed at Townsend. His greater reaction, though, was sheer pleasure at the knowledge that Malone was somewhere close.

She was not, however, in the show office. His searching glance confirmed that. He turned his gaze on the cat, wondering, but only for a moment. Trouble could not possibly have known to watch for him here. The cat must have accompanied Malone when she checked in that morning and somehow lost track of her. Unlike Townsend, cats were independent cusses. That was probably the real reason he'd ended up in Malone's rig to begin with. Cade would send Malone a quick text to let her know Trouble's whereabouts as soon as he checked in with the staff.

Big grins greeted Cade as he stepped behind the long counter. His assistant, a tall red-head with unmatched efficiency, waved a sheet of paper. "We're a sell-out, boss." Aleta's grin broadened. "You did it."

Cade smiled in return, allowing himself to enjoy the moment with her. Tried and true rodeo fans had followed them to the new venue and they'd added new enthusiasts, doubling the potential profits for their sponsors. That would lead to increased sponsorships down the road. After a brief exchange with the team, who had a whirlwind few days in front of them as contestants arrived and checked in, he asked which office was his and was gestured toward a corner door. He headed that way, Townsend and Trouble close at his heels.

A stack of reports waited for him in the sizeable room Aleta had selected to serve as his office for the duration of the event. He took a moment to send Malone a text concerning Trouble's current location before he settled into business. He hadn't gotten far into the first report when his assistant tapped at his door, a curious expression on her face. "You've got a visitor, Mr. Delaney. May I show him in?"

A look of affront crossed her face as the *visitor* stepped past her and into the room without waiting for an invitation.

Despite the plain clothes, Cade recognized the crisp air of authority in every aspect of the man and said, "Thank you, Aleta. If you'd close the door ..."

The young woman gave him a searching look then nodded as if satisfied by his lack of alarm.

Cade gestured towards one of the chairs pushed into a corner. "How can I help you, Officer ...?"

"Deputy U.S. Marshal James Ryder." The man said the words simply, not officiously before he handed Cade his badge, not questioning the fact that Cade recognized had him as law enforcement.

After a cursory look, Cade handed it back. He gave the deputy marshal a longer look. He judged him to be in his late thirties to early forties with a decade or two of experience in piercing brown eyes.

Ryder pulled one of the chairs closer to Cade's desk and sat down. He leaned back with a casual air clearly intended to be disarming.

"I understand you're the director here."

"I'm one of the directors of this association," Cade agreed, "Director of Operations." That title and the roles and responsibilities it carried put him in a lead position but Cade didn't see a need to comment on the fact.

"So definitely a person who'd want to know about possible criminal activity within your rank and file."

Cade glanced toward the black cat who now sat erect on the padded seat of the second chair. The tip of his tail, curled around him, twitched once as he returned Cade's look. Not possible, Cade thought to himself. The cat's movement and eye contact were coincidental and not a reaction to the comment. "I take it you don't mean the routine barroom brawl with busted tables and broken glass and maybe a broken bone or two."

"I don't, no."

"Names?"

Ryder hesitated. "Names can't be a part of this discussion. It's too early in the investigation with more unanswered than answered questions. That's what I'm looking for now. Answers." Cade had a feeling the marshal didn't give names because he didn't have them. He was fishing. "I'd like access to any information you have on your contestants and your vendors."

Cade leaned back in his chair and stifled a sigh. "I can't allow that."

"Even though you know I can get them ..." Ryder let the sentence trail off suggestively.

"... through proper channels and proper methods," Cade finished for him.

Ryder did nothing to suppress his own exhalation of annoyance. "We're not talking penny ante stuff here, Delaney."

"Well then, ask me something I can answer or give me something I *can* do."

The deputy marshal got to his feet and handed Cade a business card. "Call me if you see anything you don't like."

Cade almost laughed – would have if he weren't feeling so grim inside – at the thought of all the things he'd witnessed over the years that he hadn't liked. "Give me a clue where to focus, at least."

Ryder gave him a hard look. "Trailers intended for horses and cattle can carry a hell of a lot more than livestock."

"Drugs?"

"That's the trail I'm following."

"So why would a U.S. Marshal be involved in something typically handled by the DEA?"

"Because it's tied to another investigation involving arms trafficking."

"Which is the province of the ATF," Cade prodded, knowing he was pushing his luck but, to his surprise, Ryder answered.

"Yeah, but I believe we can connect those crimes to an individual who's eluded capture for nearly a year. And that one's mine."

This time Ryder didn't wait for a response. Just nodded, turned and walked out the door.

Cade sat for a moment, wondering what in blazes had just been dumped in his lap with the worst possible timing. This event – these contestants – commanded and deserved every bit of his concentration and effort. Now this. Damn.

HERE WE GO, *then. The hunt for the villain is on. Mr. Silver Eyes thinks he has clue number one handed to him by a pithy U.S. Marshal. My suspicion is that elite status belongs to the mysterious phone call from Tyge 'whoever' that left Ms. Rodeo so unnerved. Somehow, I must ensure she shares her alarm so these two can begin to piece their knowledge together. Which, of course, is why I waited here for his arrival. The more I know about his habits, the easier my work. And I believe it will be up to me to determine if somehow Joss doesn't figure into this as the true clue numero uno. That is Italian for the number one for those less erudite than I. Not to be confused with the crass, common day usage for expressing one's self interest.*

I can sense the anger building as Mr. Silver Eyes taps the lawman's business card against his desk. He gives me another of those steely, questioning glances as if he wished he could read my mind. As do I, when dealing with non-felines, so many times. Alas, mind-reading isn't an ability in the humans I am called to assist. However, there are other means of communication and I am adept at finding those means at the appropriate place and time.

I suspect that Townie senses the tension as well. He watches his master and his tail swirls.

Ah, good, our man is standing and reaching for his hat, a fine western piece of attire in grey that carries the same cool tone as his eyes.

And out the door we go. Time for a bit of reconnoitering, a bit of action at last. Oomph! Well, my word, the Aussie is crowding me through the exit, his hair actually brushing against me. I pause to deliver my most imperious glare. Of course, it goes unheeded as the clumsy canine bounces onto the sidewalk with complete lack of finesse. He brushes against me once again and I growl softly. He hesitates at the warning then wags his tail with unwarranted enthusiasm. Hmph. Townie, indeed.

CADE STROLLED around the grounds with no particular destination in mind. The deputy marshal had given him far too much to think about and he needed to clear his mind. For now, the traffic remained light. In a day or two every available inch would be taken, vehicles would get blocked, problems would need solving, and tempers would need soothing. Fortunately, that coordination wasn't his job. His was to ensure there were sufficient and competent staff whose job it was. He greeted the early arrivals by name but didn't linger with any of them until he bumped into one of the stock contractors who'd been with the association at its inception.

Asa Morrissette had been one of the top steer wrestlers for a decade, taking the title three years running. A vehicle wreck had derailed his career and stolen his daughter from him. Afterward, he'd taken over his father's ranch, turning the focus from beef cattle to stock contracting for the sport he loved more than anything, even the wife who'd given it her best shot before leaving for a man who had never been on a horse.

Cade and Asa weren't bosom buddies but had that long-standing kind of friendship that allowed them to meet up after months, share a beer and a steak, and swap stories. They could comfortably enjoy each other's company for an hour or two and part ways until the next time.

They exchanged greetings while Asa propped against the fender of his stock trailer and watched his oldest son ramrod the unloading of strong looking bulls with glossy coats and bright eyes. Unlike Asa who was rarely without a sports coat and button-down shirt paired with impeccable jeans, the younger Morrissette wore a long-sleeved tee-shirt with the name of a rock band blazoned across the back. His jeans were strategically faded with frayed hems over sharp looking boots.

"Joel has turned into quite a hand," Cade commented. "How's your father doing? Did he come with you?"

"No, not this year. He's ornery as ever." Asa sighed and added, "Failing a bit, though I don't like owning up to that. He's enjoyed his retirement so much, sits a horse as well and as often as ever. And he keeps a keen eye on my boys as they work, teaching them all he knows about cattle and loves doing it. But he's lost weight lately and that worries me though doc says he's stronger than most his age. Still, this is the first time he didn't make this trip with me. Just ain't like him, you know?"

They chatted a bit more about Asa's dad and Cade's parents before Cade circled the conversation closer to where he wanted it to go. "What do you think about the new group, Carlisle Contracting? Had much interaction with them?"

"Hauls the broncs only?" At Cade's nod, he said, "They seem okay. Quiet bunch. Mostly gals, did you notice? Found that odd but guess that's my age talking. Girls are taking over the world these days."

Cade laughed. "Probably do a better job with it than some of us have, but, yeah, that's the group. We signed them on less than a year ago. I've been trying to keep tabs on them. Haven't heard any complaints from the contestants but don't want to assume all is well simply because of that."

Judging from Asa's expression, Cade knew he hadn't heard any complaints either, at least no more than the run of the mill gripes from those whose rides hadn't turned out well.

Asa confirmed that with a shrug and said, "Seem to be providing solid, healthy stock. Don't think you can ask more than that. At least not if their paperwork is clean."

His tone and his glance turned questioning with that last comment and Cade was quick to reassure him. "Nothing of concern there. Business is legit and so are their dealings. They want a shot at the finals next year," he added by way of explanation. "They're on my 'wait and see' list but I haven't ruled them out." But they were the newest of the contractors and Cade knew the least about them on a personal level. Of course, Ryder had mentioned contestants as well as vendors but the association had hundreds of members. It wouldn't be possible to dig into each one of them. All Cade could do was question where he could and keep his eyes open as the lawman had suggested.

Before Cade moved on, he said, "I heard the BlackJack has a mean porterhouse these days. Thought I'd check them out tonight."

Asa smiled broadly. "Hot damn. About seven?"

"Sounds good. See you there." Cade turned to leave but stopped when Asa spoke again.

"Uh, Cade?"

"Yeah?"

"Townsend's looking good but when in blazes did you get a cat?"

Cade turned to glance at Trouble who was looking decidedly bored. "He belongs to a friend."

"Well, huh." Asa rubbed his jaw thoughtfully. "Didn't picture you for a cat-sitter. See you at the BlackJack."

Cat sitter! How offensive. The dog receives a compliment and I am tendered an affront. I suppose that simply indicates the low level of intelligence to be found in some humans. It is most fortunate that it is time to resume our excursion.

I find all things of some interest but bovine only in a limited capacity and only for a brief time. They have not the nobility of the equine. But they do have their uses and, by way of most excellent example, steak tartare is one of those.

It's time we checked in with Ms. Rodeo so I must guide this entourage in that direction. With a nudge and a bump at Mr. Silver Eyes' leg, I take the lead. Ahhh, it is so satisfying that he allows me to do so, following obediently in my wake. No doubt about it, he is coming to accept my elevated level of intelligence.

Good, he has spotted our rig – and I do find that an odd terminology for a truck and trailer. His step quickens and I lose my lead status. However, I am not the least concerned by the fact. My supremacy is evident in so many ways that I need no superficial evidence of the fact. Townsend remains sublimely happy to merely be in the presence of his master. I, however, have no master. My lovely Tammy Lynn is my supporter as I am her advisor. Our unique talents ever complement that of the other.

Before us is the competent Ms. Rodeo. It would seem she hasn't been idle in my absence though I begin to suspect she is never truly idle. I watch as she effortlessly lifts a saddle from the back of a sleek looking animal, one of six that she has brought with her to ride here. I've learned that isn't the norm as most riders have two, three at most, that are up to this level of competition. It is a testament to her ability that her clients trust her with the best of their best.

She glances our way and gives a civil hello to Mr. Silver Eyes. Civil and patently cool, though not as chill as the front that blows from the north. I flatten my ears at the unpleasant force, grateful for my healthy covering of fur while knowing tomorrow could dawn sunny and mild. That is one of the vagaries of the southern states. With no desire to settle on cold ground, I leap to a folding chair that I doubt anyone has spared more than a minute to relax upon.

Our Joss rounds the rear of the horse trailer and I see that Mr. Silver Eyes does not at once recognize the girl with her newly, and inexpertly, shorn hair. Only a few wisps float out from under a warm cap the same nondescript olive green of her oversized jacket. She acknowledged it too large when the purchase was made but cited the extra length as her reason. Truth be told, I suspect it was the shapelessness that appealed.

Just as recognition dawns, an insistent buzzing disturbs my comfort and I realize I share space with a cell phone. The surface lights and I see 'Tyge' across the screen. This is my chance and it will be brief! In the scant moment that I have, I expertly bat the phone into the air, hissing to catch Mr. Silver Eyes' attention.

Good man! He catches it mid-air and glances at the name. I see a hard gleam of recognition in his eyes. This is a name he knows and a person he holds in distaste. I've given him the hint and the opening. Let us hope he doesn't botch the deal at this point.

"WELL DONE," Cade murmured to Trouble. He placed the phone in Malone's outstretched hand. "The phone call that made your hands shake? That was Tyge?"

"Both times," Joss offered, closing the distance between them.

Malone slipped the phone into her jacket pocket, giving first the cat, then the girl a reproving look.

Joss ignored the look. "The second call was worse. When they actually talked."

"Joss." There was no mistaking Malone's tone of voice. It was clearly a warning.

The teen stared at her patently unrepentant. "You're not afraid of anything. Nothing rattles you. I've been with you less than a week and watched you change a tire on the side of the interstate and stare down two dudes at a gas pump who tried to mess with you. But whatever is going on with this guy," she tilted her chin toward the pocket where the cell phone had disappeared, "has you edgy. Not afraid, maybe, but edgy for sure."

Cade battled with his temper before he allowed himself to cut in. "What's going on, Malone?"

"Nothing I can't handle. I've been handling things for a long time, Cade, all without help."

She said the words quietly and evenly. He wasn't sure if it was meant as a dig, but he felt the bite of it all the same. He was wise enough not to argue but he'd be damned if he wasn't going to hunt Tyge down and make him understand a few hard truths. And the thought of Malone facing down two guys bent on mischief chilled him to the bone. He couldn't discount the fact that, yeah, she'd been on her own a long time. Couldn't discount the fact that he'd been forced to put her out of his mind for a long time, that or go crazy. But he'd never been entirely successful there. He'd tucked her away as a memory and a regret. But she was back in the here and now, within reach.

He wasn't sure what he was going to do about the fact but he damned sure wasn't going to ignore it.

CHAPTER SEVEN

*T*he BlackJack wasn't fine cuisine but neither was it a hole-in-the-wall. The small, non-chain restaurant boasted a top-of-the-line chef who also happened to be the owner. Beer and wine were on the menu but the offerings were good quality. If you wanted a cheap drunk, this wasn't the place to come. Which was why Cade was surprised to see Tyge stroll in when he was half way through the perfectly seared steak on his plate.

They hadn't crossed paths in several years and Cade noted the changes a dissolute lifestyle had brought about in the other man. A slight paunch carried above the belt buckle had replaced the hard, lean muscle of a pay-window cowboy. His face sagged more than his age warranted. Tyge bypassed the scattering of tables with their neat tablecloths and napkins folded around dinnerware in favor of the bar. His gaze passed over the corner where Cade sat facing Asa without any sign of recognition.

Cade watched from the corner of his eye as Tyge took an empty barstool next to a small group of cowboys. He recognized some of them. Frank Roberts was a competitor, the older half of a father-son rope team. Somehow Cade wasn't surprised when

Frank got to his feet shortly after Tyge took the seat next to him. He doubted the two had much in common to talk about. Tyge was a has-been. Frank had kept his competitive edge through some twenty years by working hard and living clean. Tyge said something Cade couldn't hear but Frank shook his head and walked toward the door.

Cade wished, honestly wished, for a few minutes in which he could be just another rodeo contestant instead of a director. A brawl of any sort wasn't something he could afford though it was something he damn sure wanted. Tyge was due a fist or two for all he'd the misery he'd dealt Malone.

Looking up from his plate, Asa asked, "Something wrong with your steak?"

Cade picked up his fork. "No, for a second I thought I saw someone I knew. The steak here is as excellent as I remember. Glad the owner added porterhouse to the menu."

"Yeah, it's gotten hard to find most places."

They finished their meal in companionable conversation and parted at the front door of the establishment. Asa was parked out front, Cade in the back. The night was starkly cold though the earlier wind had dropped making the temperature less unbearable. Beyond the glow of the street lights, the dark was absolute with the thick layer of clouds hugging close to the earth.

While Asa pulled away from the curb, Cade made a slow circle around the restaurant and walked right back in the front door to the small bar where two or three lone patrons ate first class steak and drank first rate beer. The bronze pendants over the bar cast a warm glow across the inhabitants. Tyge didn't look half as disreputable in the hazy light.

Cade slid onto the one empty stool, right next to Tyge. Quietly and on a hunch, he said, "I hear you're in a tight spot."

Tyge tensed, cut a glance his way, then relaxed his white-knuckled grip on his beer. "Someone been talking? Malone, maybe?"

Pretending ignorance, Cade asked, "Is she someone I need to chat with about this?"

"Nothing she can tell you."

"Who can, LaMonte? You?"

The other man hunched his shoulders. "Nothing to tell. And, even if there was, ain't none of your business."

"Well, now, being that you're a member of the association and I'm a director of same, I'm afraid it is my business."

Tyge turned to face him. "What do you want, Delaney?"

"I want you to keep your nose clean and stay away from Malone."

"So, it was her. Should've known. No loyalty anywhere anymore."

"Really?" Fury ripped through Cade. Quiet, deadly fury. "How many times has she taken you back when your luck and your money ran out? A half-dozen? A dozen? And, with losers like you, the luck always runs out, isn't that right?" Cade has seen it too many times. Despite the strides the sport had made, he supposed there would always be one breed of rodeo cowboys who drifted from one woman to the next, eating their food, sleeping in their bed until they either made enough at the pay window to move on or got kicked out only to do it all over again with the next.

Tyge snarled and got to his feet. "I did for Malone what you wouldn't do. I helped her make her dream and I helped her live it. Yeah, man, I screwed up plenty and I lost her. But you screwed up first. You lost her first. Now, keep the hell away from me."

Despite the sucker punch of truth, Cade stood firm. "I'm serious, Tyge. Stay away from Malone. You're not going to use her again. If you're down on your luck, find yourself a hole to crawl into but not anyplace near her."

"Hell, a man can't even have a drink in peace." Tyge threw a twenty on the bar and headed for the door.

Cade squelched the urge to follow him. His foremost thought

as he got in his truck was that Malone wasn't going to be happy with his interference.

H*mmm*. *Although there's plenty of bustle around the barn even at this late hour, it seems an odd time for play. And I might add that I find this particular human-canine pastime incomprehensible. The Aussie, trembling with happy anticipation, waits for his master to throw some kind of stick – not a run-of-the-mill chunk of wood, mind you, but a carved stick made to look like a large bone – so that he can race to retrieve it only to have it thrown again.*

I don't believe the positioning of their game is by chance as it is within viewing distance of our equipage. We moved the truck and trailer from its earlier check-in location to a place with hook-ups for plumbing and electricity. Much nicer than the din of the generator, though that proved useful as we traveled cross-country. Numerous security lights hold the dark at bay. The horses are all snug inside the barn area with its entrance to the climate-controlled arena where, last I checked on her, Ms. Rodeo hand-walked each of her equines in turn. That action made me a bit nervous as so many other contestants appeared to be riding in close proximity rather than walking, and some on animals who were not behaving as well as they might have been.

It seemed to make Joss equally nervous as she hovered, placing herself between her mentor and the riders as much as possible. That Ms. Rodeo also noticed the protective movement was evidenced by her half-smile at each occurrence.

And here comes Joss now so the horses must be settled and Ms. Rodeo on her way. Yes, she emerges from the barn in conversation with the young man who has had an eye for Joss though Joss wants nothing to do with him or with any human male creature. No doubt her experience at the hands of some of that species has not been kind, leaving her with a deep mistrust. She does, however, seem to have accepted that Mr. Silver Eyes is not a threat.

She's a pretty girl and I've watched her play with face products some evenings but she washes the color enhancements away at bedtime and never wears any outside of the living quarters of the trailer.

Townie has grown fond of her and, on his next fetch, races toward her with the stick rather than returning it to his master. Her face lights up with a smile as she accepts the wooden piece, which must be rather repulsively damp by now.

As interesting as it is to observe these humans, none of this moves my investigation forward. It is the essential but boring part of my work, waiting for the next clue to emerge and deducing the method by which to convey that clue to the humans entrusted to me. They can be stubborn about receiving the information so I must always be clever about my delivery.

Now, while my current humans are all accounted for, I believe I'll take a turn about the grounds. There's information to be gathered and hints of nefarious deeds to be revealed and I'm confident I'll learn little of consequence by loitering here amongst friends.

Although this isn't my first rodeo – hehe, pun intended – I've only recently come to realize that professional rodeo is a very nomadic existence. I'm sure the contestants gathered in this place all have a home base but it seems the more successful of them don't get to spend much time there.

The barn is lively and I pick my path carefully so that I'm in no danger of being trampled or of stepping into some disgusting pile of droppings. No doubt Townie would relish the opportunity to roll in some nastiness but not *moi*.

Not all of the liveliness is horse-related. I pass a boy chatting up a girl and then a couple in a rather heated disagreement. Oh, the drama of romance and of human romance in particular! They are, by no means, a peaceful species and youth seems to aggravate the worst of their characteristics. I pause near a small gathering of cowboys who stare into a pen of muscular horses with lustrous coats and point out which are most rank to one another. As best I can tell from their conversation, I don't think rank used in this regard is meant to describe something malodorous. Further along, the bull riders are involved in much the same stance and conversation as they gaze at rather large bulls with wicked, long horns. The eyes of the cattle hold a glint that seems, at least to me, to contain a certain cheekiness.

I'm about to give up my quest, at least for this evening, when I hear voices around the next corner. They carry a darker undertone, not quite anger but certainly no idle pleasantries. I edge closer, keeping to the shadows, so as not to be noticed. It is likely to have become apparent that Ms. Rodeo is traveling with one sleekly sophisticated black cat and I prefer to remain inconspicuous for the moment lest my reputation precedes me.

Hmmm, the tête-à-tête seems to be about money. My studies have given me a great understanding that money – or its lack – is at the root of many human foibles, frequently resulting in the failure of friendships, partnerships, and marriages. There is something about the voice of one of them that catches my attention and I move a bit closer. Unfortunately, I can't see them, their faces or expressions, unless I round that corner and risk exposure which, I believe, would not be my best course of action.

"You owe me for last time. I need the money and I want it now."

"You'll get it after the next job. I promise. And a bonus with it. My word on that."

"Your word?" *That snarl speaks volumes.* "There won't be a next. Not for me. I told you I'm out and I mean it."

"There is no 'out' for any of us. You knew that walking into this."

"The hell I did. You changed the game and the rules halfway through the last load. If you'd been anywhere around when I found out what I was hauling, I swear to God, you wouldn't be standing here, now, running your mouth. Forget it. And forget me."

"You're making a mistake, cowboy. A dangerous one. This isn't a game and the rules are what they are, when they are. You need to remember, I'm not the one calling the shots. I'm not the one you're going to answer to when you don't show up at the next load point."

A wealth of menace is carried in those words and that tone. The cowboy he threatens – whoever he is – had best watch his back. It is his voice that nags at me, but I'm not sure why that is.

"I won't be there. Tell your boss and you can also tell him that his 'enterprise' won't last long if gofers like you keep pulling tricks on drivers like you did with me."

A soft laugh conveys anything but humor. "You don't get it. It wasn't me who 'pulled the trick' as you call it and you aren't the first sap to get dragged deeper into the spider web. All I do is tell losers like you where to be and when to be there. I'm curious about something though ... what pulled you out of hiding?" *He chuckles as if he knew the answer before he asked the question.* "You went to ground and then you show up here. What's the draw, cowboy? Did I push the right button?"

"You can go to hell."

The voice is further away and I ascertain this conversation is over. Now if I can just get a glimpse of the men and figure out which is which. Alas, as I slip around the corner, both are walking away, angled in different directions. The shadows which provide such excellent cover for me allow me to discern little in turn. I can tell only that both are similar in build, average height and slim-hipped with broad shoulders. Both wear jeans and boots and western hats as do a hundred other men here. I could never identify them in a lineup. Only their voices will distinguish them to me should I encounter them again.

With all that said, I have no means of knowing if this exchange has anything to do with the deputy marshal's investigation. I heard no real proof of wrongdoing, though my suspicions are strong. To be honest, my mission seems a bit murky at the moment. My concern began with a glimpse of jeans and boots disappearing into a trailer unbeknownst to its owner. But Joss is no threat and seems to carry no threat with her. Though she remains fearful of recognition, we are far from her point of embarkation in Lake Charles, Louisiana. Beyond that, it is unlikely anyone could have trailed her successfully through our crisscrossing of many states. Her arrival is a coincidence and therein lies the needle that pricks at my thoughts. I do not trust happenstance.

And while it's true there's an investigation of some sort of crime in or around the association to which Ms. Rodeo belongs, it doesn't seem to involve her, even on a peripheral or happen-stance level.

The only hint of trouble surrounding her seems to be related to the telephone calls from her former amore, who seems to have gotten himself in a bit of a bind with some less than reputable business partners. Ah-ha! The voice on the speaker phone! That was the hint of familiarity I heard in the conversation just past! And, as they would say in some penny dreadful, the plot thickens. And was her cell phone number the 'right button pushed'? Had the threat of danger to her drawn the cowboy from his safe lair?

Oh, the frustrations of not being able to concisely communicate all that I know to my humans. I will find a way as I always do but I will need the right moment, the right opportunity, as I did with the cell phone. In the meanwhile, I have much to keep me busy if I'm am to discern what skullduggery is afoot, all the while keeping my humans from harm.

CHAPTER EIGHT

Malone leaned against the railing of the warmup pen where she and Trouble watched Joss long trot one of the horses Malone had placed in her charge. Joss had proven herself a tireless worker with a gentle but firm hand with the horses. Barrel racing and rodeo were new to her but she was a fast and willing learner. She'd confided to Malone that she preferred her new surroundings to the roughness of the horse track but Malone knew both sports had their seamier side. Joss had seen the more sordid aspects of horse racing before finding herself in the upper ranks of rodeo. But there could be no 'upper' anything without an equivalent 'lower'. Malone would protect Joss from that if she could.

Not that Joss considered herself in need of protection. In fact, in the past day or two, Malone had felt herself shepherded between Trouble and Joss so that she was never alone. The fact interested as much as it perplexed her.

A soft sound from Trouble had Malone turning. She hadn't yet deciphered all of his sounds and signals but knew he was as good as any watchdog when it came to letting her know she had company. She smiled a greeting as a man stepped closer and propped his arms on the railing beside her.

"Frank, how are you? I saw Luke last night. He said y'all came to the finals holding fifth place in rankings. That's wonderful."

Frank and his son, Luke, had more than enough earnings to secure them a place in the circuit finals as her own winnings had done for her. She liked the duo and was always pleased to see them. She hoped they'd do well here and that they'd make the association finals at the end of the year.

Malone didn't see a need to mention to Luke's dad that their conversation centered more around Joss and his son's attraction to the girl. The questions he'd asked about her had been aimed at determining her age and whether or not she had a boyfriend.

Frank smiled at her. "We've had a good year. I enjoyed roping with my older boys, but I'll tell you, my Luke, he's something else. I taught him everything I know and now I'm learning from him. A seventeen-year-old. Go figure."

Malone chuckled and turned her attention back to Joss who was swinging out of the saddle and walking their way, leading the horse. Joss gave Frank a questioning look and Malone fought the urge to roll her eyes as she made introductions, including the fact that Frank was Luke's father. Surely that would reassure Joss that he wasn't a threat.

Her introductions didn't include any particulars about Joss. Not only because she had so few - although Joss had admitted she would turn seventeen in January – but more because the few that she did have weren't hers to share and could well put Joss at risk from a past that had yet to be resolved. If it ever was.

Only a little reassured by the introduction and Trouble's lack of alarm at the visitor, Joss moved off to hand walk the horse around the pen a few times. Because the animal was in no need of cooling out, Malone realized Joss had no intention of leaving Malone on her own with this man while she returned to the barn for the next horse on her list to ride.

"I heard you might be relocating, changing circuits next year." Frank's voice held more than a hint of disappointment. "What's prompting that?"

"If I make the change, it will be earnings, plain and simple but I haven't made any final decision. For now, I'm competing in both, spending most of my time in Oklahoma, Texas, Arkansas, and Louisiana where some of the best payouts seem to occur in clusters. Our circuit has probably the largest single payouts," she admitted, "but the distances in between are greater and I've had some prospects open up for me in the southeast that I don't have further west." Malone had made a name for herself through sheer hard work. Because of that, she'd been offered horses to ride that were out of her price range to purchase. She'd leave her current home base in Oklahoma with a pinch at her heart but she had no family to speak of and friends in nearly every state from Georgia to California. "If I do, it will be a business decision."

Frank removed his hat and rubbed his ear. It was a gesture she'd seen him make when he was thinking hard about something. "Means I'll only see you once or twice a year unless I can persuade you to some other opportunities."

Malone shook her head and smiled. They'd had this conversation more than once.

"Damn, woman, you're a hard one. Can I take you to dinner tonight, to celebrate both of us making the finals again this year?"

With a rueful smile of friendship, Malone turned him down, as she had in the past, but his quick grin and the shake of his head said he'd be asking again.

As he walked away, she found Joss looking from him to her. "He's a nice-looking guy for an older man. Why won't you go out with him?"

"His wife died three years ago. He's lonely and looking for a replacement. I'm not it."

Joss snorted. "From the way he was looking at you, he doesn't see you as a 'replacement' for anyone. He sees you for you."

"Maybe. But I'm not interested in a relationship. They don't work for me."

Joss turned to lead the horse back to the gate and barn. "*One* didn't work for you," she tossed over her shoulder. "Doesn't mean all of them won't."

Malone didn't bother to correct her. Besides, she couldn't really call her past with Cade a relationship. They'd been best friends, she'd *thought* once, and moving toward something more, she'd *hoped* once. Anyway, what she'd gone through with Tyge, before and since their breakup, was more than enough to keep her unattached. She was amazingly happy with her life and darn well planned to keep it that way.

And though she didn't say it, Malone also felt a bit pleased that whatever bad things had happened to Joss hadn't turned her against men and relationships, at least if they didn't involve her. Joss continued to keep her distance from Luke but Malone couldn't blame her for that. Her bruises had faded and were all but gone, but the memories would likely last a lifetime. Malone knew she wasn't trained or equipped to give the girl the expert help and advice Joss needed, but she was wise enough to know that, for now, the girl was in a good place here with her, simply feeling safe and welcome. And, again for now, that would have to be enough.

CADE WORKED in his office as long as he could stand it. Tonight was the first go-round for the competitors. Excitement was running high and tension was running higher and the noise level in the business office had ramped up right along with it.

Grabbing his hat, he stepped into the open area behind the counter, saw a line of contestants, each of which would have a different question, a different need that should have been asked, identified, and resolved much earlier than this morning. People were people and some would always leave things to the last minute. Even important things. Cade sighed and looked around for his right-hand administrator.

Aleta grinned and rolled her eyes when she caught sight of him. "Escaping?"

"Maybe for a little while. Everything under control?"

"Yes, believe it or not."

Letting some of his tension ease away, Cade headed through the glass door on the customer side of the counter. Aleta would have let him know if she needed him to stay or intervene with anyone or anything. He greeted several contestants by name on his way out but didn't slow for a chat with anyone. Even Townsend seemed to be in a hurry to escape the building as he matched Cade step for step.

The wind was an unexpected slap in the face. It had risen since the pre-dawn hours when he'd stepped into his office. But the breaking sunshine was a welcome sight. He knew he'd be dragging by the end of the day but sometime around three o'clock that morning his mind and his worries had awakened him. He'd taken a risk in moving the location of the first of the title rounds and done everything he knew to do to ensure this event was a success. Failure wasn't an option but success wasn't a given. That fact left him somewhere between 'this had been a sound decision' and 'what the hell had he been thinking'.

Cade didn't have a destination in mind but acknowledged he was hoping to run across Malone and wish her well for her run tonight. She was a skillful rider with talented horses. He wasn't sure which of them she would be astride for this first of six go-rounds but he knew she would have each of those six runs plotted and planned. The ground would be as perfect as the arena crew could make it but barrel racing in and of itself held danger. A horse could slip or stumble or spook. Fans who were also competitors would know and hold their breath start to finish. Fans who weren't would see the splash and sparkle of tack and wardrobe and think it all a wonderful show. Which it undoubtedly was. Cade hoped the spills and thrills stayed with the rough stock riders. They expected, trained, and prepared themselves for it even as they hoped to avoid it with their skill and their luck.

The thought of seeing Malone, even if only briefly, had Cade whistling lightly as he strolled around the corner of the bronc holding pen.

Oh, posh and bother, what is it with these male humans? Can't this dullard see that Joss isn't interested in his attentions? I hope I don't find it necessary to intervene but if she gets any more uncomfortable, I'll be forced to toss my hat into the ring, as it were.

"Come on, honey, pull that old thing off your head and let's see that pretty hair. I'm betting with all that green in those eyes of yours, you're a true blonde, right? Or maybe a red head. I'm partial to red heads."

Does the pillock think that grin and wink are disarming the object of his attentions? She's growing more and more tense, backing away from him but she's backing herself into a corner and hasn't realized that, quite literally, her back will soon be against a wall. And, as he takes another step toward her, she takes another step back.

Blimey. I do believe it will be necessary for me to intervene.

"Back off, jackass!"

I turn as does Joss' tormentor to see an admirer of a different ilk leaping over the fence railing to get to her. I recognize Luke whose attentions have been nothing but polite and admiring toward our girl these past few days.

"Get lost, Roberts. Busy here, in case you didn't notice."

And isn't this just lovely with the two chaps facing off for a kerfuffle and Joss looking like she wants to lose her lunch.

"Walker." The tone of Luke's voice gives fair warning. "I mean it. Leave her alone."

"I don't see no ring on her finger or through her nose."

"You also don't seem to see that she wants to be left alone."

The pillock shrugs and turns his back on Luke, implying he perceives him to be no threat. He smirks at Joss. "That right, sweetheart? You really don't want to let me see what color your hair is under that ugly hat?" He dares another step closer.

Well, that's all it's going to take it seems. Luke's hand reaches out and spins the young tosser about. Luke doesn't land the first punch as the tosser comes around swinging and connects right solidly with a cheekbone. However, Luke does land the second and, if that crunch isn't a broken nose, I'll be much surprised.

I look across at Joss. Her face is ashen and devoid of any expression. This is all quite, quite enough. It's time I take matters in hand. With my customary strength and agility – which I will admit sometimes surprises even me - I leap into the fray, finding purchase on the thick shoulders. His build resembles that of a young, strong bull as does his current state of rage. I sink my claws deep in warning. He grabs for me but I fear not for myself so much as for Luke who almost certainly doesn't have the killer instinct I sense in my target.

"What in the hell *is going on here?"*

Thank goodness. I recognize that booming voice. Mr. Silver Eyes has arrived on the scene and Townsend with him growling with a menace quite unlike his normal peacefulness. I believe there may be more to the canine than I first suspected. And, if the fury in his voice is any indication, Mr. Silver Eyes will soon have this matter in hand. Thank goodness the two have sense enough to respond to the tone of authority and drop their hands to their sides before another punch is thrown.

While the matter of fisticuffs is dealt with, I must attend a very shaken Joss.

CADE LOOKED from one battered face to the other. He recognized both of them. "Either of you care to answer my question?"

"He was upsetting Joss," Luke finally answered.

"Bullshit!" Walker glared and rubbed at his shoulder where Trouble's claws had been buried. Blood trickled from his busted nose. "I was just flirting, just having a little fun with a good-looking girl."

Townsend growled again and Cade spoke quietly to him. Townsend reluctantly sat at Cade's heels, ready to enter the fray if allowed.

"Fun at her expense, you jerk. Didn't you even care about the look on her face! She didn't want you to pull her cap off."

At Luke's words, Cade glanced at Joss and anger churned. Cade pulled out his cell phone and started making phone calls, his hard glare daring either combatant to take a step in any direction. The first call was to Malone and all he said was "Joss needs you," telling her where to find them. The second call was to Luke's dad. He hesitated on the third call, looking at Walker. "You're one of Asa's hands, aren't you? Roland Walker?" He got a sullen nod in response and placed the third call.

When Frank and Asa arrived within moments of each other, he told all of them not to go far because he had things to say and decisions to make. Then he focused on Malone who came into sight at a sprint, taking in the scene and putting Joss behind her protectively and turning her glare from one battered face to the other just as Cade had done. But her gaze held as much disappointment as anger when it settled on Luke who looked down at his boots.

Cade walked over to Malone and spoke softly. "I'm sorry this happened. I'll deal with it and check on Joss as quick as I can."

Malone hesitated, very much looking as if she'd like to throw some punches herself. Cade had no doubt she'd make them count. Fortunately for all, like Cade, she knew that wasn't what Joss needed from her.

Cade was surprised when Trouble, after glancing from him to Malone, chose to stay behind as Malone put her arm around Joss' shoulder and steered her away. Maybe the cat wasn't done with the two combatants either.

After a brusque, "Come with me," Cade led the way back to

the show office, leaving Asa and Walker in the waiting area while he spoke privately with Luke and his dad in his office.

Trouble perched upon a window ledge behind the desk, while his Aussie took point midway between the desk and the door, sitting at attention as if ready for anything untoward. Cade didn't expect any problems but then he hadn't expected to come upon Joss looking ill while two young men swung fists at one another either.

Looking across his desk at the father and son seated in the most uncomfortable chairs he'd ever seen, Cade knew he had a hard decision to make and he wasn't entirely sure what he was going to do. He frowned at Luke. "You know the rules about fighting on the grounds, about physical violence of any kind."

"Yes, sir."

Frank scowled and opened his mouth as if to protest or defend his son, then closed it again. He knew Luke faced expulsion which would put an end to both of their hopes and dreams for these circuit finals as well as the association finals later. Not just for this year but indefinitely into the future.

Cade was glad Frank held his peace and let the boy make his own path through an unpleasant and potentially devastating set of circumstances. The simple, quiet response impressed Cade. Luke wasn't going to make any excuses for himself. Nor was he going to apologize for coming to Joss' aid.

Trouble appeared equally impressed. He leapt from the window sill where he had positioned himself upon entering and walked to sit down beside Luke. He met Cade's glance and Cade almost felt reprimanded. At the least, he felt challenged. He repressed the smile that wanted to emerge. The cat's antics and perceived judgement on events might be entertaining but the situation they were in was anything but a smiling matter.

"I gathered from your comments earlier that your intent was to protect Joss from Walker's unwanted attentions. You happened on a situation you didn't create and you reacted to it."

Luke hunched his shoulders and said again, "Yes, sir," adding, "I didn't throw the first punch but only because he beat me to it." He looked up and met Cade's gaze evenly. "I would have. I wanted to hit him."

Frank hung his head at his son's admission.

"Fair enough." Cade leaned back in his seat. "Ever been in trouble before, Luke? School? Anywhere?"

"No, sir."

Again, Frank looked like he wanted to speak and Cade decided to give him that chance. "You got anything you want to say."

Frank sighed. "I taught my boy to take up for himself and for others. I won't fault him for what he did and I won't blame you for what you need to do. But I will say this to you and anyone else, Luke's a good kid, no trouble – just like he told you. God's truth on that. He's a straight A student and works harder every day after school and all summer than half the men on my payroll." He looked at his son. "And I want *him* to know that I'm proud of him, right here, right now, for coming to that girl's aid. Damned proud."

"I am, too." Cade said it so softly that it took a moment with both of them for the words to sink in.

Luke's head jerked up. "I can compete?"

"You can compete. Rules are rules for a reason, though, so you'll pay a fine. One hundred dollars of your money, not your dad's."

"Thank you, Mr. Delaney." Though Luke didn't smile, relief shone in his eyes and his shoulders no longer looked as if they bore the weight of the world.

Cade stood and walked with them to the door, shaking Frank's hand before he opened it. As they walked out, he gestured for Asa and Walker to come in. He didn't miss the dark look that Walker aimed at Luke.

Cade rubbed the back of his neck as the two took the same

seats across from his desk. Asa looked disgusted but Walker's expression was plain pissed-off.

Walker was likely only a few years older than Luke, but he was hardened by work and experience. Cade planned to be fair to both but took a different approach with Walker than with Luke. "Tell me what happened, Roland."

"That punk roper threatened me."

Cade kept his expression neutral. "Why would he do that?"

"Reckon he's got the hots for that girl works for Ms. Malone. Didn't like me flirting with her."

"Was she enjoying your flirtation?"

"Huh," Walker seemed to sense a trap and stalled for time. "What do you mean?"

"Just what I asked. Was she enjoying your attention, smiling at you, flirting back?"

"What did that little jackass tell you when he and his dad were in here?"

Walker's tone had turned belligerent. Trouble hissed. Townsend made a throaty sound that was not quite, but almost, a growl.

"Shut up, Roland, and answer the question." Asa looked disgusted.

Walker hunched his shoulder. "Maybe she would have if Roberts had stayed out of it."

"And maybe she wouldn't have. What then?"

"Aw, hell." Walker leaned back in his chair, crossed his arms over his chest. His glare made it plain that he didn't plan to answer any more of Cade's questions.

Cade looked at Asa. "You're an old friend. A good one. I won't tell you who to hire and who to fire. That's your call. But I will tell you to send this one back to the ranch if you plan to keep him on. I don't need him here."

Walker stood up before either of the older men had a chance.

"You're going to be sorry about this. I didn't do anything wrong. And that punk Luke's going to be sorry to."

"Shut up, damn it." Asa's tone brooked no argument as he stood and slapped his hat on his head. He shook Cade's hand and thanked him. He placed a hard hand on Walker's shoulder, propelling him through the door that Cade held open for their exit.

Cade had that feeling of being watched and turned to find Trouble taking his measure. When the cat stood and stretched, Cade suspected he'd passed some kind of test.

CHAPTER NINE

Malone fit her western hat a bit more snugly on her head and took a deep breath. She fought the urge to dismount and check her girth or the wrap on the front boots. She'd checked both only moments ago. So much was riding on this moment, so much preparation and hard work for this talented gelding's owner, for Malone herself. They were as ready as they would ever be. Malone heard her name on the loudspeaker as being next to run. Another deep breath and it was time to move into the alley. No time, no need to check anything. Time to go.

The gelding held tight in the turns, flicked his ears and listened to every quietly spoken request, heeded every light touch on the reins, every easy nudge of a booted heel. Malone marveled that, even with the stakes this high, she was relaxed, thinking and acting rather than reacting. It was a good run. She knew it before they reached and rounded the third barrel. Their time was going to be good, something to be proud of, and, if she was blessed, something that would result in another paycheck.

As she passed the timers and slowed her horse, she sensed rather than saw the cowboy step from the side of the alleyway just beyond the gate and, for a moment, her heart lifted and she felt like that teenaged girl again. But it wasn't Cade who reached up to put a steadying hand on the gelding's reins.

"Great run, Malone."

She sighed, irritated at her own disappointment, and swung down from the saddle. "I thought you were in hiding."

Tyge gave her a familiar lopsided grin that did nothing to hide the look of strain in his eyes. "Too much unfinished business."

For a long moment, Malone said nothing as she studied his face, the lines that hadn't been as deep the last time she'd seen him. She'd cared a lot for him once upon a time. A part of her would probably always care – at least a little. But that was a road she wouldn't travel again. "Just keep me out of it, will you?"

"That's what I'm trying to do, babe. I promise."

Malone turned to walk away.

"I need you to call me if anybody bothers you."

Swinging back on one heel, Malone felt an all-too-accustomed and unwelcome rise of tension. "I have a feeling if you stay away from me, I won't have any problem."

Tyge looked at her a long moment. "If I thought that was true, you'd never have to lay eyes on me again. I swear to God. I need you to be careful. Please?"

Malone could feel his stare on her back as she led the gelding away. Joss caught up with her halfway to the barn, her face flushed with excitement and admiration. "You're holding the lead, Malone!"

Despite the exchange with Tyge, it wasn't as much effort as Malone thought it would be to smile at Joss' enthusiasm. "There's a few more super nice horses to go," she cautioned but, still, it *had* been a truly good run.

She ran her hand along the gelding's neck as she and Joss walked companionably. Malone crooned her pleasure to the horse and smiled her thanks to those she passed who congratulated her on having a fast, clean pattern.

"You have a lot of friends," Joss commented as they reached the barn.

"We're as much family as friends, I think. We compete in the same circuit, spend a lot of time on the road together. There's always someone to lend a helping hand. If somebody needs me, I stop what I'm doing and help where I can."

"But you're competing against each other."

Malone chuckled. "Not really. Not most of us. We're competing against the clock. Or ourselves. I'm never out to beat any other barrel racer, just always trying to beat my own last performance."

Joss fell silent and Malone supposed she'd given the girl food for thought. Going for casual, she said, "I didn't get to watch the calf roping. How did Frank and Luke do, do you know?"

"Third, I think. That's good, isn't it?"

Well, that answered her question. Joss had cared enough to watch Luke rope and enough to pay attention to the other times to figure out where he was sitting in the go-round. But all she said was, "Just *being* here is good. Pulling a check for third place is pretty fantastic."

They turned a corner in the barn and Cade straightened from his comfortable prop against the stall, Trouble and Townsend at his feet. Malone felt that lift again and fought to quell it.

"Nice job." Simple words.

Malone smiled. "Thanks."

"Shall I unsaddle?" The hint of impatience in Joss' tone made Malone wonder how long she and Cade had been standing there staring at each other.

"I've got this," Malone said. "Why don't you start getting ready for the reception?"

Joss frowned at her. "I'm not going."

"Of course, you are. All of the contestants and their families go." Malone had thought Joss was adapting to the family atmosphere of the rodeo crowd and was dismayed at her refusal.

Besides that, Joss would be better with her than alone in the trailer half the night. When Joss' expression turned mulish, Malone tried tempting her. "Luke will be looking all over for you."

"I'm not a contestant or family."

"You're my family at the moment."

Malone was almost surprised when Cade broke in. "You'll be with the two of us, Joss. It will be fine. It's a fun event, food and a band and it only lasts a couple of hours. You'll enjoy yourself. I'll make sure of that. Go get ready. I'll help Malone."

And just like that, Malone realized, he'd paired them together. That didn't set well with her but now wasn't the time to argue the point. She wanted Joss to be comfortable enough to go with her. Besides, there was something in Cade's tone that caught and turned her attention. He wanted to talk with her about Joss, most likely this morning's incident.

Joss wavered, looking from one to the other. Her gaze came to rest on Malone. "I don't know what to wear."

Malone tilted her head, thinking through the clothes she'd brought on the trip. "Find some leggings or jeggings. There's a long emerald green sweater in one of the drawers or the closet. You'll like it and it will look great on you. I'll be there soon."

As Joss turned to go, Malone noticed Trouble leave his cozy position in the stall shavings to follow. She thought he gave Cade's Australian Shepherd a supercilious look but she had too much on her mind to dwell on that.

She tied the gelding and began untacking him. "What happened with Joss?" She had deliberately not asked the girl any questions and Joss wasn't ready to talk about it.

Cade sighed as he lifted the saddle from the gelding's back. "A punk cowboy messed with her a little. Wanted to see her hair and apparently got a little obnoxious in his insistence."

"Apparently?" Malone fought to keep hold of her temper.

"Either that or Luke over reacted. When I got there, they

were taking swings at each other. A couple of them connected. Joss was pretty shaken up but not harmed."

"Who is he?"

Cade laughed softly, "And at the end of that question, I hear the unspoken death threat."

Malone laid her forehead against the gelding's warm neck. That was exactly what she was feeling but she didn't say so. She felt Cade touch her hair.

"I'm almost sorry I can't turn you lose on him. Roland Walker is one of Asa's hands. I told Asa to get him off the grounds and out of here. It didn't matter if he fired him or sent him back to the ranch but he wasn't working the event."

She stepped back. That should have prompted Cade to drop his hand but he twined his fingers in her hair and tugged gently until she moved closer. For a moment, she let herself lean against his chest. With a deep breath, she straightened and said, "Go away, Cade. This isn't going to happen."

"It just did," he told her softly before he let her go.

She wouldn't let herself watch him walk away. But she wanted to.

IT WOULD BE MOST *helpful if I had more information. But, alas, so it is at the beginning of any investigation. I must start with nothing, putting little together with little more, and produce amazing answers and astounding deductions. It is, quite simply, what I do. And I do it well.*

But a starting point is critical. Unfortunately, I have more than one, and everything appears to be unrelated. As much as I enjoy the tempting layout of food, I must take this opportunity whilst competitors and rodeo staff are entertained to nose about a bit. But one last visit to the Amazonian brunette manning the generous display of roasted meats would not be amiss, I'm sure. And isn't that an interesting spin of words. Why did humankind not coin the word 'womanning' when describing a person who attends to the success of a certain task? In general, I've found the female of the species to be a bit more cognizant of the critical aspects of such an undertaking.

Ah, see there! She has noticed my proximity to her post though I approach from a side angle and without fanfare. She lifts a plate and begins arranging the most delectable selections, nothing dry, nothing unappealingly spiced. Barbeque sauce, I shudder at the thought. Intuitively, she allows nothing of that nature to touch my plate. She places it on the floor beneath the table at her feet, ensuring I will not be trampled by the masses. Hers is the most popular table, though I'm not certain if that is because of the prime rib or succulent pork roast or the lovely Amazon herself.

If she treats every 'repeat' customer with the dignity, recall of preferences, and eye for comfort and safety as she does myself, then that would be explanation in itself.

Now that I am fortified, I must brave the sharp chill of late night and continue to earn my name as one of the foremost in the tomes of famous detectives. I don't aspire to replace my father who is at the very lead, but I shall not rest until I feel myself worthy of being regarded as his equal. Humankind may have placed me there, as I have heard it said, but there's no resting upon those laurels. I must earn that title in my own estimation.

I wait at one of the entrances until it opens to a pair of nicely booted feet. They are wearing the luxury of Lucchese, I do believe, that most famous Texas brand founded by Italian emigrant, Salvatore Lucchese in the 1800's. That brand has been worn by some of the most famous personages throughout the 1900's and is sought after to this day. I'm pleased at what I recall from my research into my current environment. Knowledge is power.

With a sense of fortitude, I exit and move forward on light feet toward the less traveled, business end of the facilities where stock contractors load and unload their prized animals.

I have given significant amount of thought to information Deputy Marshal Ryder shared. He implied that more than horses and cattle were being moved from place to place by some elements of the rodeo world. Drug and gun trafficking from Mexico is well-known to be heavy along the corridors that cross the lower United States. We're central to that here, *however, certain addictions are thriving throughout the continental states and drugs must reach those far flung places by some means. What better method than the ever-popular rodeo which has found a place in nearly every state if memory serves - as mine always does.*

One never knows what one might learn when humans are otherwise occupied. The odors of heroin and the like are each distinct. I'm confident in my ability to detect the smallest whiff. While humans have elected to train canines to perform certain tasks, including drug detection, I believe that is only because they have accepted the fact that felines are not amenable to learning tricks. Admittedly, it did cross my mind to bring Townie along, but only for a moment. He's a nice enough chap and not without a certain intelligence but clumsy in my estimation and this is a situation that calls for stealth.

I've no doubt I shall fare much better without his presence.

STEPPING out of the trailer with Joss, Malone acknowledged a pleasant sense of anticipation for the night ahead. There would be camaraderie and banter and laughter. And there would be music, though she had no intention of dancing. She'd loved it once and probably still did if the truth was told. It just wasn't a thing she indulged in anymore. There were many idle pleasures she no longer allowed herself. Life's lessons had been hard but she'd learned them well and felt no bitterness for the fact. Life was good and tonight she was eager to see old friends she hadn't seen in a while.

Before they'd gone more than a few steps, Joss slowed then stopped. Malone glanced her way, prepared to offer encouragement for the festivities ahead. The color had faded from the girl's face as she stared at a point just over Malone's shoulder.

Malone tensed as she turned to look. Roland Walker stood opposite her trailer, his back propped against a light pole, arms crossed in front of his chest. But where Joss undoubtedly felt fear, Malone felt only fury. "Wait here."

Joss shook her head and opened her mouth to speak but, before she could protest, Malone said firmly, "No argument."

Malone strode to where the cowboy waited with a sneer on his face. He straightened slightly when she showed no sign of stopping until she was in his face. "You moron! You complete and utter idiot."

"You'll want to be a little careful with those insults."

"No, you'll want to be a little careful, you jackass! You've got about five minutes to disappear and I'd better not ever see you so much as looking sideways at Joss again."

"What's that girl to you?"

The effrontery of the question surprised her but she didn't hesitate. "I'm not sure what you're asking me or why you think you have the right to ask but I'll tell you she's in my care. Ask someone who knows me what that means. Now get out of my sight."

For just a moment, she thought he might challenge her, but he pushed away from the pole, gave a last look toward the trailer, then turned and walked away. His footsteps echoed on the pavement as he disappeared into the dark beyond the soft glow of the security light.

CADE WALKED into the open area that had been set up for the opening night reception. The outer perimeter was distinguished by at least a dozen tables. Each was draped in black linen and laden with appetizers, meats, seafood, vegetables, or bread. Aleta had outdone herself in her instructions to the caterers. He noted with amusement that the meat tables outnumbered the remaining tables by half. Wise woman.

The DJ played a familiar country artist at an acceptable sound level but no one had taken to the dance floor. He knew they might not. Most cowboys preferred more than a couple of drinks before braving the dance floor and, though Aleta had made sure to have a good offering of higher class beer and wine available, he knew there'd be only moderate alcohol consumption tonight. This was a highly motivated group of competitors and their focus this week wasn't hard partying. They were here to win, and that meant nothing to excess. But they all enjoyed the appreciation for their hard work and their support of the association that the reception was intended to convey.

As his gaze swept the room, Cade didn't try to pretend to himself that he was doing anything but looking for one brown-haired, brown-eyed drum runner. He'd missed her for so many years it had turned into a dull ache. He'd pushed thoughts of her to the back of his mind and heart while he earned a living in the sport he loved, vacationed in places most people only dreamed of, and drifted through several long-term relationships that never quite went anywhere. And now he knew why they hadn't and none ever would. Having Malone at the back of his mind had only meant she was deeply rooted and always there. He finally accepted she always would be and he was determined to get it right this time. He only hoped she wouldn't prove just as determined to deny him that chance. Malone was one hard-headed cowgirl.

It was her hair, the rich shimmer of what should have been just brown but was so much more, that caught Cade's attention and pulled his gaze to Malone. Her back was to him and her shoulders were squared for a fight. She had Asa Morrissette in her line of sight. Cade started their way.

Asa looked as miserable as any real gentleman would be as he tried to fend off the fury of her comments. Cade heard a few of her castigations as he got closer. He understood her distress, but he also understood an employer couldn't necessarily screen his help for negative personality traits. Some, like Asa and other stock contractors, had to focus on knowledge of livestock and physical ability. They also needed hands willing to labor long, hard hours in temperature extremes from sweltering summer to winters of ice. Sometimes that came with honesty and integrity and a well-mannered disposition and sometimes it didn't.

Asa saw him coming and his eyes widened with relief. "Cade."

Malone turned at the sound of his name and Cade gave her a quick, appreciative glance. She'd traded jeans and boots for a long turquoise tunic of some sort, belted at the waist, over leggings that – while they looked warm – also looked sexy as hell. She said 'hi' but he couldn't tell if she was glad to see him. She was much too angry with Asa for any other consideration.

"Malone, all I can tell you is I'm sorry and there won't be any more trouble from Roland."

"Really? Then why was he watching my trailer when Joss and I came out tonight?"

Asa stared at her. "Are you sure? I sent him to the hotel right after it happened, told him to pack his bag and head back to the ranch at first light."

"Apparently, he didn't listen. You should have fired him, Asa."

Asa rubbed his brow. "Now, Malone, I can't fire every cowboy that acts stupid over a pretty girl. I wouldn't have anyone left to work for me except a few old timers who learned their lessons a long time ago and most the hard way. Roland acted stupid but he didn't mean any harm."

Cade suspected Asa wasn't going to get far with that argument. Nor did he like the idea that Roland had been anywhere near Joss after he'd been warned by both Cade and Asa. He'd have plenty to say to Asa later.

"Well, you'd better figure out a way to keep them in line and Roland away from Joss."

Looking disgusted, Asa jammed his head on his head. "I'll take care of Roland tonight, Malone. He won't bother you or Joss again. I can promise you that."

Malone tracked his departure with a steely gaze.

"Hey," Cade said softly. When she turned to look at him, he was pleased to see her temper fade.

"Hey, yourself."

"Joss wouldn't come?"

"No, not after seeing Roland."

"I'm sorry, Malone," and he was, "but Asa wouldn't have had that happen for the world."

"I know but, darn it, Roland Walker isn't a teenager. He's a grown man and Joss is a kid. He could see that as well as anyone. I want to pound some sense into his head."

"And Joss is more fragile than most girls her age in similar situations. She has a history Walker doesn't know about."

"I'm not sure he would act any better if he did," she said darkly.

Cade couldn't argue the point. He wasn't sure of that either.

From the speaker, he heard the tempo of the music shift. The dance floor was empty but, on impulse, Cade took a risk – a big risk – and swept Malone into a cowboy waltz. For a moment, she stayed stiff in his arms though her feet instinctively found rhythm with the music.

When he murmured in her ear, "I've wanted to do this since the wedding at Summer Valley Ranch," Malone relaxed into the dance and Cade found himself grateful to the long-ago girlfriend who had talked him into taking dance lessons with her.

Glancing down at the curve of her cheek, Cade felt a contentment he hadn't known in too many years. He had no intention of giving that up, not without a fight.

With a final slow spin as the music faded, he stopped them at the edge of the dance floor and nudged Malone so that her gaze followed his. Joss stood near the doorway, looking pretty in green, but also looking shy and a bit uncertain. Her hand was grasped by Luke who didn't look unsure in the least. Apparently, he'd done what Malone hadn't been able to do and convinced Joss to join the fun.

CHAPTER TEN

The back of the facility is no less well-appointed than what the fans see from their box office seats surrounding the competition arena. It is well-lit and properly maintained with stout railings for the livestock that it shelters. Unlike the highly trained athletes of the barrel racers and ropers and steer wrestlers, these animals are bedded down in small herds. They are no less well-tended than their counterparts but definitely not as pampered by separate lodgings.

I will say, although it looks as if serious effort has been given to cleanliness, the odor of droppings scooped up and placed in bins around these pens gives rise to the likelihood that the scent of illicit drugs would remain undetected in this area. At least to the uninitiated.

The first animals I pass are what the rodeo announcer called the broncs, though I cannot distinguish the saddle broncs from the bareback broncs. The next are bulls with wicked horns. As fierce as they seem, their manner is peaceful – with one another at least. The only restive group is the last, the young bovine for the calf-roping event. I cannot at once ascertain the cause for their fretful behavior and circle closer. Perhaps they're hungry and anxious to be fed. But, no, fresh hay fills multiple racks along the railing.

Fresh hay, fresh water, no predators. I deduce, then, it is their youth *that prevents them from settling. Those of us with some maturity understand the value of a good night's rest.*

Hmmm, not a hint - or a scent - of illegal narcotics. I won't say I've wasted my time but I must admit my efforts have produced nothing.

I turn to leave and catch a glint, a suggestion of something shiny, not in the pen but on the other side, close to the block wall of the rear of the building. I circle around to investigate though it doesn't appear large enough to be of much significance. But it's been a boring sojourn, after all, and I always strive to nurture the more inquisitive aspects of my nature, so important to a top detective.

As I draw near, an underlying odor tugs at me but I see nothing untoward. The glint that caught my eye proves to be an abandoned spur, not too fancy, with a bit of black filigree inlay, and otherwise much the same as I've seen on the competitors. Just your garden-variety, blunt-ended spur with a leather strap worn through. But I don't turn back. The smell has become all-prevailing and I realize the malodorous droppings have hidden more than the possibility of unlawful trafficking. They covered the scent of death, one so faint, as yet, that humans would not likely have detected it. But – surprising to a sleuth accustomed to the investigation of murder, mayhem and the like – there is no accompanying reek of blood.

I follow the airborne trail around a corner and find the body propped upright between two beams. This is not good. I recognize the young cowboy. There's no sign of a struggle but, as I tell myself, the chap certainly didn't break his own neck, now did he? I check to ensure the presence of an intact spur on each boot and make a mental note of the lone, abandoned one as possible evidence.

I do hope Master Luke has a good alibi as his altercation with the deceased, one Roland Walker, received much publicity. Time to find Mr. Silver Eyes and make known the death of the cowboy.

MALONE PREFERRED NOT TO ACKNOWLEDGE, even to herself, the sparkle of awareness that zinged through her every time her glance met Cade's And that seemed to happen all too often.

They'd danced, sure, and it had been nice – more than nice – but she'd 'been there, done that' with him. She didn't plan for a repeat even though they were two very different people now. And that - the differences - was part of the point. Her life had moved on from Cade and it confused her that he wanted to revisit a past that had been so hurtful, at least for her. She never thought of herself as a coward. She'd taken on and won some of life's hardest challenges. She'd carved success and happiness out of what appeared, at times, to be solid rock. But, with all that, some things took more courage than even she could boast.

Cade's popularity as director of the rodeo association gave her easy opportunity to put distance between them and she'd taken advantage of that. She found a glass of water and carried it as a buffer between herself and any other offers to hit the dance floor. Although she had no problem telling the cowboys no – she'd done it for years – it softened the refusal to claim thirst and a need to catch her breath as if she'd been dancing every dance. She wondered sometimes why they continued to ask at every opportunity.

As she chatted in a corner with long-time friends, a glimpse of black fur caught her attention and she gave a second look. Trouble wove his way through denim and leather. There was intensity to his movement that caught her eye. She chided herself he was always similarly focused in his quest for food he thought worthy of him, though she would have thought he'd had plenty earlier. When it became clear he was making a bee-line for Cade, she excused herself from the conversation and made her way back across the room where Cade was deep in conversation with one of his staff.

She'd had several conversations with Tammy Lynn since leaving the wedding and each had ended with an admonition to pay attention to Trouble. He knew things. He was with Malone for a reason. She had only to wait and he'd prove that to her.

If she believed all that, then Trouble's determination to seek out Cade should have irritated her. Instead, all she felt was resignation that fate seemed determined to keep them together tonight.

The cat reached Cade seconds before her. He stretched upward and placed his paws on Cade's jeans. Without missing a beat in his conversation, Cade idly rubbed the cat's ears and found himself swatted for his effort.

Malone smiled despite herself. Trouble had a way of making his intentions known. "Come on, Trouble, I'll go see what you've found."

Cade glanced her way, then back at Trouble. Malone was surprised by the look of acceptance in Cade's expression. It seemed they were both coming around to Trouble's unique abilities. "Why don't you wait here and I'll check out what's bothering him?"

"Nope. He's with me ... he seems to have forgotten that at the moment."

Trouble appeared to have caught a hint of the tartness of her tone. He looked up at her and blinked slowly. She wasn't sure if she should take it as an apology but it would have to do.

After a quick look around the room reassured her that Joss was well-occupied on the dance floor with Luke, Malone walked to where her jacket hung from one of the many coat racks placed near the door. She wasn't surprised when Cade's Australian Shepherd met them there. She'd noticed that, even when the dog appeared to be in solid slumber, if his master moved, he knew it.

Trouble led the way out of the warmth and music and into the beauty of the night. The wind had died with the onset of dusk and stars had overtaken the sky. It was cold but not bitterly so.

Her pulse leapt as the streak of black took them toward the barns, then settled as Trouble bypassed the one where the competitors' horses were stalled. She felt Cade's occasional glance her way, but neither had spoken since leaving the reception hall.

They passed the bucking stock and Trouble slowed his pace.

For the first time, Malone felt a slight sense of dread. Something wasn't right but she couldn't have said for sure how she knew that. She wished for a flashlight. The barn wasn't in complete dark, but the few lights that burned high along the walls weren't enough.

Trouble sat in the middle of the hall and looked up at them with a sound somewhere between growl and rumble. When he had their attention, he batted at a spur barely discernible in the dark. Cade hesitated. It could belong to anyone. Competitors lost equipment every day, a broken hook, a broken strap were common mishaps. He'd likely never find the owner. But Trouble thought it was important. Cade picked it up and slipped it into his back pocket.

Blinking, Trouble stood and led them around another corner.

Malone felt shock hit the back of her throat in the form of nausea and she swallowed hard. Cade said the ugliest word she'd ever heard him utter before pulling her into him so that the young man's body with its grotesquely twisted neck was hidden from her sight.

CADE MADE a calculated decision and hoped it wasn't a wrong one. The first call he made wasn't 911. It was to Deputy Marshal Ryder. 911 was next. His third call was to Asa Morrissette.

While he waited for the authorities to arrive, he hit Aleta's number.

"What's up, boss?" he could hear the surprise in her voice.

"I need a favor, more than one."

"Sure."

"Wrap things up and get everyone out the door as soon as you can. Tell them I hope they all rest well and wake ready for a successful round two." He checked his watch. "It's only a quarter of an hour early so hopefully no one will question."

"I'm questioning," Aleta said.

"You question everything and I'll answer – but later. I also need you to make sure the girl traveling with Malone gets to their trailer safely. Make sure she locks herself in and tell her Malone will be there soon."

"Something bad has happened, hasn't it?" Aleta's voice held gloomy resignation.

"Yeah."

"What else, boss?"

Beside him Malone's teeth chattered, though he suspected that was due more to shock than cold. "See if you can scrape up a thermos of coffee or two. All hell is fixing to break out here and we're going to have plenty of company."

He told her where they were and smiled faintly as she said, "On that, boss."

Because it had been nearly time to close the festivities for the night, he hoped he might get lucky enough that some contestants didn't hear about the death until morning. The police had been asked to come in the back entrance without lights and sirens. He'd emphasized the need to avoid panicking the livestock, but not being surrounded by several dozen contestants and event workers would be a definite benefit.

I DID NOT SUFFICIENTLY APPRECIATE the efficiencies of Mr. Silver Eyes' assistant. That was remiss of me. The statuesque red-head arrived not only with two flasks of coffee, she also brought a small offering of cream, with the chill nicely removed, for me. Even Townie wasn't forgotten, being gifted with a thick beefsteak bone.

Tsk-tsk. Ms. Rodeo cradles the coffee in her hands for warmth but seems frozen in place and does not drink. I can sympathize. I recall all too well my first glimpse of violent death. It leaves an aura not easily dispelled.

Although I don't think Mr. Silver Eyes is immune, he remains stoic as he orchestrates the comings and goings of various entities, giving directions and providing information as needed and making phone calls when requested. Periodically, he turns his gaze on the woman beside him. Whatever he is thinking remains unspoken.

An ambulance is backed with care into the narrow opening not too far from where the body, now strapped to a gurney, awaits transport. Pictures have been taken from every conceivable angle. Surfaces have been dusted for fingerprints. I have no doubt a multitude will be found with none relevant to the case. This was no clumsy deed done in a fit of rage. It takes skill to deliberately break a human neck. Skill and a cold-bloodedness that mercifully few possess. But there are benefits. It's quick. It leaves little trail. No murder weapon to discard. No blood which could be carried away in tell-tale sign.

Asa Morrissette looks as if he's been gut-punched. As Walker's employer, and with no family present, he signs the paper on the clipboard that is handed him by the ambulance driver.

As the ambulance pulls away, an officer walks up to Mr. Silver Eyes. "I'll need to speak with a Mr. Roberts now."

So at least one of the hangers-on who drifted in has told a tale out of school. I sigh. Humans rarely realize the ill effects of their gossip.

"Aleta, would you ask Luke and his father to come to my office? We'll join them there."

"I don't need his father," *the officer protests.*

"Luke is seventeen. You won't talk to him unless his father allows. Or I can go ahead and call an attorney now." *There's steel in that tone though he has been nothing but polite until now.*

The officer yields and we all troop back to the show office building. Mr. Silver Eyes places his arm around Ms. Rodeo. She doesn't lean against him but neither does she push away. I flank them on one side, Townie on the other. The canine continues to display some limited uses, I acknowledge.

Within moments, we are all crowded into one small space. Aleta quietly closes the door on us. To my surprise, though the officer glares around the room once as if counting heads, he asks no one to leave. At Mr. Silver Eyes' discreet nod, Luke's father has agreed his son can answer a few questions. I understand that reasoning. It is often these preliminary forays that set the tone for the real investigation. That twisted neck is the work of a cold-blooded - and likely professional - killer. The sooner the authorities realize that Luke doesn't fit the bill, the sooner they will direct their effort more appropriately.

The officer flips open his notepad and begins asking questions any decent mystery writer could have crafted. Why had Luke and the deceased traded blows earlier in the day? Had they known each other previously? When was the last time Luke saw the deceased? Where was Luke during the two hours prior to the body being found?

With his father's hand resting upon his shoulder, Luke acquits himself well, remaining quiet-spoken and polite and without hesitation in his responses. His youth comes through as surely as the unlikelihood that he had the skill or the bulk or the sheer ugliness of nature it had taken to break Walker's neck, much less the time. He'd been with his father or friends during a timeline he was able to recount without hesitation. The only response that draws even a hint of consternation is when Luke told of being with Joss, talking her into attending the reception and escorting her there.

The officer glances around in resignation. "I suppose this Joss is also seventeen."

"Sixteen," *Ms. Rodeo says,* "And asleep." *I surmise her concern. If questioned by the authorities, Joss may well disappear in a panic.*

The officer closes his writing pad at last and looks around. "I'll expect to have all of you here and available for any additional questions in the days to come. And Ms. Joss as well."

I peek around the corner of the door as he exits and am not in the least surprised to see the ever-efficient Aleta hand him a thermos and what looks to be two nicely wrapped sandwiches to take on his way. His surprise turns to gratitude and I note the lines of weariness on his face as he thanks her.

Mr. Silver Eyes sends the Roberts off to get some rest then nods to his assistant. "You can show Ryder in now."

"Thank God." *I detect a wealth of feeling in those two words. I gather the good deputy marshal has not been the most patient of visitors.*

Ah, well, one down and one to go.

RYDER GLARED AT HIM. "What does that mean? The cat found the body? I asked what you and Ms. Summers were doing, both of you dressed for the festivities you abandoned, strolling through the barns where a dead guy just happened to be?"

"We weren't strolling," Cade said patiently. "We were following Trouble. I told you, he came to get us."

"Bullshit."

The urge to grin took Cade by surprise. Nothing funny about death and even less about murder, but Ryder's expression was priceless. Cade suspected the other man was more than a little irritated that he'd had to wait his turn to grill Cade and Malone. He wasn't on the scene officially. He was there because Cade had been cooperative enough to call him. He owed Cade that, plus the spur with the leather strap which could prove to be worth something or nothing at all. Trouble had seemed to think it was evidence of something. Cade wasn't convinced either way.

Ryder looked from Cade to Malone and back again before his gaze flicked to the black cat in the window sill.

"You think this dead guy has something to do with my investigation?"

"I don't know if it does or not. You asked me to call you if I saw anything I didn't like. I damned sure don't like what I saw in that barn." Cade could feel Malone's gaze on him and knew she'd be demanding explanations of her own as soon as they were alone.

"So, you don't believe Walker was killed because of a fight over a girl? That's what was being hinted out there among some of the other contestants."

"I have no idea why he was killed, but I'm confident Luke Roberts wasn't the person who broke his neck."

Malone straightened at that. "Luke didn't kill anyone. He's a good kid."

"But he punched the daylights out of the guy earlier today."

These were all questions they'd already answered. Multiple times. The answers weren't going to change with retelling. Cade stretched his back and shoulders and rolled his neck, trying to relieve some of the tension. It was hours past midnight after an already long day. He knew Malone must be exhausted.

He got to his feet, forcing Ryder to do the same. "Look, I've told you everything I know. Just like I told the police everything I know. Now I'm going to ask you to go do your job and let me do mine which has little to do with a murder investigation."

CHAPTER ELEVEN

Malone opened her eyes and froze. Joss! It was full daylight and she was alone in the trailer. Well, not quite. Trouble sat at the foot of the bed where she'd collapsed fully dressed too few hours ago.

She let herself relax. The cat had proven a good barometer. Joss was someplace safe and Malone had horses to tend. She glanced at the clock, relieved that it was still early and that she felt more rested than she would have thought.

Minutes later, dressed for the morning chill, she opened the door of her living quarters. Joss rose from one of the two canvas folding chairs she'd placed close to the door. She handed Malone a thermos and a wrapped sandwich. Her large, expressive eyes were troubled. "Horses are fed. I hand-walked Diablo but he'll need to be ridden."

"We'll ride everyone lightly except Scoop. I'll hand-walk him." The sleek sorrel would be her competition run tonight.

Malone opened the wrapping and bit into warm bacon and cheese and eggs with real pleasure. Most of the time she cooked in her tiny kitchenette but this was a welcome treat and time was valuable considering how much of the morning she'd lost. Although, it appeared Joss had made up for that on her behalf.

Because Trouble didn't bat an eye as she savored her food, she knew he'd been happy with his breakfast. He'd probably had two of the croissants to her one.

"How did you decide who you're going to ride which night?"

"I ran Diablo first because he can handle just about any ground but he skims across the top of fresh dirt easier than some of the others who like to dig deep. And, yes, he always needs to be ridden the morning after a run. It settles him back down. This ground is going to get deeper every night, not in a bad way because the crew will keep it good for the finals, but some deeper. Because of that, I'll run Jaz on the last evening because she digs in hardest. The ones in between were pretty much a toss-up."

She finished her breakfast and opened the thermos, sighing with real pleasure at the deep, rich aroma of it. Not coffee. A latte. "Thank you for this."

Joss shook her head. "Luke brought it." She hesitated then added in a rush, "He didn't kill that guy."

"Of course he didn't."

The teen's shoulders relaxed visibly and Malone studied her over the rim of the thermos. "All of this is going to be okay, Joss. It's truly ugly and I feel more than bad for Roland Walker's family but the police will figure it out." She hesitated. "But I'll need you to be careful until they do. Stay close to me and keep the trailer locked when you're inside alone."

Joss looked at her with those young-old eyes and Malone remembered she was talking to a girl who'd probably seen things that would make Malone shudder. She *hoped* that one day Joss would trust enough to share. What she *feared* was that one day Joss would disappear as soundlessly as she had landed in Malone's life. For now, though, she was Malone's to protect.

Trouble accompanied them to the barn where things were busy for the next few hours. Malone was pleased to realize that

Joss no longer ducked and turned away when acquaintances stopped to speak with them.

After one such exchange, as they rode two of the horses at a quiet walk, side-by-side, Joss said, "You're popular."

"I've been round longer than many and made a lot of friends." A few enemies, too, she acknowledged to herself, but it had never been intentional.

"The tiny blonde on the huge roan, that's who beat your time last night, isn't it?"

"Yep. She's ridden that mare to the finals three years in a row. They're an awesome duo."

"But ...?"

Malone chuckled. "But nothing as far as the competitor or the competition here goes. Courtney works as hard as anyone I know and gives everything she's got every time and she's friendly, always willing to extend a helping hand. It would scare me to have everything pinned to one horse. She's got a couple of young horses she started hauling this year and they're showing promise but she keeps them on the back burner. The others she has here are loaners she's barely ridden. She'll probably ride her good horse every other night which isn't too much – only three runs but it would make me nervous."

"She seemed a little snooty to me. I was watching everybody when you were warming up. When the other girls tried to talk with her, she would cut them off and move her horse away."

"Most of that is nerves. You'll find a lot of competitors want to be alone with their horse right before a run. It helps them focus. Others would rather be distracted with conversation. Courtney is actually very friendly, not snobbish at all. But she gets tense when the stakes are higher and the circuit finals are almost as high as it gets."

"I don't care. I still hate that she had the fastest time."

Malone laughed and shook her head. "No single competitor is

going to pull first place at all six goes here. I've never seen it done in any of the events. I'm not done, Joss, no worries."

As she eased the horse beneath her to a canter, she was aware of Joss heading back to the barn for her next mount. She felt pleased she hadn't even had to tell the girl what the horse had needed in pace and duration of this morning's ride. Joss was picking up more and more regarding the animals Malone had entrusted to her.

For a little while Malone was able to shake off the nightmare of the murder but as she slowed Diablo to a trot then a walk, she felt a gaze fixed on her. She glanced around but all she saw were fellow competitors, walking, talking, or otherwise focused on their own tasks. No one who appeared interested, much less overly interested, in her.

The feeling stayed and she wasn't surprised to find Tyge waiting for her when she led the untacked gelding into his stall. A bit unnerved, perhaps, but not surprised.

Tyge rose from a crouched position in the corner of the stall and moved to the opening as she maneuvered the muscular horse around him. So, he wasn't afraid to be seen. But when she gave him a searching glance, she could see that his eyes were shadowed. Haunted, even.

"What have you done?"

"I didn't kill Walker."

She sighed. "I know that." And she did. Just as she knew Luke had not. Tyge skated the line on respectability but there was no meanness to him. There never had been. She slipped the halter off and watched as Diablo shook vigorously then moved to his hay bag. Too many thoughts crowded her mind.

"But you're involved. Somehow." She didn't make it a question and he didn't answer.

"Not with murder. That's not me, Malone."

Wordlessly, she picked up the bucket that held Diablo's

grooming gear and brushed past Tyge. He moved out of her way while she secured the stall door.

When he fell into step beside her, she whirled on him in exasperation. "What do you want from me, Tyge? You called me in a panic, warning me to be careful, begging me not to tell some nameless someone where you were. Then you're here in the wide open and not hiding at all. And a man is murdered. Murdered! What the *hell* is going on?" Instead of rising, her voice had gotten lower and lower with the apprehension that held her in its grip, so low the last few words had to be forced past the constriction in her throat.

Tyge put both hands on her shoulders and, for one brief moment, she saw a different man, a man who'd once been front and center in her world. He'd cared about her hopes and her ambitions as much as he'd cared about his own. And he'd had them. Tyge was going to be a world champion. He had the skill and the physical ability and the mental determination. And he'd been close, so close. Malone had respected that man, shared her dreams with him, trusted her future to him.

That trust had long since turned to dust and been swept away with the wind.

For a moment, she thought he'd walk away, just as he'd always done before. That was Tyge. Take the easiest way out.

He surprised her when he didn't. "Sometimes a man has to be more than he thinks he can be. More than the woman he loves thought he ever could be. I'm in trouble. I'll admit that. And I don't want you dragged into it. I'm here to make sure that doesn't happen. I didn't kill Walker. He wasn't a threat to me. But I'd kill for you, Malone."

She felt no warmth at his declaration. She couldn't be moved by words of caring from him. Not anymore. Not ever again. Particularly when coupled with mention of murder. Instead, ice touched her spine. Tyge wasn't loquacious or eloquent. If he bothered to speak, it was with intent. Something bad was going on around him and he'd brought it close to her and to Joss.

Frustration made her feel harsh and the harshness was reflected in her tone. "Maybe if you disappeared again, any threat to me would disappear as well."

"If I believed that, Malone, I'd make it happen, no matter how much money they owe me."

Money. She tried not to think of all the things that could be tied to money and murder.

She took a deliberate step back and Tyge's hands dropped from her shoulders. His look of regret spoke volumes.

As he turned away, she sighed and shook her head. She had things to do and no time to worry over things she couldn't control.

She started forward but was stopped in her tracks as the large black cat stepped into her path. She'd been so intent on her exchange with Tyge, she hadn't been aware of Trouble's arrival. He swung his green gaze from her to Tyge's retreating figure and back again.

Trouble growled softly and she said, "Yeah, me, too. I don't like it one bit but there's not a damn thing I can do."

Oh, dear, I take that to mean she has no intention of sharing this exchange and that could be a serious mistake. I do understand not taking it to the authorities. She has nothing concrete to offer, after all. Nor do I think Mr. Silver Eyes more astute or better able to solve this mystery. I do, however, suspect that each will have different pieces of this puzzle and will need to work together to fit them all together for the final analysis.

Most unfortunately, this is all as I suspected. There's a very real threat here and the danger is tied to this Tyge and to the chap who got his neck broken. Or rather the person who broke it for him. Joss' precipitous arrival on the scene, which is what occasioned my involvement in the lives of these people, appears to be nothing but a twist of fate and, yet, something warns me to remain wary of happenstance.

My senses are on hyper-alert but I believe all is safe for now. It is daylight and Joss is extraordinarily vigilant for a young human female. That is most certainly due to whatever dark deed sent her our way initially. I think if I am to learn much of anything for now, I'd best tag along with Tyge. Ouch. I can only wince at that feeble alliteration though it was certainly not intentional.

The air is more enjoyable this morning, crisp and clear without the wind clawing at my fur. More what I expect on a nice autumn day. Which reminds me that the holidays will be upon us soon and it behooves me to solve this case so that I may return in time for my favorite festivities. I have fond memories of batting Christmas ornaments from low-hanging branches, always careful to discern the unbreakable from the breakable as I was never a destructive kitten. These days it's not the bright-colored décor that most appeals, although I do enjoy the twinkling of colorful fairy lights. No, for me, the pleasures of the season have become the edible delicacies, the slivers of tenderloin, the tidbits of well-spiced ham, and even, on occasion, pâté. I prefer mine warm but humans seem to have a preference for it chilled. Fortunately, my Tammy Lynn caters to my preferences.

Equally enjoyable, now that I am coming into maturity, is the convivial gathering of old friends with new. On occasion, we have guests who stay a night or two. I eagerly anticipate those who bring with them some of my favorite female felines. There's healthy pleasure in sharing a cozy corner of a loveseat on a night where the windowpanes reflect winter's chill. But I grow indelicate.

And rather far off topic from my mission ... although I do anticipate Ms. Rodeo and Mr. Silver Eyes numbering among those I'll see at the occasional future holiday gathering, whether paired or individually though I have my thoughts on that. And, for those merry reunions to occur, I must ensure their safety through the perils to come.

Upon my word, this Tyge appears to be ambling with no direction in mind. The layout of the structure is well suited to that, I might add.

Whoever designed this barn may have had method to his madness, but it eludes me. The twists and turns are that of a rabbit warren.

In the same moment I realize we have circled the same space over again, I comprehend that Tyge's gaze is searching and far more keen and intent than his ambling steps would imply. It may be that his goal is to 'accidentally' cross paths with someone. It is inexcusable in me that I didn't pay attention sooner to more than his boots dawdling along.

And, there! Tyge hesitates then moves toward a cowboy who wears jangling spurs and a belt buckle that – as they say – is bigger than Texas. The cowboy moseys just ahead, a cell phone to his ear. Mosey is a nice cowboy word I heard on the television and I do like to stretch my vocabulary. Tyge takes advantage of the cowboy's inattention. With hand to shoulder, he turns him about with a sharp aggression and the phone goes flying from the other's hand.

"You owe me," *Tyge says angrily.*

No mincing of words with Tyge this morning.

"Only thing you got comin' to you is an ass-whooping."

Tyge bristles a bit like an English bulldog at those words. "You want to try, asshole? Go ahead." *No one's fool, but equally no one's epitome of gentlemanly engagement, Tyge doesn't wait for the first punch to be thrown after issuing the challenge. And he makes his first strike count. The 'jangling spurs' cowboy staggers and puts a hand to a nose that is no doubt as broken as it is bloody.*

"You bastard."

"Yeah," *Tyge taunts,* "that's me, a son of a bitch of a son of a bitch. But quit whining and bring it."

Unfortunately, it appears that the cowboy will have help 'bringing it'. Without warning, there are two additional pairs of hands, one on either side, holding Tyge immobile as the cowboy swaggers close.

Tyge has two things in his favor. He has shown a tenderness for Ms. Rodeo, which must carry weight with me, and I have an affinity for symmetry, even in fisticuffs. Three to one is not symmetrical. Adding another will not even things out but will bring it a bit closer, especially if that other is me.

My leap, quite agile I feel I may boast, lands me squarely against a thick neck. I dig my claws into a meaty shoulder and close sharp teeth on a vulnerable ear. The bellow the thug emits can only be likened to that of one of the rodeo bulls as it exits the chutes with an unwanted rider on his back. As thug one spins in confusion, I make the leap for thug two and am disappointed as I miss my intended point of landing. My claws dig for purchase through hair in need of a good soaping. The squall that erupts is satisfying, as I sink into a correspondingly unwashed scalp.

I spring to a fence railing and watch as Tyge takes advantage of the pain and confusion I have inflicted with my distraction. He wades in with both fists flying and is soon given the gratification of seeing all three hoodlums fleeing.

To my complete disappointment, Tyge gives me no credit for my intervention. Though he stands there with abrasions that are bad but not as bad as they could have been, he sneers at their flight then turns away, somewhat unsteadily, but on his feet. And not so much as a thank you do I get for coming to his aid!

All I can do is remind myself that I didn't intervene for Tyge as much as for Ms. Rodeo. Even so, I cannot help but feel the sting of insult as I stalk away in determination that my path will cross Mr. Silver Eyes. Perhaps he has found something of more import than saving an ungrateful wretch from a beating that was likely well-deserved!

CHAPTER TWELVE

"I want to put an undercover agent on your staff."
Cade's instinctive response was an abrupt refusal but he tempered his words to Ryder because the man had a job to do and Cade respected that. "I don't have a place or a function for another person. My team would be suspicious."

A car whizzed by and Cade snapped his fingers to bring Townsend a bit closer to heel. They were on the sidewalk between the perimeter of the expansive grounds and the very busy streets of the city.

When Ryder had called at an early hour, Cade had agreed to meet but away from his office. The deputy marshal could no more hide his military bearing than Townsend could shed his canine nature. Roland Walker's death had left everyone on edge and Cade needed their attention focused on the event and not the investigation that swirled around them. Distraction made for mistakes and mistakes made for failure and sometimes injuries. The contestants had worked hard to get here. They didn't need to meet with inefficiencies in the event staff.

"Deputy Armand is twenty-eight years old and looks ten years younger. She's been around horses all her life. You'll introduce her with intentional vagueness as some veterinary student who is kin to one of the city officials. You've just been advised she's always given part-time work at any large equine events in the area. She'll take care of the rest of her disguise and her investigation."

"You want me to lie to my team."

"Damn it, Delaney. You've got one dead body here. You're just as likely to have another. But those are the bad guys and I'm not real concerned with their well-being. So, yeah, I want you to lie to your team if it will help me nail the guilty and protect the innocent."

Cade rubbed the back of his neck, feeling the pressure of what he was being asked to do stack up with the pressure inherent to directing an event that was the culmination of a yearlong effort for the finalists. He and his team were dedicated to ensuring the event itself created no hardships that might hinder their drive for success. But Ryder was asking him to help with something that could put a murderer behind bars and more. Ryder's investigation couldn't prevent, but it might at least slow, the distribution of drugs and the untold suffering that came with that distribution. And if it were guns, rather than drugs, the stakes were even higher.

Hell. "Alright. Send her."

His phone buzzed in his pocket. Aleta. Hopefully not with a problem. He turned away from Ryder as he answered.

Aleta went straight to the point. "There's a plain-clothes officer here. I verified his credentials. He's in your office." He heard the hesitation in her voice as she added, "He's got Malone Summers penned up in there, apparently planning to grill her. He asked me to wait about thirty minutes before calling you to meet with him."

Good for her Aleta and her unswerving loyalty. "Thank you for not waiting. I'm on my way." All sides of law enforcement were on the job early today. He turned back toward the show grounds and Ryder fell into step with him.

"Problem?"

"Nothing unforeseen. Our local investigating officer has shown up."

Ryder grinned unexpectedly. "He wouldn't be happy to see me here. The locals get a bit touchy about jurisdiction."

"Aren't you going to need any information he can gather?"

"Not much for him to find, is there? No weapon, no trace, not even potential fingerprints. Possible DNA under the victim's fingernails, if he had a chance to fight, but nothing to match it with. But, yeah, I'll want to see what he comes up with but desk jockeys can deal with transfer of information. I'll be on my way for now but I'll be in touch." When they reached the parking area, the marshal simply stepped away between the rows of trucks and trailers.

Cade wondered wryly if the man had intended that last comment to be reassuring. It was anything but. Cade supposed he could add juggling two opposing law enforcement agencies to his tension level.

Keeping his stride long but easy, Cade made his way across the grounds, threading through and greeting contestants and staff but not stopping. He wondered if any of the familiar faces hid ugly secrets that would come to light in the next few days. It sickened him to think that people he knew and trusted might be involved in hauling drugs or, even worse, guns. He'd worked with most of the riders, competitors, and stock haulers for years. He liked to give people the benefit of the doubt, but drugs ruined lives and guns ended them. If anyone he knew was caught up in Ryder's web, he'd help expose them if he could but he prayed it wouldn't come to that.

Aleta gave him a concerned look as he stepped behind the counter of the outer office. Seeing her distress, he gave her a slight nod and a reassuring wink. He didn't feel the least surprised when Trouble stood up from a curled position on the counter and muttered at him.

Without hesitation, he opened his office door and stepped in, focusing on Malone's expression and ignoring that of the plainclothesman who stood as he entered and snapped, "You'll need to give us a while here."

Cade tamped down his anger at Malone's haunted look and said "You're in my office." He kept his voice easy but added, "Uninvited." He held out his hand, "Cade Delaney, Director of Operations for Twin Circuit Rodeos."

The officer squared his shoulders and pulled in his slight paunch as he shook Cade's hand but retained his officious expression. "Detective Hendrix."

Careful to keep the upper-hand, Cade invited the detective to be seated, gesturing to the other side of his desk. He was pleased to see that the man, who looked to be near retirement age, wouldn't stand out in any crowd, medium height, average weight, ordinary features. His shirt and slacks were neat but not crisply tailored. He'd blend in anywhere, a typical Joe.

"What can we help you with?" He aligned himself with Malone and allowed himself a sideways glance at her. Although her lips were no longer compressed into thin lines, she hadn't relaxed into her chair but kept the same faultless posture with which she sat a horse.

Hendrix sighed. "I was just having Ms. Summers walk me through finding the body."

"For the third time." Malone's impatience was clear in her voice.

Cade swung his gaze to her and kept it there a moment. There was the faintest hint of humor in her eyes and that relieved him. He turned back to Hendrix. "And did you learn anything different during the second and third round?"

"You don't want to interfere in this investigation." The detective added a scowl to his words.

"I don't. A young man who should have been safe in this city is dead. I've got a rodeo grounds full of contestants who should feel safe at this facility and now they don't. When the city council approached me about moving this event from Little Rock to Montgomery, I was assured this was becoming one of the safest cities in the south. I expect your department to be quick and efficient in making an arrest."

"Even if that person is associated with your organization?" Hendrix jabbed.

Cade pierced him with a deadly cold look. "Even if."

As if sensing he'd met his match and even been slightly bested, the other man took the seat he'd been offered, not bothering to ask Malone to leave when he told Cade, "I'll need your statement and as much as you can recall of last night's events."

"Certainly." And Cade talked him through every aspect of the evening except the moments he'd waltzed with Malone, holding her close as he'd once given up all hope of doing.

Hendrix had fewer follow-up questions than Cade expected. Either his own observations from the previous night had filled in any gaps that Malone's had left or their memories were so aligned, the detective couldn't find any gaps to close.

He looked dissatisfied but resigned when he closed his notebook and put away his pen. "I need to talk with Luke Roberts and, yeah, I know his father needs to be present. Maybe the girl, too. I don't have her name but the one that witnessed the two fighting."

Cade got to his feet. He had no intention of allowing Joss to be questioned but he'd fight that battle if and when it came to that. "I'll have my assistant contact Mr. Roberts and Luke and bring you some coffee. Feel free to wait here. It may take a few minutes for her to get in touch with them."

As a surprised Hendrix murmured his appreciation for the offer of coffee, Cade stepped around his desk and held out a hand to Malone who took it and rose gracefully from her chair.

When he opened the door, Cade noted that Townsend moved to stand beside him but Trouble simply stared at Cade and blinked. Apparently, the cat preferred to sit and listen to the next exchange. For a moment, Cade's total acceptance of Trouble's unique characteristics struck him with amazement then he mentally shrugged. He couldn't ignore what he'd observed and experienced with the cat so far.

He glanced at his watch. Barely lunch but close enough. With any luck, he'd convince Malone of that. As they walked out into the reception area, he said her name before she could slip away and she turned to look at him. "A minute?" The hesitation in her eyes was evident but she nodded and stayed close to the outer door as he spoke with Aleta.

"Hendrix wants to talk with Luke. I'll need you to call Frank to bring Luke over to meet with him. I told the detective I'd make sure he got some coffee so I'd appreciate your help with that. Make it a full carafe."

Aleta nodded. "Why don't I send someone to the deli to pick up lunch for all three of them?"

"That's a good idea. Do you have someone you can spare?"

At her nod, he said, "Get enough for you and your team, then. Maybe a few platters of cookies to set out for any of the contestants who drop by this afternoon."

His assistant was smiling as she turned away. The stream of contestants with requests – some urgent, some petty – was never-ending. Cade knew his staff would be appreciative of the lunch as a small gesture of thanks for their patience and something as simple as an offer of a cookie could take the edge off a contestant's irritation or complaint.

He felt a little guilty that he'd withheld a part of this morning's conversations from his assistant but it would work to Aleta's advantage in the end. He'd allow Ryder to ensconce Deputy Armand in his team before he told Aleta she was an undercover agent. That would ensure Aleta's initial reaction to an unexpected staff addition was natural in front of the others. He didn't suspect any of the office staff of wrongdoing but he could take nothing for granted.

He didn't keep secrets from Aleta, but neither Ryder nor Armand needed to know that. Aleta he would trust with his life and anything told her in private would go with her to the grave.

He planned to tell Malone over lunch. If she would go with him. Big if.

CADE HELD the door open for Malone and she walked out into a day that seemed far too bright and beautiful. A man had been murdered in a violent, ugly way. Somehow it felt wrong that the sun was shining and the air crisp and cool. Yesterday's overcast sky would feel more appropriate.

Cade was silent as they left the office but, when she angled toward her trailer and the next task on her mental list, he took her hand and tugged in the opposite direction. "I was going to the café a block over for some lunch. Come with me. Please?"

For a moment she had that same swept away feeling as the evening before, when he'd taken her with him into a cowboy's waltz. Instinctively, she started to resist then thought, why should she? After all, they'd been best friends once upon a time. It wasn't inconceivable that they could be again. "Is it lunch already?" she asked, admitting to herself she might be stalling a bit. It had been so long ago, that time when friendship had turned to a crush, a silly school girl crush. She didn't know him now at all. And he didn't know her.

"I missed breakfast so anywhere in between works for me." But the searching look in his gaze told her his thoughts weren't on food any more than hers.

It could be a mistake, she knew, but she nodded and fell into step with him. Some clocks couldn't be turned back. And she was not nearly as brave as that young girl Cade had once known. But she *was* content and at peace, a hard-won peace at that. Even more, her life, everything about it, made her happy. Would she be willing to risk that? Maybe not, but neither was she quite ready to reject the possibilities.

The walk to the café was short. Cade signaled his beautiful Australian Shepherd to wait at the door as they went inside.

As soon as they were seated, Malone felt uncomfortable and wished she hadn't come with him.

Cade seemed to sense her shift in mood and smiled at her. "Relax. It's just lunch."

"This is awkward for me."

"It doesn't have to be."

"We're not the same people."

"Thank God for that."

His fervent comment drew a soft laugh from her that caught her by surprise and some of her tension slipped away.

"Were we as bad as all that?" she asked.

"You were hardheaded as hell and I was arrogant as hell. So, yeah, pretty much we were."

The arrival of a waitress to take their order provided a brief interruption and just long enough for Malone to decide not to evade the conversation.

"I wanted you to believe in me," she said softly.

Cade leaned forward, resting his forearm on the table. She wasn't sure how eyes the color of a frozen lake could hold so much heat. "Malone, I did believe in you. You were bright and talented. I didn't doubt you could do anything you set your mind to but you were only seventeen and there were so many possibilities in front of you. I wanted those possibilities for you."

"You never said."

"No. I said all the wrong things." He checked them off one finger at a time. "You were too young. You were acting like a brat. You didn't know what you were doing. You were dumb as dirt to walk away from a full scholarship, that rodeo would be waiting."

"Seventeen-year-olds aren't known for their patience. I didn't want rodeo to be waiting for me. I wanted it right then, right there. So, I went after it." With Tyge. And left Cade far behind.

Cade leaned back in his chair, some of the intensity leaving his expression. "And maybe you were right to go."

His admission surprised her and she wasn't quite ready to explore what he meant by the words. "Grandma knew I was leaving. I don't know how she suspected and I don't know if she told Grandpa. She came into my room while I was packing what little I took and gave me two hundred dollars. Probably that week's grocery money. I was just selfish enough to take it."

"She would've been heartbroken if you hadn't. And your grandpa knew. He was the one who told me not to go after you – that the time wasn't right for us then, maybe someday, but not then. He said if I went after you as angry as I was, I'd break the bond we had. Possibly forever."

The revelation stunned her. "I never knew you and he had even talked about me leaving ... about us." The *us* that had never really been.

"He was disappointed in some regard but he was proud of you, too. Said you were strong and knew your own mind. Told me to let you go until you were ready to come back."

But she never had. In fact, she'd fought against even the idea of it.

She shied from that thought, from the look on Cade's face. "I always felt bad, afraid that my dad would blame my grandparents for not keeping closer watch on me that summer. If he ever figured out they'd known and let it happen, he would have gone on a rampage. And I missed them horribly." She'd missed Cade, too, but she wasn't ready to tell him that and knew she might never be. The first time she'd clocked a major win at a professional rodeo, she'd thought of Cade, longed to tell him. Not once had she considered he might be thinking of her too. And maybe he hadn't. Maybe he'd put thoughts of her aside until their paths had crossed on their upward climb through the world they both loved. But she wasn't going to ask him. Not yet. Maybe never.

It was almost a relief when their lunches were served.

Malone kept the conversation light as they ate and Cade followed her lead.

When they'd both declined the waitress' temptation of dessert, Cade paid the bill. "I'm glad you came with me. We said some things that needed to be said." He took her hand as she rose to stand beside him. "But not everything."

It sounded like a challenge but she left that one alone. She knew some words were best left unspoken. "But, for now, I have things to do and so do you."

"True. My event director is efficient but I don't like being away from the arena once the morning rounds start. This investigation has taken too much of my attention."

Malone felt a pinch of guilt as well because every competitor was expected to be at the arena when the colors were carried in. Even the fact that she'd been hemmed up by Detective Hendrix didn't dispel that sense of being somehow truant through the national anthem and invocation.

Only when they were halfway back to the grounds, did Malone recall the questions she should have been asking Cade during lunch.

"The marshal – Ryder – what's he investigating?"

"Murder, for one thing."

"And before the murder?"

"I'm surprised you let those questions go unanswered as long as you did," Cade admitted.

"Might be a little of that patience you thought I'd never learn," she said lightly, even a little teasingly.

And, there, on the open city street, Cade did what he'd never really done, what she had longed for him to do all those years ago. He gathered her into his arms and he kissed her, long and hard and deep. And she really, truly wished he had not, for there went the friendship hypothesis. Beyond that, her response had been too swift, too intense, too obvious. At least to her.

Cade's release was as slow and reluctant as his embrace had been swift and urgent. He rested his forehead on hers and said, "It appears you gained what I lost. I meant to wait on that, to go slow and not scare you away."

Malone thought of all the things she could say in that moment, and all that left her lips was, "I'm not afraid." But she was also wiser than she'd once been, wise enough to know she needed time and space. "I'm also not forgetting the question I asked. What is Ryder investigating?"

When Cade told her, she was almost sorry she'd asked.

"Drug smuggling? One of us?" As large as their organization was, most of them were family of sorts. The idea that someone she knew, someone she saw rodeo after rodeo and talked with as easily as she talked with Cade now, might be involved in something so vile was alien to her. As was the thought of a federal agent in their midst, posing as part of the staff and spying on them.

"Drugs or guns. Ryder's been rather cryptic with his information. Regardless, I gather he's trailing a drug ring that has ties to a gun ring with connection to some king pin who's managed to evade the law for a while."

"And he thinks that's why Roland Walker was murdered?"

"I suspect it's a possibility in his mind, at least."

"Is it a possibility in yours?"

"I wish I could say no, but, yeah, a possibility ... maybe even a probability. Ryder was already looking our way and he's suspicious enough to plant one of his team in my staff. Maybe it was coincidental that Walker happened to get his neck broke at the same time. I'm just not much into coincidences."

CHAPTER THIRTEEN

*H*mph. Staying behind to listen to the Detective Hendrix question Luke Roberts once more proved a complete waste of my time. The detective learned nothing of consequence, if anything at all. Therefore, neither did I. Not that I think Luke had anything to do with Roland Walker's broken neck, but there are times humans know more than they realize and a question or two can bring it to the forefront. My role model Sherlock, as skillfully portrayed by the highly esteemed Cumberbatch, was adept at that method of discovery. A word or phrase here, a tangible clue there. Weave it together and – voila! – a mystery is solved. I've become adept at the same methods but am too often hampered by my inability to pose questions to the humans who are central, whether knowingly or unknowingly, to the mystery.

I had suspected I'd gain nothing from this interrogation. Nevertheless, it did behoove me not to miss an opportunity where I might. The work of a detective, even one so skilled as I, can be tedious but the rewards in enduring that tedium are great.

Much of detective work involves intuition and mine tells me that Tyge's encounter with those thugs is somehow linked to young Walker's death. It is, of course, possible that there's more than one set of bad guys on *the scene and that the two are unrelated but my mind does not lean in that direction. I believe there's a link and, if it exists, I will find it.*

For now, I've been too far and too long from my charges.

MALONE MOVED her bucket of brushes and combs and sprays to the next stall. Everyone got at least a half hour of grooming every day. Joss made it easier than it had ever been for her to give them that time and attention. The girl seemed tireless, constantly making rounds to clean and refill water buckets and scoop droppings from shavings to keep their stalls as clean as possible. Malone had told her, only half-joking, that she was going to have to find a gym to stay in shape if Joss kept doing the hardest work. Joss had just smiled and shook her head and kept going.

Trouble joined her halfway through the grooming, moving languidly from stall to stall with her as she worked. With each relocation, he chose to sit upright in the open stall door, either careful to stay out from under sharp hooves or careful to sit where he could watch the hallway and the approach of any human. Malone wouldn't have bet against either probability.

As she ran a brush over a sleek red rump, she said a soft prayer for that horse as she did for each of them as she worked. Scoop was her partner for tonight's performance. He was a quiet gelding, neither flashy nor fiery so he rarely drew much attention outside of the arena, but inside, oh my, could that boy run and turn with a smoothness that deceived all but the timer. Malone wished again that he belonged to her, but then she wished all of them did. Scoop's real human partner was in her first pregnancy and had called Malone as soon as she'd seen the evidence on the pregnancy strip. The amount she offered Malone to take him for a year had been generous and Malone had been honored by her trust in asking.

"We're going to surprise some people tonight, for sure. There's more to you than they've seen and the ground couldn't be more your style. All I have to do is stay out of your way." That was the hard part of riding so many different horses. Some needed a little help, some needed a lot, and some – like Scoop – needed her to sit as quietly as possible and 'do no harm' as it were. His one quirk was the last two or three strides of his run. If she wasn't careful to gather him up firmly at the right moment, he would express his exuberance at what he'd just done with a quick series of bucks before prancing from the arena. His owner had warned her and, so far, Malone had been careful to avoid any unwanted pitching.

As she worked, Malone listened to the announcer call names and times for the steer wrestling. There was a speaker in every barn and warm-up pen so that contestants could gauge the various times they needed for each stage of their preparations as well as to keep up with the successes of their friends and family. So many of the contestants were kin, father-son, brothers, mother-daughter, sisters. And some not related by blood felt more like family than those who were. Malone had fought with them and for them, knew them, loved them, despaired of them, but – yeah – so many of them were the family she didn't have.

Finishing her work, she decided to head back to the trailer to rub some oil into the saddle and tack she would use tomorrow. She'd done the same with Scoop's tack the day before. Only two of the horses could wear the same saddle and none of them wore the same breast collar or bridle or pad.

Halfway there, she was hailed from one of the practice pens and changed directions to talk with a long-time friend and competitor. Janie had started down the rodeo path a year or two before Malone. Side-lined by a hip replacement, she was there for her daughter who was every bit the rider her mother had been. These days Janie's primary role was to mentor and cheer on her daughter while keeping her two-year-old grandson out of the path of horses' hooves.

As Janie's daughter rode from the practice pen, giving Malone a friendly wave, a pair of ropers moved into the pen, a team who'd been making a name for themselves the past year, moving up fast in the rankings. Janie scooped up her grandson and said her farewells, hurrying after her daughter. Malone stood a moment, admiring the fluid twists and turns of the horses in an unusual but effective warm-up pattern.

"Malone." She turned at the familiar, gravelly voice and smiled at Asa Morrissette. He removed his hat in that polite way he had of always acknowledging the presence of a lady. It was old-fashioned and maybe even archaic, but she preferred that to having tobacco spit at her feet.

"Hi, Asa. How's it going?" She could see the shadows in his eyes and knew the death of one of his hands had hit him hard.

"Could be better," he admitted.

"I'm sorry about Roland." Regardless of her opinion of Roland Walker as a man, he'd been Asa's employee.

"Yeah." He sighed. "A hell of a thing." He stood in silence for a moment, watching the ropers in the practice pen then pushed back from the fence. "I don't suppose you'd accept a dinner invitation."

It wasn't the first time Asa had asked her for a date. "That answer is still no and the invitation is still regarded as a compliment."

"I'll keep trying, you know."

"I don't know why."

He gave a grunt of laughter.

She tilted her head to look at him. Asa was a good eight inches taller, with thick silver hair worn a bit longer than fashionable, a mustache the same shade also longer than fashionable. Any sane woman would consider him a catch. She was just sane enough to appreciate the fact, but she'd never found herself interested in him that way and wasn't going to give him any hope that would change. And not for once had she ever believed he wanted it to.

The sad truth was, after the failure of life with Tyge, she'd never found herself interested in any man that way, not with Cade always somewhere in the recesses of her mind to compare to. And she was surprised that she was admitting as much even to herself.

"Asa." She spoke his name on a sigh. "All these pretty ladies giving you the eye everywhere you go. All you have to do is look around you."

"I don't want to look around." Blue eyes held a hint of sadness though he kept the slight curve of a smile on his lips.

Malone didn't kid herself that the sadness was on her account. Asa had never fallen out of love with his wife though she'd left him years ago. The death of their young daughter in the truck and trailer wreck that had put Asa in the hospital for several long months had devastated the woman. Asa had buried his grief in the stock-contracting business which kept him close to rodeo although he could no longer compete. His wife blamed the sport of rodeo, the long hard hours of hauling for both her daughter's death and Asa's distance and had given up hoping he would walk away. When he wouldn't, she did.

A part of Malone had always believed Asa kept asking her out because he knew she would keep saying no. Another woman might make the mistake of saying yes. She suspected Asa would have nothing to give her.

Trouble grumbled, pulling her attention away from Asa momentarily.

"Malone, I've always wondered ..."

At his hesitation, she looked back at him and waited.

"If it hadn't been me, if I hadn't been the one ..." Asa's voice trailed away.

"To tell me about Tyge?" About the money he'd borrowed from Asa and others and couldn't pay. About the other women. She shrugged. "I don't know. I don't think it would make any difference in my feelings now if it'd been someone else."

"But you can't say for sure."

"I don't feel any differently about you than I did before you told me, if that's what you're asking. We were and always will be friends."

"But you think about it sometimes when we're talking."

She sighed. "Yeah, sometimes I do." But she'd never had a harsh thought toward Asa for being honest with her.

It had been a hard, hard moment for her. She'd been living in denial; she knew that now. Tyge had never been someone she should have depended upon and someone she'd been learning not to. There'd been too many times he'd stayed gone a day longer than planned, too many times he'd hit ignore on a phone call and not said why. She hadn't asked. She wouldn't be one of those women. If there wasn't trust, there was no reason for them to be together. No wedding bands, no certificate, no children.

For those reasons, and others, she'd trusted. For too long. Stupidly. And too many people she'd once thought friends had let her. She'd begun to wonder. And then Asa had asked to talk to her, had brought her a cold, hard truth.

"Asa, I'll always be grateful you were friend enough to tell me what I needed to hear."

The smile he gave her was relieved but rueful. He placed his hat back on his head. "I'll be watching your run tonight, Malone. Good luck." He gave her a wink as he turned away. "And I will ask again."

She chuckled, feeling as if they'd passed some kind of relationship crisis. Asa was a decent man who deserved better than life had dealt him. She'd be sorry to lose his friendship over anything, much less over something she could neither change nor prevent. The 'more than friendship' he professed to want was not something she had to give him. Nor was she certain he really wanted it.

WELL, *hmmm. It appears the gentleman would like to give Mr. Silver*

Eyes some competition in the romance department. Could I speak, I'd advise the latter to step up his game.

But the crudity of human speech isn't a talent I can profess, nor – I can truthfully say – is it one I covet even though it would make some of my discoveries much easier to reveal to those I'm here to help. Not that there's been much in the way of discoveries on this case. Well, I suppose a dead body is something and there was the spur, which I'm convinced is tied to the deed. Even so, it has been remarkably hard to get to the heart of the matter. The wankers who pummeled Tyge are underlings. Of that, I'm certain. There's a mastermind behind whatever dodgy doings have entangled that miscreant cowboy. And I'm not certain about the nature of those misdeeds though the smuggling of drugs remains high on the list of possibilities.

Nor can I find anything to tie that 'lost and found' spur to any person of interest. Certainly, I've seen no cowboy walking around with one spur, nor cowgirl. And, yes, I must at least admit to a cowgirl as a possibility. I've seen some with sufficient bulk and muscle to twist a man's neck with lethal force. The female isn't always the gentler of the species as previous of my cases have proven.

I've lowered myself to crawl through what seems a multitude of cattle trailers that are in need of a good cleansing, hopeful that I'll sniff some aroma that is out of bounds with the locale. Although I'm no canine, thank the good Heavens above, I feel certain I could detect the more common drugs I've encountered. If marijuana or heroin or the nauseous smelling crystal meth has been aboard any of the conveyances I've traversed, I would have detected them.

There remain several I haven't investigated and it's difficult to keep up with what I have and have not inspected. The silly humans move them from one point to another on the grounds for reasons I cannot fathom.

Nor can I content myself with scrutiny of bovine transportation. It must be allowed that one of the fancier equine trailers in such abundance here could be used for the same purpose and with possibly greater success. How many inspection points would wave on a lovely young woman who is rodeo-bound? Lovely young women can also be guilty of great evil. I *saved Ms. Gorgeous from just such a one during my sojourn at Summer Valley Ranch.*

No, indeed, I've much to do and few clues to guide me. I will ensure all is well with Ms. Rodeo and her foundling and let them know my need for decent sustenance. Then I shall renew my search.

As I turn to go, I hear sounds of an approach behind me, then voices, at which I move politely to one side of the wide corridor.

"What do you mean you're going to walk? Are you crazy?"

"Maybe, or maybe I'm coming to my senses."

Uh-oh, two arguing humans, and young males – once again – are headed my way, hopefully nothing more than a bit of entertainment in the offing. Well, yes, I'll confess to enjoying a bit of fisticuffs as long as I'm an observer and not a participant.

I'll take a small leap and move to the sidelines to let them pass by. I can defend myself better than most hand-to-hand ... er paw-to-paw ... when I need but there's no reason to draw attention to myself without that need. That is a detective's first rule of thumb. And I've already made a name for myself as a combatant coming to the Tyge's aid as I did. But there was no help for that. A cat must do what a cat must do.

And there they are, of an age and a size and a swaggering look about them that brands them – at least to my discerning eyes – as among the rough stock competitors. They all have that same shoulders back, loose-hipped walk.

One strides a bit ahead, his cowboy hat shading his face, as if in a bit of a hurry. "I'm getting out, Dawson. If you're smart, you will, too. This shit will get you killed."

The other grabs his shoulder and spins him around and I expect a blow to land.

"Damn it, Quinn, bailin' will get you killed faster. These bastards take care of business. Look what happened to Roland."

The two stand face-to-face and I grasp that they are not at odds with each other despite the quarrelsome sound of their voices, which hold less anger than fear. "That wasn't about him getting out, that was about him getting greedy. I ain't greedy and I didn't want in to start with."

"Yeah, but you took the pay-out and spent it. Kept your mouth shut just like I did."

"And wish to God I never had," *the one called Quinn turns and starts walking again.* "I'm going to finish the week 'cause my luck with the broncs is holding, then I'm disappearing back home for a year or two."

"You think you can hide in them Louisiana swamps?"

"Damn right. I'll be with the snakes and the gators until I'm forgotten."

"You're kidding yourself!" *Quinn doesn't turn around at the rising level of the voice behind him.* "That bastard ain't ever going to forget your name or your face or the fact that you know too much."

The second cowboy waits in vain for a response then throws a costly-looking hat to the ground and kicks it. I sigh at the wastefulness of the young and almost miss his last rejoinder, spoken with a soft, rueful anger. "And he knows we're kin, you jackass."

Which fact would put the remaining cowboy in some serious danger of retaliation, particularly if this outfit is being run like some kind of godfather gang.

Convinced as I am that these two are a part of the criminal element that the Deputy Marshal is looking to find – mention of the dead Roland Walker is proof enough of that - I have nothing solid to lay before Mr. Silver Eyes. Yet.

CHAPTER FOURTEEN

In spite of her mood, Malone smiled as she stepped into the trailer. Joss sat on the sleeper sofa with a handful of the brighter shirts from Malone's closet scattered around her. "I'm choosing for this performance," she pronounced, then asked, "Where've you been? Where's Trouble?"

As if on cue, a familiar bump at the door signaled the cat's return and Malone opened it wide enough for him to slide through. He leaped to the counter of the tiny kitchen area.

"Hungry, are you? Or thirsty?"

"He shouldn't be hungry. Luke brought him bacon and eggs for lunch."

Malone gave Joss a curious look.

A faint color tinged her cheeks. "I like him."

Malone heard the hint of defiance at the thought that Malone might object to Luke's continued attentions. She tried to remember how she would have felt at that age, to imagine what Joss was feeling now. She couldn't. Beyond a doubt Joss was as headstrong, as strong willed as she had been. She wouldn't have survived, either emotionally or physically, if she hadn't been. But

Joss had experienced things that had molded her in different ways than Malone's own life had done for her.

In the end, Malone nodded. "I've known the family for years. Frank and his wife did a good job raising him and his brothers."

"So ... where've you been? Luke brought you something to eat, too."

Now it was Malone's turn to blush. The soft heat that hit her cheeks surprised her. Where had that come from?

"That was sweet of him but Cade and I had some things to talk about so we grabbed a bite at a café just down the street."

Joss studied her face for a moment, then grinned. "I'm sure his parents did a good job of raising him, too."

Malone rolled her eyes but refused to take the bait, deciding simply to be glad that Joss had gained enough security in their roles to tease.

Joss' smile faded. "That Tyge came looking for you."

Malone studied her face. "What did he want?"

"I don't know. I was reading and had the door locked. I didn't open it but I recognized his voice from the phone call."

If Malone could choose differently, she wouldn't have listened to Tyge's message on the truck phone where Joss could overhear, but then neither would she have dreamed that he would get himself in what appeared to be a very dangerous situation.

"Luke said somebody must have beat the sh ... stew out of him. His face is pretty banged up."

All Malone could do was hope it had nothing to do with Roland Walker's ugly death and be honest enough with Joss that she remained cautious. Not that Malone thought there was much chance she wouldn't. "You did well not to open the door. Tyge wouldn't hurt you. I'm sure of that. But I don't know what he's been into and who he's been running with the last few years. I'm guessing they aren't the nicest people in the world."

"He must have been a lot different when you were together."

"Well ... yes and no ... Tyge always had a bit of an edge to him, a wild side that tends to appeal to a teenage girl. I didn't give him a second look the first time I met him. He was a few years older, muscles all over from riding rough stock, so good-looking. On the other hand, he was also a bit drunk and had a cute little red-head hanging all over him. He came after me, though. After that night."

"And you fell."

"Not at first. I made him work for it, but rodeo after rodeo he was there, helping me saddle, waiting for me after my run, cheering me on." She heard her own voice soften with memories. Cade had once done the same, but Cade had been away at college by then, chasing his own dreams. "We didn't travel far competing – grandpa and me – just stuck with local runs. The small payouts looked big to me then. I found out later, Tyge let his buddies go on without him, following the big money, so he could chase after me."

"He loved you."

"He wanted me for sure," Malone said drily.

"What did your grandpa think about him?"

"Not much. He never said so flat out but Grandpa had a way of saying a lot in a very few words."

"You miss him."

"Always and forever. Grandpa and Grandma, both." And home. And she had yet to decide what she would do about home.

"Well, looks like your grandpa was right." Joss gave her a quick look. "And you still need to stay away from Tyge."

"I plan on it. Now we need to get ready."

An hour later they stepped out of the living quarters with Trouble at their heels. "Why don't you go inside where it's warm?" Malone suggested.

"I'd rather come with you." Joss' tone was firm and Malone didn't argue. She was never sure if Joss was staying close for her own protection or Malone's.

"It's another hour before barrels. You aren't dressed very warm."

Joss ignored that. "Why do they stick to such set times? It'd save a lot of time if they started one event right after another."

"Mostly for the fans, so they know what event is happening when. Some people care more about watching roping and maybe steer-wrestling. These are usually fans of the sport and not the thrill. There's a bigger crowd for rough stock riding, a lot of those are people you'd as easily find at monster truck jams and motor cross. They like the excitement of knowing that someone could get hurt."

"Sounds sick to me."

Malone laughed. "Not necessarily. It isn't that they *want* someone to get hurt. Some wish they had the courage or freedom to risk themselves for a sport they love. It takes them out of what can seem to be a dull world."

"Do the sponsors follow the fans more than they do the competitors?"

"For the most part. Sponsors as well as the vendors who pay a hefty fee to set up at these events, but it brings in the sales, now and later."

"Sure are a lot of them. You can buy anything and everything without ever leaving the place. From hats and boots to jeans and jewelry."

"You see something you like?" Malone asked.

"Every time I turn around," Joss admitted, "but nothing I need."

Malone made a mental note to find a reason for a shopping trip.

"I did think I'd walk a few blocks south of here in the morning. I used your cell phone to look up a salon that specializes in short cuts. I made an appointment." Joss hesitated. "I guess I should have asked first."

"Of course, you can use it. But . . . are you sure? Your hair is gorgeous and you've already cut so much of it."

"I like it a lot better short. It's easier and ... cute. I haven't been allowed to cut it for a while. And I, for sure, need someone to straighten out the mess I made of it."

The implications of that saddened Malone while Joss' wanting to look cute – for Luke? – heartened her. "Will you give up wearing a cap all the time?"

Joss gave her an *almost* smile. "Most of the time, anyway."

"Did you happen to notice if they did nails?"

"I think so."

"Good, I'll try to get an appointment close to yours and then we'll have some lunch away from here."

"Lots of choices right here on the grounds," Joss said.

"And none of them really healthy, now, are they?"

Joss hesitated. "I'll need some money."

"You know where your money is. I've put it away every day."

"I haven't earned it yet. I haven't finished paying off the clothes you bought me – I kept every tag so I'd know - and I know how much I eat."

Malone shot her a look. "The money is yours." She left it at that.

They reached the barn and Scoop's stall and Malone started laughing. "*That* is why you've earned your pay. I *hate* braiding manes." The sorrel's mane wasn't simply braided, it was woven into a fancy lattice-work of hair. Malone did the bare minimum necessary to keep from grabbing flowing mane rather than reins in her run, but she had to admit Scoop looked 'photo ready'. And she always bought one of the professional photographs of herself during a performance. Most were at the first or second barrel going into or coming out of the tight turns but she had a few where she and her horse were breezing for home, hair, mane, and tail flying.

"Hey, beautiful." Malone turned, startled at Cade's voice

behind her. Before she could speak, he waved his hand negligibly in her direction. "Not you. This gorgeous creature."

Stepping forward, he ran a hand over Scoop's gleaming red shoulder.

And Malone laughed again, glad that she could with all the drama that had happened in the past few days, with all that had – and hadn't – happened between the two of them over the past many years.

I AM a creature of instinct rather than habit. I believe I came by the trait naturally both from my feline heritage as well as from my father's examples and teachings. And instinct advises me that my plan to stick close to Joss this evening may not be needed.

With a slight signal, Cade attaches Townie to Joss' heel as we all part ways. That Aussie, like most dogs, is bound by habit as I am not, but more, is bound by obedience as I most definitely am not. With Cade accompanying Ms. Rodeo and Townie guarding Joss, I find myself free to surveil the premises. Yet again, I'm forced to concede the canine has his uses.

I start in outlying areas, looking for anything that is untoward, and drift closer to the action in the arena as all remains quiet on the perimeter. Besides I hear the announcer declare the end of the steer wrestling, a silly event in which a cowboy leaps from a speeding horse to grasp a steer by the horns and force him to the ground. I am familiar, now, with the line-up of events. Bronc riding will be next with barrel racing behind it. I shall not miss my barrel racer's performance.

My next area of surveillance will be behind the bucking chutes. Rough stock riding is not my favorite rodeo sport. I cannot fathom the incredible stupidity that causes a human to climb aboard a massive package of muscle determined to unseat him.

However, more to my purpose, I've noted that the contestants tend to leave their duffle bags lying open in what appears to be a trusting, if careless, manner. I don't know what, if anything, I might find. Most of them are as studious to their craft as the ropers and bulldoggers and barrel racers but, beyond a doubt, their ranks have been infiltrated by not just the undesirable but the unlawful – and perhaps even the deadly.

As I make my way from one end of the coliseum to the other, the clowns assume position on the arena floor for a brief comedic act while the rodeo announcer proclaims the gate will soon be opening on the first bronc rider of the evening. I listen as he begins his spiel about bronc riding being the more potentially dangerous of the rough stock events despite the hazards of a bull's horns.

I watch said broncs trot down an alleyway that runs parallel to the corridor I traverse, within touching distance should I be so inclined. With a little 'cowboy encouragement' of yipping and yaying – which sounds are not just on the movie screen after all – they make their way into a series of holding pens rather than milling about in a mass. I peer into eyes that, while watchful, do not seem the least wild and rank. In fact, most appear to hold a spark of interest in their new surroundings. However, the man on the loudspeaker assures his audience that many broncs have an inclination to turn dangerous hooves upon a rider once he is down, making me wonder if that is perhaps a precursor to the metaphor to 'kick a man while he's down'.

His patter helps the antics of the clowns fill the void, although I suspect die-hard fans of rough stock riding are more inclined to use the facilities and buy another alcoholic beverage than they are to get bored and leave.

I relegate his voice to background noise, as I suspect so many spectators do. My attention must remain on greater things though I will remain in tune sufficient that I do not miss the end of bronc riding and the barrel racing that will follow.

Despite my own expectations on the subject, I have found barrel racing to be a sport I can admire. The equestrians are dedicated and skilled, their horses athletic and talented. The bursts of speed and fast turns combine for a breath-taking performance that thrills the crowd.

I find a spot to perch and allow myself to watch the bare bronc riding to ensure I don't miss the event that follows.

As the gate is flung open for each bronc, the whooping and hollering of the cowboys around me is deafening. I feel heartened that they appear to be cheering each other on rather than hoping for defeat of what must – many times – be a competitor who stands between them and a paycheck. I suspect it will be the same with the bull riders.

Observing the bipeds, it seems, each competitor has a posse – in the common vernacular – of two or three fellow competitors. These trusted mates help him settle upon the broad back of his ride and ensure his rigging is secure before the tip of his hat signals the opening of the gate. Once the animal makes his explosive escape from the narrow chute into the arena, they continue their support with shouts of encouragement which the rider cannot possibly hear over the blare of the speaker and the snorts of his draw.

I have not long to wait before bronc riding – both bareback and saddle – concludes, followed by another intermission. At last, Ms. Rodeo enters the arena on the powerfully built horse called Scoop, which name probably makes perfect sense to someone somewhere. He digs into the ground as effortlessly as a train steams along its track, heeding signals that are invisible to the uneducated among the spectators. I, however, have educated myself, watching her daily routine as she does what she calls 'tuning'. Her slow work in the practice pen mimics the moves she makes at incredible speeds during a performance. And the signals vary from horse to horse. A stride or two from the barrel, she sits in preparation for the turn. One horse will require nothing more to slow than that subtle signal. One will need a softly voiced 'whoa'. Yet another will require a soft 'bump' of the reins. It is a fascinating art. Absolutely fascinating. And the horses – at least the ones Ms. Rodeo rides – all enjoy their jobs. That is evident in their eagerness to enter the arena.

I experience a strong feeling of pride as she exits the arena after a flawless performance. She is, after all, my human for the present. I hear the announcer declare hers as the time to beat so far tonight but cautions there are more outstanding horses and riders to come. Hmph. Perhaps that is so but they will have to work hard for their money.

Now to the task at hand.

I'm sure there are those who find the bawling of cattle a familiar, even welcome, sound. I decide that could only be true for those equipped with something less than my highly attuned sense of hearing. It's a most unharmonious din though the bulls themselves do not seem to realize the fact.

Neither do the contestants seem bothered by it. That may be because the clatter they make, combined with the noise of the loudspeaker, is equal in decibels. I'm careful to skirt those contestants, keeping to the periphery of careless boots. Fortunately, most in this vicinity cling to fence railings or climb up to sit in precarious positions for a better visual of each ride.

I'm careful to keep my movements discreet but hesitate at the sight of Tyge with his back propped against a corner post. He seems more interested in studying the faces around him than in the arena action and – as Luke described to Joss – his own mug is rather badly 'banged up'. To both my chagrin and relief, his gaze skims over me without recognition. I should not be surprised. Past actions have made it clear that a cat, regardless of my commendable defensive action on his behalf, is beneath his notice. I'm not certain the nature of his quest but I deduce it must be a mission that has him so markedly quiet and still, almost as if he is hidden in plain sight. I keep my attention at least partly with him as I make my way from duffle to duffle. I'm adept at appearing nonchalant so that even the most observant human is unlikely to notice my search. The first few bags hold nothing untoward, just ropes and gloves and containers of rosin, a substance the cowboys use on their ropes.

Something dark and metallic catches my eye in one and I circle from a different angle to catch a better look. What appears to be the short barrel of a handgun gives me pause but I must accept there is nothing to be done about it now. By the time I find Cade and convince him to follow, the duffle and its owner could be long gone and I will have missed any opportunity to determine its owner.

As if to prove that probability, the announcer strikes up once again while the first of the bulls are moved into the bucking chutes. "Ladies and gentlemen, like the broncs, these bulls are more powerful and muscular than even a decade ago. They are the result of selective breeding. Their physical attributes have been pulled to the fore by genetics. Watch as their hoofs hit the ground with incredible force, as they jump to extraordinary heights then twist and turn midair with amazing agility."

After a moment, I tune him out. Interesting, but not my mission. I resume my perusal of cowboy gear but see nothing more that appears problematic. I'm careful to note which cowboy retrieves the bag with the handgun. I don't recognize him but I will in the future, and not just because of my photographic memory. The scar low on one jaw, though barely visible in the dim light, is distinct in appearance, almost a tiny starburst. If that saw a surgeon's hand, it was a most unskilled one.

With my focus still partly on Tyge, I'm aware that he shifts positions as the cowboy in question passes him by. Shifts and stares but makes no other move. Unlike myself, the cowboy does not notice. Humans are so incredibly unobservant.

Tyge watches as the space around us empties then refills with bull riders. Some contestants trade the number previously affixed to their shirts for a different one, close one duffle and open another. The implications are obvious and amazing. It must take a special kind of stupid to choose to ride both bulls and broncs.

Despite my scrutiny, other than the handgun which isn't all that uncommon these days, I see nothing more among the collection of cowboy gear that I'm inclined to think noteworthy. I can only deduce that I've unearthed all that I can here and it is little enough. Too little.

I cast a last glance toward the chutes before seeking sustenance worthy of my efforts and hesitate. I realize the first cowboy up is Quinn and his lead posse member appears to be the "kin" who argued with him earlier. I swiftly alter course, hoping to glean at least one tidbit of information from tonight's work. I listen to their banter. Whatever rancor was between them seems to have dissipated, but that is the way of humans, unpredictable in their emotions. For now, they appear to have set aside their difference of opinion as kith and kin often do. Perched atop a wooden rail, I can now better see the arena. I hear the excitement in Quinn's voice as he climbs up the chute and peers down at the bull.

"Dawson." Catching the cowboy's attention, Quinn hands his bull rope to the other and climbs over to settle on the broad, muscular back of his ride.

I almost miss the sleight of hand that follows because I'm watching Dawson's face. Yet it is because I note his faint, but discernable, look of regret that I catch the cowboy's surreptitious movement. Quinn's bull rope is dropped to the ground as Dawson pulls a substitute from a bag lying at his feet. A feeling of dread sweeps me and I yowl a warning that my intellect tells me Quinn cannot hear above the clamor around him and wouldn't understand if he did hear. This cannot end well for Quinn.

I leap from the rail, darting through the cowboys in my path. I reach the chutes, but I'm already too late. The gate is swung wide. I hear shouts of dismay and a thud. The bull is spinning free and riderless in the arena. Quinn is crumpled on the ground half in, half out of the chute. I cannot tell if he lives and cannot help him regardless. I focus my attention on Dawson who is crouched beside him and – had I not witnessed the exchange of the bull rope – I would believe the anguish on his face to be genuine. And Dawson's guilt, too, I can do nothing about. At least for the moment.

What I can do is find the evidence of the crime, for I have no doubt a crime of monumental proportion has been committed. There! The switched bull rope lies in the dirt beyond Dawson. His back is to it and to me as he focuses on Quinn.

I snag and drag the rope under the chute. I'm confident I am not noticed as I bury it close to a corner post as deeply as speed allows. Fortunately, there is a mix of shavings and sawdust everywhere. I must keep it safe until I can bring it to the attention of Mr. Silver Eyes.

CHAPTER FIFTEEN

Cade moved quickly in and out of the crowd as the ambulance, lights flashing but siren off as requested, pulled as close to the back of the chutes as possible. The announcer was assuring the crowd that emergency assistance was at hand as a team was paid to be at each and every performance throughout the event. He urged everyone to please keep their seat while the cowboy received the best possible care.

But Cade had seen Quinn Rivers hit the chute with a force equivalent to an unseat-belted passenger ejected from a car in a crash. If the bull rider lived long enough to get that care it would be a miracle.

Since he'd been at the far side of the arena, he reached the bucking chutes as a stretcher was being placed on the ground beside Rivers. The bull rider's twisted torso brought a sick feeling to Cade's stomach. This wasn't a case of a cowboy concussed and momentarily unconscious. Rivers could not have gotten to his feet regardless.

Cade's gaze swept the scene and found nothing to explain what had happened. Rivers' glove was still fastened to his hand so the force of the bull's leap, twist, and turn hadn't caused it to tear lose. Cade suspected, if he checked, he'd find rosin had been carefully applied providing just that much more grip. Rivers wasn't some yahoo rough stock rider. He was a year-end finalist in a multimillion-dollar association. He knew what he was doing.

The EMTs stabilized then maneuvered the cowboy onto the stretcher with as much finesse as possible given the circumstances. Cade tried to read their expressions but they were professionals and their faces gave nothing away of their assessment of his condition. One spoke into a small headset before they lifted the stretcher and began easing their way back to the ambulance.

Cade was pleased to see his staff keeping the milling cowboys shepherded back and out of the way. Only one competitor hovered beside the stretcher, then one of the flank men placed a hand on the cowboy's shoulder gently urging him aside. When he turned to stare at the stretcher as it was carried away, Cade recognized him. Dawson White was another bull rider, one he'd seen frequently in Rivers' company. It would be unimaginably difficult to see a friend in that kind of shape. Harder yet to climb on a bull's back moments later and complete a successful ride. But that's what these competitors would be required to do moments from now, knowing that Rivers was being sped to the hospital, not knowing his fate. Cade made a mental note to speak with Dawson before his ride.

Even as the lights of the ambulance disappeared from sight, the announcer was sweeping the crowd back to the performance, reminding them that every cowboy who'd ridden a bronc earlier or would step down onto a bull in this event put himself – life and limb – at risk.

Cade moved into the crowd of cowboys and made a split-second decision to do something he'd never before had occasion to do. Signaling them to move away from the chutes and the blare of the loudspeaker, he waited until they quieted and focused their attention on him.

"What just happened was rough. Bad. I know you're all rattled. What I want to know is whether you want to move forward with this event tonight or if you want to push it out." The crowd would be disappointed and some sponsors might complain but his primary concern was the safety of the contestants. If they couldn't focus, the risks of them climbing on a bull became exponentially greater.

After some shuffling of feet and whispers amongst themselves, one said quietly, "We'll ride."

Cade took a moment to search their faces, then nodded. He understood and respected that decision. He looked for Dawson among those gathered and didn't see him. For a moment, he wondered if Quinn's friend had followed the ambulance. Then he saw him close to the bucking chute that had been the scene of the accident.

He walked over as the cowboy kicked at the dust in the chute. As Cade neared, one of the staff called. "Here it is, Dawson. I've got it."

Dawson reached for the bull rope as the staffer handed it to him.

"That Quinn's?" Cade asked.

"Yeah. He'll want it." Dawson studied the rig in his hands a faint frown upon his face. He glanced at Cade then turned away abruptly. "I'll put it in his bag and get it to him at the hospital when I'm done here."

"You going to be okay to ride?" Cade knew Dawson hadn't heard the question he'd put to the others, suspected he'd be the most shaken among them.

"Sure. Yeah. Sure."

And even though Cade himself wasn't sure how 'okay' the cowboy would be, the choice was his to make. He watched as Dawson walked away with Quinn's bull rope, twisting and turning the rig in his hand as he looked down at it. Probably wondering what the hell had gone so wrong in that chute when the gate swung open, Cade thought, just like they all were.

Cade said a quiet prayer as he propped himself against a post. He'd watch from here until this event was over. He'd seen all kinds of wrecks through his rodeo years, seen competitors injured, even killed, and most had been due to some freakish but explainable incident. He had no explanation for what had happened to Quinn. He hoped the cowboy survived and, if he did, maybe he could provide an answer of some kind.

The second cowboy out of the chute completed his ride without incident, but Cade suspected he'd be disappointed with the less than stellar performance that was reflected in his score. No doubt his head wasn't in the game and with good reason. As the gate opened on the next ride, Cade heard Trouble's yowl in almost the same moment he felt a firm tug on the knee of his jeans.

He glanced down at the black cat and had a moment's confusion. The cat sat amid a tangled length of thickly braided rope. Recognition dawned as he caught sight of the cowbell, whose weight allowed the rope to fall off the bull when a cowboy's ride was over. The rope was a bull rope and the rosin that had been applied had picked up a significant amount of sawdust and shavings, probably as Trouble had dragged it over to him.

When he bent to pick it up, Trouble sat back on his haunches with a satisfied air. Cade could almost see the 'finally' as a cartoon bubble over the cat's head. But he suspected this particular bull rope signified something far less funny than a cartoon. That suspicion was so strong he was almost hesitant to put his hand on it. Trouble's vigilant stare didn't allow for that as an option.

In the heartbeat of time that he straightened, rope in hand, he saw it. The handle, braided into the center, had been severed nearly in half at one end. The smooth edges of the cut sides told a clear story. The edges on the other side were frayed where they'd given way to the g-force of the bull's bulk twisting and turning in the air. It had been carefully thought through, skillfully done by someone who knew the sport intimately, knew and was known by the rider. Onlookers would have been unable to see the damage and unlikely to notice even had it been obvious. The cowboy, himself, would have checked his gear earlier, handed his rig to someone he trusted to have his back so he could focus his attention on the bull whose number he'd drawn.

Cade wished he were wrong, wished like hell he wasn't seeing what was before his eyes.

He met Trouble's steady gaze and gave the cat a nod. What the hell. One or both of them was a loony tune. Or maybe it was neither. On that possibility, he pulled his phone from his pocket and made the call to Ryder.

Ending the call, he looked up and found Tyge watching him from a distance away.

AT THE END of the night's performance, Cade waited patiently while competitors and staff assembled around him on the arena floor. The space was remarkably quiet with the announcer on the floor with them. Even the din of the ever-present animals was muted in the background.

Aleta, who'd put the word out for him that everyone was to gather for a brief meeting, stood close to his side, clipboard in hand, alert and prepared as always. His gaze sought and found Malone and he realized she centered him in a way no one ever had. She was the missing piece of his life. He put that thought aside to address the crowd.

Though he didn't turn on the mike he held in one hand, his voice carried clearly, even echoing faintly. "Thank you for coming. I won't keep you long. One of our own was hurt tonight and each and every one of you handled yourself and the unfortunate accident professionally and respectfully. I want you to know how much I appreciate that fact, how much I appreciate each one of you."

Cade hesitated. Even now, as he was calling it an accident, he was convinced that Trouble was right. It was no mishap that had sent Rivers in an ambulance speeding through the city.

"I know you're waiting to hear how Quinn is doing. All I can tell you is he's in surgery. I'm headed to the hospital when we finish here and I'll share what I can as soon as I can. Over the next few days, Aleta will have updates in the show office as we get them." If the cowboy lived that long. The thought lingered in his mind but those were words he wouldn't say.

Stepping back, he handed the microphone to a steer wrestler who also frequently held Cowboy Church services when on the road. The man led them in prayer and asked them to continue praying for their fellow competitor and his family in the days to come.

Aleta waited with him while the staff and contestants dispersed. "What else, boss?"

"I won't know more until I get to the hospital."

"Wait," she put a hand on his arm as he turned away. "That veterinary intern you want me to keep busy? She's not worth crap for office work. What am I supposed to do with her?"

In as few words as possible, he explained, watching as her eyes widened. He ended with, "Bottom line, I suspect she needs an excuse to get out and about the grounds. So, without letting her know you know, explain some of the staff functions and tell her you'd like for her to be productive while she's here and not just another pretty face." He paused. "If she is? Pretty that is." The comment could be unfortunate if she were not.

Aleta nodded. "Very."

"Anyway, ask her what she can do to lighten the load you have and then allow her whatever latitude she takes."

"And I'm supposed to explain that to the rest of the staff, how?"

Cade shrugged and answered even as his gaze and thoughts tracked Malone across the arena. He wanted her to go to the hospital with him. "However you can. That's why you're my right hand and lead staff member and why you're the only one of them who's going to know who and what she is."

Aleta rolled her eyes and started away from him but decided to have the last word. "You'd better hustle, Malone is getting away."

Cade stifled both a retort and a curse word as he saw Malone exit with Joss at the far end of the arena.

Aleta's soft laugh, still holding a tinge of sadness from the night's disastrous ride, drifted over her shoulder.

CADE'S LONG, focused stride reached Malone's trailer almost before she and Joss did. Townsend had been forced to trot to keep up. Malone turned with a look of surprise as he called her name.

"Go to the hospital with me?"

Joss raised her brows and Cade gave her what was intended to be a quelling look. She proved it totally ineffective when she lifted one brow, crossed her arms and leaned against the side of the trailer.

Malone nodded. "I can do that. Let me grab a jacket."

As she stepped inside, Cade turned his attention to Joss who still wore that knowing look. "I'm leaving Townsend with you and Trouble. Keep the door locked until we get back."

"I will." Joss let go of the half-smirk as a hint of worry crept into her eyes. "I'm sorry for the cowboy, real sorry, but don't keep Malone out too much later. She's tired."

"We won't be long."

Townsend gave a soft woof as the black cat strolled into view and sat at Joss' boots. The cat gave Cade a look as if to say 'I've got this'. And perhaps - just perhaps - Cade thought, he did.

When Malone stepped back out, she wore a crimson jacket with a soft black fur collar that appealed to him on every level, even the fact that – knowing Malone – he suspected the fur of being imitation. The vivid color, the woman, the brush of fur against her smooth neck drew a visceral response.

Giving Cade a final look of warning, Joss stepped inside with Trouble and Townsend. Once they heard the sound of the deadbolt sliding home behind Joss and her companions for the evening, Malone and Cade were on their way.

With a click of his remote, Cade started his truck from half a parking lot away. It wouldn't make it entirely warm when they got there but it did help remove a bit of the chill before he opened the door on the passenger side for Malone.

She had her seat belt secure before he slid in on the driver's side. He felt her watching him as he pulled up the address of the hospital on the truck's navigation screen. "What's going on, Cade?"

"Show that much, huh?"

"Maybe not to everyone."

It surprised him a little that she'd admit it and pleased him even more. "I'm not sure Quinn Rivers' accident was accidental." He told her about the rope that Trouble had brought to his attention. "It sounds crazy, I know."

"I'm sure it would to the authorities," she said dryly, then added more slowly, "but there's something about that cat."

"Yeah," he agreed, "but not something easily explained. Ryder's going to think I'm a nut case."

"You called him?"

"He's meeting us at the hospital." Cade had second-guessed himself ever since he'd made the call, but he didn't know what the hell else to do. Lives were at stake.

When they walked into the crowded waiting room, Ryder wasn't the only lawman present. Detective Hendrix stood propped against a wall near the entrance, glowering. He straightened as soon as he caught sight of Cade. His scowl deepened.

Ignoring the scowl and the movement, Cade moved Malone past him, toward the huddle of Quinn's friends and fellow competitors. Some lifted red-rimmed eyes to nod at him, others sat with head down as Cade touched a back or a shoulder. They didn't know and didn't care who offered comfort. A few stood as motionless as sentinels, their backs to the wall, staring outward with thoughts focused inward.

Cade could almost read those thoughts. Life was short. Life was sweet. Sure, they took risks. Every day. It was what they loved, how they earned a living, some of them with families to feed. They knew the penalty for failure, but ... it wasn't supposed to be like this. This was never really supposed to happen.

There was one girl among them but not part of them. She twisted and retwisted the straps of her purse, staring down at her high-heeled boots. Cade couldn't see her face, just the fall of blonde hair that hid her features from sight. He would have comforted her but was too wise to believe that he could. He sighed and turned to face the business at hand, callous as that seemed. But he had one murder on his hands, already, and he couldn't be sure Quinn wasn't an attempted murder. If he was, Cade hope liked hell the 'attempted' aspect stood firm.

Hendrix waited in the center of the wide exit to the hallway as if he suspected Cade might flee. Cade sent a questioning look toward Ryder who shrugged and grimaced. It was clear he wasn't enjoying the detective's presence. That didn't enlighten Cade as to who had alerted the local authorities to the injury but it did clarify that it hadn't been the U.S. Marshal.

With a last glance at the cowboys scattered around waiting for news on Quinn, hoping against hope, Cade motioned to the lawmen to follow him out into the hall. He kept a protective arm around Malone, drawing her with him when she might have lingered in the waiting area.

The detective was first to speak but he, at least, kept his voice low. "You want to explain why a federal marshal is here?"

Taking a chance – one he considered a fairly safe bet – Cade said with equal quiet and much less belligerence, "Have you tried asking him?"

"Said he got a tip." Hendrix's irritation was blatant.

"I can speak for myself," Ryder said with a grunt. "I get lots of tips. Some pan out, some don't. If I start giving away my sources, I won't have to worry with wasting time on the ones that don't. Then again, I won't have the benefit of the ones that do either."

"Did your source happen to link the cowboy in surgery with a broken back to the one in the morgue with a broken neck?" His tone was as blunt as his words. And as ugly.

Cade felt as much as heard Malone's sudden intake of breath. He sent the detective a heated glare.

The detective glared right back. "What? You don't even think this was suspicious, Delaney? I'm telling you now, you got anything says this wasn't an accident, you'd better lay it out. I've already heard the whisperings in that room. His friends aren't buying that it was an accident. Said Rivers was as good as they come and had his butt tight as a tick on that bull." He nodded what passed for an apology at Malone. "Their words not mine."

He waited a moment and when Cade didn't answer, snapped his fingers as he threatened, "I'm that close to arresting your ass."

"For what?"

"Obstruction of justice."

Abruptly, Cade decided it might be time to take himself out of the middle. He trusted Ryder to find answers more than he did Hendrix but the association couldn't afford the bad press of their operations director being arrested. It might only be for a short while so Hendrix could have his moment of revenge but it could have lasting impact on the association. As long as Ryder heard the information at the same time as Hendrix, the federal agent could get his hands on it through other means.

"Well," Hendrix pressed, "do you have evidence of foul play?"

"I have a bull rope that appears to be tampered with but I've no idea whether or not it was Quinn's." That was a flat-out lie. He had a good idea that it was Quinn's. Just no proof.

"And it was at the scene of the crime?" Hendrix almost pounced on Cade's admission.

"I don't know that there was a crime." Cade gave that a moment to sink in then asked, "Do you?"

"If there was, I'll find out. And I don't need help from the feds or obstacles from you. Was it close to the fallen cowboy?" He didn't even pretend patience with the question.

"Not when it was brought to my attention." Cade wished he could enjoy baiting the pompous idiot but the reality of Quinn's injuries was too close, too raw.

"Brought to your attention? By who?" He clearly didn't enjoy pulling information from Cade.

"By Trouble."

"Trouble?" the detective almost sneered. "Is that some cowboy nickname?"

"No nickname and no cowboy. Trouble is a cat, a black cat who travels with Ms. Summers here."

Cade chanced a glance her way. She was looking at the local officer with her chin tilted and her brow lifted, daring him to say anything derogatory. Even so, Cade caught her sidelong look his way. She was no doubt thinking he was crazy and maybe he was. The expression on the detective's face spoke volumes.

"Damn it, Delaney. I want to know who the hell brought you that rope."

"I told you. The cat brought it to me."

"You have a rope that wasn't by the chute where Quinn Rivers was hurt. That may or may not be his. And it was brought to you by a cat."

With feet planted, Hendrix had leaned closer toward him with each word, so much so Cade thought he might topple over.

"I don't know where it was when Trouble found it." Tired of the game, Cade kept his voice quiet but as taunting as Hendrix's. "It may or may not have been by the chute. It may or may not be Quinn's. But it was brought to me by the cat."

Ryder actually chuckled and Cade didn't trust himself to look at him and keep a straight face, but Hendrix shot the deputy marshal an evil look before turning his attention back to Cade. "Where is this rope now?"

"It's in my truck. I wasn't sure what to do with it. It looked like it had been buried in the dirt so I didn't want to drag it in here." He lifted a brow, questioning Hendrix's next move.

"I'll walk out with you and take a look at it, but Delaney, you'd better figure out what kind of outfit you're running here – or I'll figure it out for you."

"I've got nothing better to do," Ryder inserted smoothly. "I may as well join y'all."

Cade looked at Malone and she shook her head. "That girl in the waiting room ... I think she's Quinn's fiancée. I'll go sit with her awhile."

He touched her cheek softly, mentally daring Hendrix to say an impatient word at the delay. "I won't be long."

CHAPTER SIXTEEN

Unfortunately, Cade was gone five minutes too long. When he returned, Malone looked at him numbly over the shoulder of the weeping young woman, hearing but not absorbing the curses of Quinn Rivers' friends. The doctor had been brief, but compassionate, though his face had revealed what he thought of a sport that had taken a young man's life.

Cade's face was just as reflective. Malone knew the moment he realized the shift in the waiting room from fear and hope to grief and fury. The only thing she saw in the gaze that never left her face as he crossed to her side was sorrowful regret at the ending of a life.

She released Quinn's fiancée to the arms of a trio of girlfriends who had entered on Cade's heels. They had undisguised shock etched on their faces as they realized the worst for Quinn had transpired. Malone never believed that death *was* the worst that could happen to a person. There were things she would not want to survive.

Thoughts tumbled through her mind as Cade pulled her in close to his chest and pressed his lips to her forehead. "Let's go home."

For a moment, she let herself wonder what it would be like if she could do just that. Go with Cade to a home that they shared, the home she'd once dreamed about. She shook off the thought as they walked through the silent halls of the hospital. She had other dreams now. Bigger dreams, but not – perhaps – sweeter ones.

Townie bumps into me yet again with his restless pacing and I swat him with sheathed claws. He is a nuisance but I understand his agitation. There's something about the atmosphere beyond this cozy abode that is unsettled. At this time of night, the area is normally filled with voices and laughter as contestants return to trailers and settle in. Now the doors of vehicles and living quarters slam shut and echo across the asphalt unaccompanied by human voice. A dog barks once and is quickly hushed. Townsend lifts his head and pricks his ears at the sound then subsides without his usual low response.

Death does that and Quinn's demise has affected many. I'm as confident that Quinn has died as I am that he was murdered by his own kin. Hopefully the clue of the bull rope I was able to seize and deliver will help convict the killer. My next mission is to identify him to Mr. Silver Eyes. Though I am confident that will not be an easy task, a resourceful feline such as I will always find a way.

I watch as Joss lies down on the sleeper couch and Townsend seeks permission to join her with a steady stare. She pats the coverlet and he leaps up to settle beside her. I take a vigilant position beside the front door ready to attack and defend should the occasion arise. I do not anticipate that it will and certainly hope that it will not. I am a master sleuth, after all, not a warrior. With that said, I can, in any case, hold my own in a kerfuffle and shan't be caught unprepared in the event a bout of fisticuffs is brought to me.

Despite Joss' reclining pose, I sense her tension. She looks my way from time to time and I try to look as nonchalant as I can but she is not reassured by the fact that I begin my nightly grooming. After all, even in the midst of crisis, it is important to maintain one's appearance. Joss, however, is not fooled by my façade, proving herself, as the old adage goes, wise beyond her years.

At a rap on the door, her indrawn breath is sharp and deep. Her eyes widen as she stares at the knob. I know terror when I see it. Townsend growls deep in his throat but she places her hand on his head and he does not bark. Good canine.

"Malone?"

Tyge's voice. Fear gone, Joss rolls her eyes. But she makes no move to open the door nor does she answer him when he calls out again.

His boot heels strike hard on the pavement as he stalks away. In the silence that follows, I ponder his persistence in wanting to speak with Ms. Rodeo. Have his enemies threatened to harm her? Does he fear they believe she has some knowledge of their wrong-doings through her association with him? And are his enemies and Quinn Rivers' the same? If I were a betting feline, I would place money on a 'yes' there.

Little time passes before a key turns in the lock. As Ms. Rodeo steps in, I slip out. Time enough for a nap a bit later. For now, I am restless with the sense that events are escalating and that danger encircles 'the Tyge'. Saving him from himself could be a by-product of my efforts. My focus is on protecting my charges from becoming collateral damage.

MALONE STARED down at the hand she had stretched in front of the manicurist, then closed her eyes. Although she had lost her enthusiasm for the bit of pampering, she and Joss made the trip to the salon. A little to her surprise, the tiny, rather plain entryway had opened into an upscale space filled with light and elegance. Joss was swept away by an enthusiastic woman with flaming red hair and a smattering of freckles across her nose and cheeks. Malone's manicurist was male with a shaved head and kind, brown eyes.

"You seem tense," he said as he studied her hands which she knew were pretty much a mess. Today's manicure would quickly become a casualty of her way of life. "Would you like a glass of wine?"

That surprised a chuckle from her. "It's ten in the morning."

He smiled broadly. "A Bloody Mary, then? We'll call it brunch."

She hesitated, tempted more than she would have thought. Any alcohol in the drink would be long gone before her run tonight. But she had a full afternoon in front of her so she shook her head with a twinge of regret.

When asked to select a color for her nails, she leaned back in the comfortable chair and closed her eyes. "Surprise me."

"Ah, I was right." She heard a hint of an accent in his voice but didn't try to place it. "You have a trusting soul and a brave one."

Malone returned the smile she heard in his voice but didn't open her eyes. She'd trusted too much for too many years. She suspected she didn't have a lot of trust left in her. As for courage ... she'd never stopped to consider or question whether or not she was brave. Maybe that teenage girl had been or maybe she'd just been headstrong and foolish. In the years since, Malone had simply put one foot in front of the other, digging in, building the life she wanted, creating the security she needed. The color of her nails wasn't a matter of daring. How she appeared to others was of far less consequence than how she felt about herself.

She'd begun to get that feeling about Joss, as well. There were insecurities about the girl but they weren't emotional ones. Joss had a strong sense of self.

Nevertheless, when her nails were dry and Joss walked out of the back of the salon, Malone knew her jaw dropped. The natural blonde hair that had slowly begun to emerge from cheap dark dye with each day's shower now shimmered with highlights and there was no longer any evidence of the chopped look Joss had created with a pair of barn shears. Clearly the stylist who had taken her in hand was as much an artist as Malone's manicurist had proven to be. The short locks were feathered enchantingly around her face. Joss wasn't simply a pretty, young girl. She had beautiful features that would carry gracefully into maturity and beyond.

When Malone said as much, Joss grinned. "I sure don't look like the old me."

And Malone knew that was what mattered most to the girl. That she not be recognized. Still, Malone could see a hint of shyness in Joss' smile as she added, "I think Luke will like it. Now let me see your nails."

As Malone obliged, holding them up and wiggling them in the air, Joss crowed, "You let him do tiny stars! And a moon. And little crosses. Look at the detail!"

"Well, my eyes were closed and he didn't ask so I didn't have to answer." Malone studied her nails, silently pleased. The man had proven himself an artist and she'd tipped that artistry generously as she would Joss' stylist. Her nails were a shimmery cream and the stars and moon and crosses were all a pale gold. "It will be a real shame to scrub water buckets with these hands this afternoon."

Moments later, they took to the sidewalk and strolled past several ethnic restaurants that would have seriously tempted Malone if they were having dinner. With all she had to do each afternoon, she was looking for lighter fare and allowed Joss to pull her into a little café where they ordered soup and salad.

Joss seized one of the rolls that were brought with their glasses of ice water and, after slathering it from a crockery bowl of whipped butter, ate it with the appetite of the young and always famished. The meal that followed was delicious and they chatted about the horses while they ate. Malone sometimes thought Joss had more questions than any teenager she'd ever been around.

When Joss' plate and bowl were empty, she picked up the last bread roll and offered it to Malone. When Malone smiled and shook her head, Joss buttered it, her motions slowing. Malone noted a faint frown creasing her forehead. She didn't say anything but wasn't surprised when Joss lifted unexpectedly troubled eyes to her.

"I've been thinking."

Malone waited silently.

"There's something I need to do but I'm afraid."

"Tell me."

"First, you need to know a couple of things. When you asked if I'd broken any laws...?"

Malone nodded, still silent but now concerned as well.

"I said I hadn't and I don't think I did. If you hurt someone in self-defense that's not a crime, is it?"

"Probably not but it depends on the circumstances. Before we get into that, what is the second thing?"

"Someone could come looking for me."

"I gathered that much on my own. Otherwise you wouldn't have been trying to disguise your looks. Family?" She'd asked that question once, but Joss had said there were none.

"No."

"The 'someone' you hurt in self-defense?"

"I don't know." Though she was staring down at the crusty roll she held, she didn't seem to realize she was pulling it into tiny shreds.

Malone reached across the table to still her fingers. "Joss. Talk to me."

Joss took a deep breath and dusted the crumbs from her hands. "My dad was a brush track trainer. There wasn't a lot of money in that but we always had food on the table and laughter. There was always laughter. Daddy could have made more going out on the oil rigs but he always said he'd rather be home with us and eat beans than gone half the time just so we could eat steak. He taught me to ride and I was good. I made money after school every day exercising racehorses."

Those memories lightened her face for a few minutes before she dropped her gaze. "Then mama got sick. Real sick, real fast.

She died of cancer in the spring and a few months later Daddy was hit head on by a drunk driver in the wrong lane. Daddy was pulling a trailer with four good racehorses. They all died. So did my dad."

Malone felt her heart break for Joss. She was a young girl, dealing with the grief of losing both parents within months of each other. And, then, somehow, something even worse had happened to her. Someone had failed to keep her safe. "Keep going," she said softly.

"I tried to get emancipation papers. One of the race horse owners who used my dad as trainer said he'd hire me on full time but the judge said I was a ward of the state and needed to be in school. I was put in a couple different foster homes. I was at the last one maybe a couple of months before I went to bed one night and woke up the next day lying wedged in some kind of semi-trailer with my duffle bag of clothes and four other girls."

Joss paused to gulp air. Sweat beaded on her forehead. "I started screaming and the other girls begged me to be quiet so we wouldn't all be killed. I could see daylight through the cracks in the plate metal above me, places it was worn through. It was inches above my face."

There was no doubt the girl was describing a false bottomed floor. For a moment, Malone felt as if they were in the room alone. A kind of white noise filled her ears filtering out the conversation of other diners, of servers taking orders or refilling drinks. Reaching across the table, she took Joss' hand, almost surprised when Joss gripped hers in turn. Joss had been cautious of being touched, never reaching out, never stepping into the occasional light hug that Malone had given.

"That's why you won't sleep in the bed space of the trailer." Though the mattress was king size with plenty of room for two or even three, in a pinch, a person had to sit with care of their head touching the ceiling. Joss preferred the far less comfortable sleeper couch.

Joss shuddered. "I rolled off the nasty smelling blankets so I could breathe. And so there'd be more space between me and the floor above." She spoke in a tone empty of anything she had been feeling then, might be feeling now. "The oldest girl – Carmen – said I'd been drugged. Like them. And I'd probably been given too much. She thought I was going to die before I woke up. All I knew was that I was sick as a dog."

Hearing what Joss had been through, Malone felt ill herself. She fought the bile that crept up her throat.

"I wanted to claw my hair out. It was hard, hard to keep from screaming. Carmen kept talking to me, low and quiet until I could think again. We made a plan. She said we'd be let out every few hours to pee in the bushes, always in some field or dirt road. One guy would hold a gun on us. The driver always stayed in the truck. Carmen kept telling the other girls to say nothing. All they had to do was get out of the truck and just say nothing. I could tell she was worried they'd mess it up, being so much younger and scared and all."

Malone sighed, not sure she wanted an answer to what she was about to ask. "How old were they?"

"Carmen was eighteen. The other girls were younger than me, maybe twelve or thirteen."

She'd been right. Better not to have known that there were two young girls on their own somewhere with no way to find them now. She nodded for Joss to go on.

"I was the tallest and we figured I was probably also strongest of us so, the next time the truck stopped and the three were allowed to climb out, Carmen told him I was out cold. It was close to dark by then which was good." Joss stopped for a moment. "Not moving when that trap door was opened was harder than I thought it would be. Carmen had said I should make sure all three of them were out before I moved so he wouldn't be looking in. That she'd take her time in the weeds. My knees were shaky when I climbed out of that hole, some from fear, but I knew I was weaker than I thought from whatever they gave me. I was scared, but I was desperate. The guy had his back to me, keeping an eye on the other girls, when I took a running jump from the back of that truck. I aimed for his head. It was a long way down, longer than I expected it to be. I guess he heard me because he turned at the last minute. He saw me but he didn't have time to move. I don't know what he hit when he fell but he didn't get up. That's where I got all the bruises. I crashed into him hard, as hard as I could. I knew if I didn't, I'd never get away."

She pulled her hand back from Malone's to take a long drink from her glass of ice water.

"He saw me," she repeated.

"What matters is you got away from him, from them."

"Carmen had said we should run in different directions. The men might catch up with one of us, two if the men decided to split up looking, but we'd all at least have a chance at getting away. Carmen and the two younger ones scattered, but I went just far enough into the woods to find a good tree and climbed it. I knew I could sit quiet for hours if I had to and I wanted to stay close to the dirt road we were on. At least it would lead somewhere."

"Did any of the girls get away?"

"All three, as far as I know. I hope they're somewhere safe. When the driver got out, I could hear him cussing when he found the man with the gun laid out on the ground. A few minutes later, I heard him throw stuff out of the back of the trailer and pull out. I suspected he'd left the other guy right where he found him. I knew I couldn't wait long in case he wasn't dead and managed to get up so I climbed out of that tree. I was scared to death but I wanted my clothes and the little bit of money I had tucked into a seam of the duffle bag. Sure enough, the guy was lying right where I landed on him. I didn't get any closer than I had to, but he didn't move. I grabbed my bag from the pile of nasty blankets we'd been laying on and started walking. The truck wasn't really parked in the woods, like I'd thought. Just beside a thin line of trees. Not too far past that was a parking area full of trucks and trailers."

With that Joss leaned back in her chair, watching Malone with wary eyes.

"The rodeo. Where you climbed aboard my trailer."

Joss nodded cautiously.

"You were brave. It must have been very, very hard to get back in a small, enclosed space."

Without speaking, Joss nodded again.

"You were also very, very lucky that the trailer was mine." Her mind circled back to Joss' first comment. "What is it you need help to do? Find out if the guy lived?"

"No. I don't care. I didn't mean to kill him but I don't care if he's dead or alive. But the foster parents ... I think they sold me. I went to sleep in the room they said was mine and woke up in a truck. Someone needs to know so they can't do it again."

Malone felt a slow rage simmering in the pit of her stomach and wished she hadn't eaten before hearing what Joss had been put through for greed. The girl's story explained why there had been no Amber Alert for Joss. Her disappearance had probably been documented as another runaway. If it even had been at this point. She had no idea how often agencies checked in with foster parents. "I'll help you, Joss. And I'll keep you safe. Even if I have to lay someone out on the ground."

Joss smiled faintly, looking far less tense now that she had placed her problem with an adult she trusted. "I'll bet you could, too."

In that moment, Malone knew if she never succeeded again at anything in her life, she would succeed at the promise she'd just made. Joss was counting on her and looking at her with such confidence it was almost scary.

"Do you think you could help me get emancipation papers?"

"We can work on that when we get done in Montgomery." But where Malone's mind truly went with Joss' question wasn't setting her up as an adult who had to make her own way. Joss needed a parent, at least one, who cared about her well-being. Malone wouldn't be the first single person to adopt. "There are attorneys I trust back home in Georgia."

Home. As she said the word, Malone realized that somewhere along the miles, she'd made another decision as well.

THREE HOURS LATER, Malone sat astride Jaz and watched Joss canter Gemini in ever-tightening circles. The fine-boned mare tended to be hyper and the corkscrew work-out, cantering big circles while slowly decreasing the circle size by easing her in toward the center with a steady hand on the rein, tended to settle her. Malone had learned early on if she started with smaller circles the mare fought continually for more room and more speed. Joss took instructions well and learned quickly. Which reminded Malone that Joss needed to be in school. Her future could be as bright as any other teen. Maybe homeschool if she chose to stay with Malone, then college. But they couldn't get her registered for anything until the mess that had happened to her was straightened out and, hopefully, people were in prison for what they'd done.

Maybe a name change with adoption would be safest for her. No one would ever need to know that the girl who had disappeared from south Louisiana was safe with her.

"Malone."

She turned, startled, realizing that her name had been spoken for a second time.

"Asa. I'm sorry. I was lost in thought."

Asa stepped up on the lowest rung of the tall pipe fence that enclosed the practice pen and crossed his arms along the top.

"That girl is a better hand than most of the young men I have on my payroll. I might try to steal her away from you."

"She's younger than she looks and I have to return her to her family at the end of the week but, you're right, Joss is an awesome talent. I'll miss her." Malone wasn't much for lying but Joss' safety depended upon there being no possibility of an indiscreet word here or there. And cowboys, so taciturn in movie land, were, in reality, very good at gossip. She and Joss had agreed to a story and Malone would hold firm.

A glance at Asa's face told Malone his thoughts weren't on Joss and her skill with a horse. His next words proved it. "I can't figure out what the hell is going on around here, Malone. I'm hearing whispers here and there that Quinn's death may not have been accidental."

Malone turned her gaze back to Joss so that her face was slightly tilted away from Asa. She wasn't good at subterfuge. "Why would anyone want to hurt Quinn? Besides, there were a dozen or so people working those chutes. You know the association - Cade - is super careful that the workers aren't short-handed anywhere. There're enough hazards with what all of us do every day to be careless in the handling of an event."

"I'm not saying it's true, but ... there's talk."

"I haven't heard any gossip but, then, Joss and I got away from the grounds for several hours this morning. We needed some breathing room after all that has happened." Two days, two deaths. She hesitated but Cade would need to know what rumors were floating. "What kind of talk?"

Asa sighed. "That maybe something wasn't right with his bull rope. Maybe it wasn't secure. Hell, I don't know."

"It was his rope, wasn't it?"

"Yeah, his cousin picked it up after."

"Did anything look odd about it?"

"No. But one of the flank men said Quinn's expression changed right as the bull made his leap out of the chute. Said it went from his usual daredevil 'I've got this' to real fear. The guy's swearing something went wrong, and Quinn knew it."

"Maybe something did. Or maybe Quinn got careless this once." Malone spoke softly sensing that Asa was truly upset by what had happened. They all were. But every cowboy carried his own rope and helped those working the chutes secure it around the bull. The gate wasn't opened until they gave the nod. "The bull was one of yours?"

"Yeah." Asa pushed away from the fence. "Mine."

"That doesn't make you responsible for what happened in that chute, Asa. Just like the owners of the horses I ride aren't responsible if I get hurt or killed while riding or handling them."

His expression didn't ease and she felt sincerely bad for him. He gave her a strained smile. "You be careful out there tonight. I won't wish you luck. You don't need it. Malone, you're one of the best – to my mind, *the best* – but I'm wishing you real success. I'll be watching."

For the first time, Malone wondered if the look in his eyes that she'd always passed off as pure flirtation wasn't something more than that. Watching him walk away, she hoped not. She'd rather see his attentions turned solidly elsewhere – heaven knew there were plenty of women who'd had their eyes on him over the last few years – but Malone only ever thought of him with friendship. Asa was successful in business, good-looking, and athletic in build. The low gravel of his voice was appealing and his manners made a woman feel as if she were his sole focus in conversation. He was, in fact, all most single women would want in a man. But Malone had long ago decided she didn't want the complication or the risk of a man in her life. Not again. And, if she ever changed her mind, Asa wasn't going to be the one.

As Joss rode up to the fence, Malone pulled her gaze away from Asa's departure.

"That guy's after you." Joss said knowingly.

"I'm sorry for that," Malone said honestly. "I'm not in the market."

"At least not for him."

Malone decided some comments were best left unanswered and she nudged Jaz into a walk. But she didn't miss Joss' knowing look as she made her escape.

CHAPTER SEVENTEEN

Cade walked into the show office and immediately noticed the new face. Detective Armand, he supposed. He gave her a quick nod and walked past the counter, into his office. To his surprise, she followed.

She stood with her back to the doorway, one step inside. Cade realized at once that she had placed herself where she could be seen by his staff but couldn't be heard by any casual listener. He studied her for a moment, realizing she had features that could be highlighted to real beauty but had somehow been downplayed by makeup. Interesting.

"Rivers' fiancée asked for the bell off his bull rope, said she'd had it engraved with both their names inside after he asked her to marry him. The family let her have it. She was pleased – heartbroken – but pleased to get it back."

Cade didn't ask how she knew all that. Ryder had said she was good at her job. "And the rope with the damaged handhold?"

"The locals are sharing information for now but not going public with it. Plain bell, no engraving."

"So not his rope."

"Not his rope. But Ryder is convinced it's the one that was on that bull when the chute opened. Hendrix is halfway to believing it. Give me a task I can take back out front."

He looked at her blankly for a minute then nodded as he realized her meaning. "Flowers and a card with every staff member's signature need to be sent to Rivers' family." He'd done the same for Roland Walker though the circumstances had been far different.

She nodded and walked out. Her voice carried back to his office. "Mr. Delaney said flowers need to be sent to the cowboy's family. Everyone needs to sign the card. I'll go get a card. I don't know how to order flowers or what to get."

With that she strolled through the front door, for all the world like a student intern who hadn't a clue about office etiquette.

Cade's amusement at her tactics faded. He rocked back in his chair and stared at his steepled fingers, picturing again Dawson White's face as he'd looked at the rope in his hand. Without a doubt, his expression had registered confusion. Was he trying to understand why a rope in perfect condition had failed the rider? Or was he wondering why the rope handed to him showed no sign of the sabotage he knew should exist?

What had Trouble seen in the moments before Quinn had signaled the gatemen to throw the chute wide with a dip of his head? Some sleight of hand and a fast exchange?

Or was it as simple as Quinn misjudging his readiness or the gatemen misjudging some movement for the nod that he was ready? And, if that were true, whose was the rope with the half-severed hand braid?

Cade wished he could ask Trouble that question. Even as the thought came to him, he shook his head. He wasn't crazy enough to think a cat could find a way to answer. Or was he?

Ms. Rodeo doesn't talk enough. *I thought Ms. Gorgeous was taci-*

turn but I'm finding there are new levels to that description with this case. I can't always tell when I need to follow her and when I need to be about my own reconnoitering. I'm most comfortable when she and Joss remain together but Joss is grooming horses with Luke to keep her company and Ms. Rodeo is off on some mission.

I slip into the show office on her heels, then into the corner office as she hesitates in the open doorway. Mr. Silver Eyes is engrossed in what appears to be a report of some sort. I see columns of numbers, likely financial information for this rodeo business he manages.

She's safe here but there are times the information my humans carry in their head could assist me in my investigations. Getting them to share can be a bit tricky. Perhaps someday, in the distant future, they'll evolve to my own highly honed level of unspoken communication. For now, a master sleuth must find what means he can to remain informed. I leap to my usual comfortable spot in the wide-ledge of the window sill as she taps at the doorframe.

"Cade?"

"Malone." He stands, ever the gentleman. "Come in."

He doesn't sit until she takes a seat. I've learned enough to know that he came up through the rodeo ranks as a team roper. Either these contestants are not all as rough and tumble as they've appeared to be in my sojourn here or he has gained significant polish in the years he's been in the business end of the sport.

"Do you have a moment?"

"A lifetime if you want it."

If I were human, I could not help but roll my eyes at such a response. I'm not surprised when she blinks, then opens and closes her mouth before finally saying, "It's about Joss." She must see concern in his expression because she hastily adds, "She's fine. At least for now. It's a long story."

He rises and walks to the door to close it to a mere slit of an opening. "That's Aleta's signal to run interference with anyone wanting to see me." *I win a bet with myself when he does not return to the chair behind his desk but takes the companion to the one in which she sits. They* are now close enough to touch. It will be interesting to see if either makes that move.

Time enough for such speculations later. I have a feeling she's about to impart the type of news that I need my humans to share with me.

"Is Joss upset with what's been going on around here?"

"No, it's nothing to do with them." *She hesitates.* "I think I'm going to need a good lawyer for Joss. I thought you might be able to help with that."

Not what either of us expected her to say. I would place a bet on that.

"What has she done?" *I hear concern but no condemnation. Good man.*

And an increasingly angry man at the moment. I watch his face as he learns Joss' story, an ugly one of human greed and cruelty. I've heard of such things occurring but never been called upon to solve a case involving human trafficking. An ugly, ugly business. Uglier than murder, plain and simple.

He listens and comforts and reassures. Even as she leaves us to prepare for her evening competition, I suspect she has yet to couple what happened to Joss with what has been happening around us here. But, when we are once more alone in that small office, he turns his gaze to me and I deduce, like me, he has pieced the picture together. "Trouble, I need to know who handed Quinn Rivers the damaged rope you brought to me."

He rises and takes his hat from the rack, twisting it in his hands for a moment, deep in thought. I can feel the fury strong within him, see it in his eyes. I follow him from the office, out into strong afternoon sunlight.

I will be so bold as to acknowledge how easy it would be for me to identify the guilty cowboy to him. A leap and obvious pounce upon leg or back as we stroll the rodeo grounds. But my cooler head cautions that I must be subtle. The reveal cannot be coupled with an angry man on the hunt for guilt. I don't know that he has himself in hand. It wouldn't do for me to enable the guilty cowboy to link my action to a flash of knowledge in those knowing, grey eyes. Or worse to a flash of fists. As director, he has a reputation which must be protected for his own good and the good of the association. *A cowboy kerfuffle is beneath him, as satisfying as that might be.*

For now, I shall follow and not lead. If our path takes us to the bucking chutes and cowboy Dawson, at some point, I will follow my inner wisdom in determining whether I act. Or bide my time for a better moment.

WELL, Cade thought, it's a start ... Malone turning to him for help. He'd wondered more than once in the hours since they'd stood together on that sidewalk if he'd only imagined Malone's brief response to his embrace, his kiss. He'd wondered what she'd been feeling since. He'd dared a lot in that moment and at least she'd not pulled away. But that one brief moment hadn't been enough and he knew it never would.

The first night of the competition, he'd been waiting for her at the end of the alley. But Tyge had stepped in ahead of him, a reminder of all the years the cowboy had been there for her and Cade had not. The two hadn't noticed Cade as they'd passed by deep in conversation. He'd been jealous. Hell, he still was. But she'd come to him now. He'd let her slip away once, but he'd be damned if he would again.

Unfortunately, Cade hadn't a clue how or where to begin in connecting Joss' tragic story to the murder of two rough stock riders. Yet he couldn't shake a feeling, a strong feeling, it was there. Ryder was looking for traffickers. Cade's mind had jumped to drugs, perhaps even guns, particularly in today's political clime. But humans? With people he knew, perhaps intimately, as friends and comrades and business associates?

The thought disgusted him but the facts were strong. Cade couldn't believe it was by chance that the truck carrying Joss and three other girls had been stopped next to the Lake Charles rodeo, perhaps even on the rodeo grounds. It wasn't by chance that Ryder was looking here, at the rodeo crowd. Ryder had more than hinted that he thought stock trailers, whether for bulls or broncs or calves or steers, were a possible means of transportation.

It wasn't a big leap to look at potential connections between hauling drugs and human cargo and the murders of Roland Walker and Quinn Rivers. And Cade was now firmly convinced that Rivers' death was no accident. It was unfortunate that Ryder hadn't put him into the picture of human trafficking. Something in the past few days might have caught his eye, something said or some behavior that might have a different meaning with that knowledge.

Cade wondered if agreeing to move the Southeastern Circuit finals here had been a terrible mistake. His mistake. Sometimes what looked too good to be true was just that. But the deal presented to the association had meant more pay-out money for the finalists and more savings in the future.

He'd been offered the year-old facility – all inclusive, from coliseum to barns to outside working pens to city hook ups for trailers – at a fraction of what the cost would have been at their previous venue. The benefit to the city was a five-year contract that the association would continue to use the facility each of those years at a reduced cost. During that time, if either the city or the association failed to show a solid profit, the contract could be ended by written notification. At the end of five years, it could be extended, renegotiated, or allowed to lapse.

The board of directors had been enthusiastic once they'd had time to review the potential numbers. Cade had been pleased. Theirs wasn't the largest or oldest pro-rodeo association but it was showing steady growth each year. Cade was glad to contribute to that growth. But Cade hadn't anticipated murder in the mix, not even one, much less two. Now he had to keep his wits about him and – with the help of one black cat – find out who was behind the deaths and if the crimes were connected to Ryder's investigation and Joss' story as he believed. And knowing he was counting on a cat to help him do all that made him doubtful how much of his wits he had left to keep about him.

Cade started on the outskirts, just walking, looking and thinking. He felt a little conspicuous with Trouble weaving in and out between him and Townsend. The first cold front of the season had made for a bitter and dreary start to the event but left glorious fall weather in its wake. The brilliant blue of the sky and the warmth of the sun seemed at odds with the grimness of his mood. He had to work at a pleasant expression as he greeted his members and their families.

He stopped to watch Frank Roberts working with a couple of Little Britches ropers, helping them roll up their ropes and guiding their swings so that one finally looped the horns on the roping dummy and let out a whoop of exultation. Luke sat in a folding chair half-watching, half-working rosin into his own rope.

Luke looked up watchful, undoubtedly expecting more bad news of some sort.

Cade smiled, sorry that events had conspired to make a generally happy-go-lucky young man so cautious. "Congratulations on your winnings last night. You and your dad pulled a good check."

Some of the stiffness left Luke's shoulders. "We needed it. Not the money, so much, you know. But the win."

Cade did know. A couple of other teams, equally talented and with even more experience, had had poor luck and a slow start which was proving a drag on them now. He couldn't say why adversity made some dig in and some lose heart.

When he would have walked on, Luke spoke again, softly. "Mr. Delaney?"

"Yeah?"

"What's happening here?"

Cade wished he had an answer, at least a better one than he could voice. "Whatever it is, I know there are two different law enforcement agencies teamed up to find the answer." Teamed up was probably over-stating reality but no need for Luke or anyone else to know that. "Just focus on your riding and your throw, Luke."

"Some of the other guys are getting scared one of us will be next but I don't think whatever's happening has anything to do with us or the rodeo. Not really."

Luke watched Cade carefully, clearly hoping for affirmation of his belief from someone he trusted, someone in authority, someone who'd know if he had reason to be afraid. Cade felt out of his element in one sense, but confident in another. Watching out for his members was a key component of his position.

"I think you're right, Luke. Just be careful of your surroundings so that you aren't caught up in something you don't mean to be. Otherwise, I believe you're all safe enough." As safe as anyone could be. For decades, Montgomery hadn't been considered the safest city in the United States but things were changing dramatically with the revitalization projects going on. This facility was new. Restaurants and theatres had opened. Strip malls were disappearing and burglar bars were gradually being removed from storefront windows. Progress, slow but sure.

He clapped Luke reassuringly on the shoulder as he moved on.

Frank gave him a brief nod before returning his attention to the two youngsters in front of him.

Near the first barn he passed a group of teenage girls in blue jeans and sneakers, carrying multiple bags, many bearing the names of their sponsors for the week. Good for business. A group of teenage boys trailed behind them but one of the girls tossed a smile over her shoulder and he stayed relaxed. He supposed boys the world over tagged along in the wake of girls on a shopping mission.

A man in jeans and boots stood propped against the side of the first barn. Cade hesitated. The jeans were not faded and the boots were unscathed by barn work. Not a scuff mark anywhere. He could have been a fan or a parent or merely a passer-by were it not for the look in his eyes. The sport coat wasn't out of place in the late October weather. Still.

Cade looked for but didn't see the tell-tale bulge of a concealed carry. Even so, he went on his intuition and the sudden interest Trouble displayed in the man.

Stopping in front of him, Cade held out his hand. "Badge."

"Mr. Delaney, you need to walk on."

"Bull shit. Ryder can go to hell if he thinks he's planting people on these grounds without my knowing." He had to guess between Hendrix and Ryder but suspected the locals didn't have the funding to spot extra officers for investigative purposes.

The lawman scowled as he passed his badge over for scrutiny. "Ryder won't be pleased."

"By what?" Cade commented affably. "By you not having sense enough to wear faded jeans and old boots if you wanted to blend in here? This is a private facility and under my control for the duration of this event. You're here at my discretion or not at all."

"That wouldn't hold up in court."

Cade grinned, knowing it probably looked more like a baring of teeth than humor. "Probably not, but Ryder would be even less pleased if it ended up there, don't you think?"

When the other man gave a grudging shrug, Cade handed his badge back to him and moved on. Though he wondered if there were others staged elsewhere on the grounds, he didn't see much use in questioning the undercover agent. He wasn't likely to get an answer, at least not a straightforward one.

On the other hand, the man's presence could well be a bargaining chip. Joss needed help and Ryder likely had strings to tug that could provide that help. He placed a quick call and Ryder answered on the first ring. Cade made quick work of telling the marshal that he was in Cade's debt for not blowing his man's cover and even quicker work of telling him that every favor should be reciprocated. Ryder agreed to talk with Joss after the evening performance. With the crowds pulling out and the contestants getting things squared away at the end of the day and ready for the one to come, Ryder's comings and goings weren't likely to draw much attention.

Assured of the deputy marshal's cooperation, Cade called Malone who wasn't enthusiastic about the suggestion but promised to reassure Joss as best she could that this was a good thing. And Joss, after all, was the one who had asked to do something positive from her horrid experience.

Cade's thoughts and long stride carried him closer and closer to the area where stock contractors parked their trailers after unloading. In his heart he couldn't believe that any of the contractors he'd worked with, shared meals with, lifted an occasional beer with, could be involved in the ugliness happening around him. But there were always newcomers and some of the old-timers had stepped back as their offspring – sons and daughters both – stepped forward to take over the business. For the most part those who were here he knew and trusted. But they supplied the larger venues, where the payouts were larger to the contestants and the money paid for stock was reflective of the caliber animal required for that level of competition. Smaller or newer districts, like the one in Lake Charles, were supplied by some of the minor, more local contractors. But no one had died in Lake Charles. They were dying *here*.

Regardless, Cade wanted to look at some actual stock trailers, think back to those he and his father had run, how they were built, how they might be modified to conceal illegal cargo. His effort might tell him nothing but grasping at straws was better than grasping at nothing but thin air.

The area was virtually bare of anything but empty trucks and trailers. The sounds from up around the arena and paddock areas came to him muted. Some distance away, two women held horses on lead ropes, talking quietly as they let the animals graze on the narrow strip of lush grass between the paved parking and the fence that backed the city street beyond.

Cade walked slowly between the long, empty trailers. From time to time, he stooped to examine the various undercarriages of the trailers, pondering possibilities for concealed compartments, how one could be constructed on this or that trailer design. It wouldn't be impossible to create but how easily could it be camouflaged from the Department of Transportation officers who patrolled weigh stations? Occasionally, Trouble would leap to a wheel fender as if peering inside. Each time Townsend would whine faintly until the cat returned to the pavement. In silence, Cade noted the professional logos etched with the names of the various contractors.

Dossett Inc., run by Gaylon Dossett and his wife, hauled some of the best broncs in the business to Cade's mind. He felt guilty even thinking about using Carlisle Contracting in their place next year but Dossett had raised their rates steadily and significantly over the last few years. Cade had questioned him, pushed him on it, but Dossett hadn't backed down on his pricing and it didn't appear likely he would. Rodeo was a business and, if Carlisle could produce comparable at a more equitable price, Cade wouldn't have much choice.

Morrissette and Sons. Asa always swore that if he couldn't stock quality bulls he wouldn't stock at all. Cade had never known him to disappoint. Asa hadn't had it easy the past few years but, with his sons taking more and more of the business, the lines of stress seemed to be easing each time Cade saw him these days.

Carriere Steers was based in Little Rock. The company wasn't quite a newcomer but was the most recent addition to the lineup. They carried some of the finest bulldogging steers in the United States. Cade had vetted them thoroughly before taking them on and, so far, they hadn't disappointed.

The last of the rigs belonged to Jemson Ventures. Lang Jemson had graduated with a veterinary degree, worked in the profession for five years and walked away without a backward glance to partner with his father-in-law on supplying calves to local rodeos. It was a family-owned business with a pristine reputation with the wives of the two men as invested in the business as their husbands. Cade couldn't see them involved in wrongdoing.

Hell, he couldn't see any of them caught up in something so ugly. With every step forward, he felt more and more like a traitor to the team who supported the association. Because with every step forward, he wondered - couldn't help but wonder - if there was a possibility that people he knew and cared about could be caught up in such bad business. He thought of the decade he and his father hauled calves to rodeos, how he would have felt if anyone had been looking at their rig with such thoughts at the back of their mind.

Trouble waited for him and Townsend on the hood of the last Jemson truck, looking bored. If there had been anything out of the way to find, the cat would have found it. Cade had given up pretending he thought otherwise. Townsend yipped softly and wagged his tail as he stared up at the cat until Trouble leapt down to give him a supercilious glance before leading the way back in the direction they'd come.

Cade's cell phone buzzed as he crossed in front of the coliseum. He glanced at the name and sighed.

"Good afternoon, Keena. What's up?" Other than her worries - and his - about how murder might impact the terms of their contract. He'd known the woman long before she became part of the management team for Montgomery's new equine facility. She'd traded on their friendship when she contacted him with the possibility of a deal between the city and rodeo association.

"Cade, do you have time to join me for a drink and a few minutes to talk?"

He'd rather have put this off but .... "I do if it's close and brief. I can't be far or long away from the grounds during the performances." Particularly not in light of the events of the past two days.

"I'm leaving my office. I'll pick you up in ten minutes and bring you right back as soon as you say the word, I promise."

"I'll be in front of the coliseum box office."

He left Townsend with Aleta, realizing that Trouble had disappeared on him somewhere along the way. He'd barely gotten to the curb when Keena slid her sports car to a skillful stop, smiling as she got out. She greeted him with the hug of a long-standing relationship that had survived several transitions and emerged as something less than she'd made clear she wanted and something more than he once would've thought possible.

"Want to drive?" she asked with a grin as she caught him admiring her car.

He caught the keys she tossed to him. It wasn't a car he had any desire to own, but he was a red-blooded male. Handling the sleek power under that hood was an offer he wouldn't turn down.

"WHO'S THAT?" Joss watched with quiet curiosity on her face as Cade slid behind the wheel of an electric blue car.

Malone glanced across at the couple she'd been pretending not to notice as she and Joss walked out of the show office. "Her name used to be Keena Ellis. They dated in college."

"Does she run barrels?"

"Not that I know, but I do and we have a lot to do before then." To her relief, Joss took the hint and turned the conversation to the horses and the tasks ahead of them.

CHAPTER EIGHTEEN

With a glass of wine in front of each of them, Cade listened while Keena made small talk. A local talent played light jazz with a soft touch on a keyboard. Another time he probably would've appreciated both the entertainment and the mood lighting. As it was, he had to tamp back his impatience. He'd realized during their initial meetings regarding the change in venue for the district finals that Keena hadn't changed much since college. She still took her time getting to the point in any conversation. Unlike Malone.

The simple thought of her made him anxious to get back to the rodeo grounds.

Cade took a sip of the wine he rarely drank and wished he'd ordered beer. But he wasn't going to be there long enough for it to matter. He was unlikely to finish his drink in any case.

"What's on your mind, Keena?"

She turned her glass by the stem without lifting it from the table. Her dark eyes looked anxious and he waited for whatever bad news she had to impart. "You've had a bit of publicity the last few days."

"And little of it good," he stated baldly without offering any excuses. They might as well get to the point of her conversation.

"But one was an accident," she offered. "I mean it's horrible, but it happens in any high-risk sport, right?"

He looked at her, surprised at her direction. He nodded. "Yeah. It happens." He wasn't about to enlighten her that Rivers' death was likely *not* an accident.

"And the other. It could have been a fight that got out of hand. I mean, the police don't *know* at this point, do they?"

"If they do, they aren't telling me."

"So, it likely could have happened anywhere? Any other city you might have been in if you weren't here," she pressed.

Cade leaned back in his chair. This was definitely taking a different track than the one he'd thought she'd embark on. He'd expected to be castigated for the rodeo association marring the new image the city was striving to create. But, business being business, Cade decided to press his advantage. "Maybe." He paused intentionally. "But I've been in rodeo since my teens. This is a first for me. I've had cowboys tear up bars before, cut each other with pocket knives, hit each other with barstools, get bones broken, and need stitches. I haven't had anyone murdered on the grounds."

Her chin dropped. "Yeah." She spoke the word softly, then straightened her shoulders. "Well, I want you to know that I've met with the police chief and he understands this simply can't happen again. They'll need to do a much better job of patrolling the area around the equine center. I've put a lot – a lot! – into this deal with you. And, Cade, it's paying off! The hoteliers and restaurateurs are already calling me about the dates for next year, wanting to time other attractions with it, target their approach."

Cade felt more than a little guilty for her distress. In all probability, the association had brought this trouble with them. But there was nothing he could say that didn't carry the potential to jeopardize Ryder's investigation and keep girls like Joss at risk. He wouldn't take that chance regardless.

"I appreciate your talking with them. I'd like to see this resolved sooner rather than later. I have a whole lot of nervous competitors. I need to know they're comfortable coming back next year. They need to know they'll be safe."

He didn't intend to cause Keena the tension he saw in her expression but that was as honest as anything he could offer. Regardless of the outcome of the investigation. Regardless of who was arrested. What had happened needed resolution for all of them. The less than honest part was that Cade didn't think the city police were going to be the ones to solve this case.

He glanced at the time as Keena dropped him off close to where she'd picked him up, relieved that they'd been gone barely an hour. Aleta would have called if anything ominous had happened in his absence but he was relieved to be back on the premises.

He collected Townsend from the show office and headed to the coliseum giving a brief thought to Trouble's whereabouts but knowing the cat was independent and self-sufficient to say the least.

I DON'T THINK *our time was entirely wasted in perusing the stock trailers. I also don't necessarily think it garnered us any new information. It certainly gave me no opportunity to reveal the identity of the cowboy who sent Quinn Rivers to his death. Frustrating, that. I'm not certain and cannot prove that he damaged that bull rope but I'm convinced beyond reasonable doubt that he knew the damage existed and what the consequences could be.*

To that end, I must gather up Mr. Silver Eyes and get him to the bucking chutes where we are most likely to encounter the miscreant. I've checked the show office and Townie is no longer ensconced there so I've no doubt they are on the grounds together someplace. I strongly suspect that he has sought the presence of Ms. Rodeo so, first stop, the barn area where she will be readying for tonight's barrel race.

All things considered, I shall keep my senses on alert as I navigate that distance. So many occurrences in such short order make it imperative that I miss nothing, whether it seems of immediate interest or not.

The sport of rodeo does pull a crowd and generates an amazing sense of energy. Each day the spectator parking areas become more and more crowded as the day goes along. Morning is lightest in terms of spectators and interest but the crowd grows throughout the day and peaks each evening when the barrel racing and rough stock riding takes place.

I move lightly among the coming and going of spectators, young parents pushing strollers, children tugging at the hands of their parents, adults navigating the elderly in wheelchairs or walking slowly beside them as they maneuver their walkers. Rodeo, it seems, appeals to all ages. I find the sport of interest but am not overly fond of the clowns, outside their role in bullfighters. Their skill and courage astound me. Then, disappointingly, they descend into the ignoble depths of loud noises and inept comedy routines that — for some reason — delight the crowds.

Ms. Rodeo is exactly where I expected her to be, brushing a lovely blue roan to a high gloss. I am fond of the color of this one's coat perhaps because it stands out in a world of bays and sorrels, rather like a black cat amongst the more mundane tabbies.

Joss is busy with scrubbing and filling water buckets, a never-ending chore it would seem.

I see no sign of my real target so I suppose he's tied up in the running of things, a necessary but often thankless task.

Joss moves to stand in the open doorway, watching. "How do you ride this one?"

I would think that an odd question had I not become so conversant with barrel speak. Once, I would have answered in my head with some disdain that the horse would be ridden astride with saddle as they all are.

"Frisco runs to the left which is always tricky for me. I have to be careful that I don't pull him off point. He's also a push-style so I can't sit too quick, not nearly as early as most of the others. If I do, he'll slow too soon. If I ride him right, he'll pull a check." *She stops grooming to look at Joss, giving her a smile.* "If I don't pull a check you can ask me what I did wrong."

Joss smiles back. "I won't have to."

Her faith is complete. And understandable.

Soon, the roan is saddled and ready. Joss retrieves the requisite western hat from its hook in the stall they have set up as a temporary tack and feed room. It keeps everything they need close at hand for the care of the horses. Along we go to the warm-up pen, while I keep my eyes 'peeled' in private eye jargon for Mr. Silver Eyes. I do not understand my own rising tension. I have an increasing sense of foreboding as if time and opportunity were slipping away. Though it is unexplained, I have learned not to ignore those feelings. Something as yet unknown to my consciousness is unsettling me.

Time is of the essence and action must be taken. I will figure out the rest as I go. I always do.

I veer off from the ladies, more determined than ever to find Mr. Silver Eyes and give him the information he needs, the information he asked of me.

CADE WAS DETERMINED to be waiting when Malone left the arena this time and he'd be damned if he'd yield one inch to LaMonte. He almost hoped the other guy would dare just so he could plant him one. And wouldn't that be the icing on the cake for a man who was supposed to be an example for his members. A good example.

Hell. He was losing it. He made a brief stop at the concession stand where he was handed a bottle of chilled water and his money was declined because he was recognized. Oh, yeah, it'd be real wise of him to get into a fistfight with LaMonte.

Just as he'd decided to take a seat in the stands for a few minutes, he saw Trouble prowling the broad, crowd-thronged hallway. He stopped to see which way the cat was headed when

Trouble turned and looked him in the eyes. Without hesitation, the cat wove his way through the cowboy boots and sneakers around him never taking his eyes off Cade.

When Trouble reached Cade, he didn't stop but continued on, glancing back once to be sure Cade followed. Cade did.

Trouble led him without hesitation to the bucking chutes where the first bronc rider was limping in painful victory from the arena. He'd made his ride, now he'd be praying his points would be worth the pain of the landing. Cade heard the announcer call his score as he rounded the corner. It was a good one. He felt certain the cowboy had heard as well, judging by the grin on his face.

Cade felt a sense of urgency to complete whatever Trouble's mission might be and make his way to the other end of the arena before Malone's run.

While the bronc riders were competing for their moment of glory, the bull riders were warming up with stretches and making last minute checks on their equipment. Only the barrel racers stood between them and their event. Nerves were heightened. He heard it in the ribbing each gave the other, saw it in the taut expressions on their faces, in the knee bends and elbow pulls against pipe railing around the livestock enclosures as they tried to work the tension from their muscles.

He followed in Trouble's wake, the black cat casting glances his way from time to time to ensure obedience. Cade felt a grim sort of amusement at his situation. Amusement faded as he realized who the cat had lined up in his sight.

The cowboy stood propped against the fence, his back to Cade, his bull rope slung over one shoulder, the bell hanging low. If Dawson saw the cat, he gave no evidence of it, even when Trouble moved close enough to touch him. Trouble sat on his haunches and turned one last glance toward Cade before he pushed upward and touched the dangling bell lightly with extended claw.

Something, some subtle movement of the rope, the tiny swing of the bell, or the light sound of it caught Dawson's attention, pulling it away from conversation with fellow competitors and the tension of knowing his ride was sheer minutes away. He glanced down at the cat and pushed him away.

Cade felt gut-punched as he watched the swing of the bell slowly subside. There were a multitude of things he would have liked to do in that moment. He did none of them.

Dawson turned and his glance met Cade's briefly before he gave an offhand nod and looked back toward the activity in the arena.

Cade had knowledge. He was certain of it. But he had no proof. Without proof, he had no clear path forward. But, with fury rising from the pit of his stomach, he knew he would find it. As much as he wished for action, there was nothing to be done here or now. He couldn't afford to show his hand and put Dawson on the run.

Meeting Trouble's gaze, Cade turned back the way he had come. Halfway around, he heard Malone's name over the loudspeaker and cursed. He'd missed her run. Again.

I FEAR my human was less observant in the moment just passed than I could wish. I'm almost positive he failed to see the look of fury I received at bringing attention to our cowboy. How he shielded that fury in the look he gave his rodeo director. Not that Dawson White by any means comprehends that my paw on that small brass bell was a well-planned signal, an actual ID of the guilty. Nor would he believe it, if I were able to gloat to him over the fact at any point.

But when humans are guilty they are suspicious of everything. Dawson is now suspicious of Mr. Silver Eyes, wondering why he was there, why he was watching. This exchange, however well intended, may have put my human partner at risk.

After all, two are dead. What is one more to a murderer? Or murder-

ers? Something about his exchange with Quinn, seconds before the bull rider's death, makes me doubt he is guilty of breaking Roland Walker's neck. At least not hands on ... and certainly no pun is intended.

I decide it is in the best interest of the case to see where Dawson goes after his ride. And who he talks with.

Uh-oh, I have company. Why is Tyge following us? Well, perhaps not us. I don't think he has noticed me. But he is without doubt on Dawson's tail. I don't need this complication. Tyge could gum up the works. I haven't completely dissected his role in all of this but I suspect that – for reasons of his own – he is skirting a line between the master villain and the law. And a fine, thin line it is.

I fall behind him to ensure I remain undetected. Unexpectedly, Tyge veers away. I look up to see what has alarmed him but there's nothing save the typical bunch of cowboys before us. Dawson wades into their midst with the jovial tossing of insults toward the other rough stock riders. That repartee I've recognized as a bit of stock-in-trade for their sport.

After a moment, Dawson maneuvers his way through the cowboys and continues on which is a bit of a relief to me. I apply myself faithfully to my craft but it is late and I'm as tired as I am hungry. Well, perhaps not quite as tired but close. I endure much for my profession.

Ah, a familiar pair, Dawson greets young Luke and his father who are walking slowly and seeming lost in talk. I think they fared well in this morning's team-roping competition. Likely they are dissecting what they did right and what could be improved. I have learned this rehashing is a common practice among competitors. Regardless, it is heartening to see a father and son so close. I was more fortunate than some that my sire took a real interest in my formative years. His mentoring has played no small part in my success. A certain amount of talent can be passed through the genes but my father imparted his knowledge to me as well his aptitude. I am forever grateful for the time he took to do that.

I anticipate Dawson will pass them by on whatever mission draws him. Unexpectedly, he slows his step and falls into conversation with the father-son team. They draw near the Roberts' trailer and Luke gives his dad a nod and goes inside. I'm fascinated by this nomadic lifestyle of rodeo competitors. I can't help but wonder which feels more like a home, these trailers with minute quarters in which they live and travel for weeks, even months on end, or the houses to which they return.

To my surprise, Frank and Dawson prop against the rear bumper of a truck pulled close to the trailer, as if settling in for a bit of conversation. Feeling more comfortable now that I am amongst friends, so to speak, I leap lightly to the hood of the truck then on to the cab. Dawson pays me no mind. Frank casts a curious glance my way before losing interest as I curl into a ball. As I am determined to wait this out until Dawson continues on his way, I may as well take the opportunity to rest a bit.

I am quickly disabused of that notion as Frank glances towards the closed door of the trailer before turning a hard look toward Dawson. "What the hell do you think you're doing?" His voice is low but as unwelcoming as his expression.

So much for a friendly chat.

"You worried because your precious son knows we're out here talking?"

"Shut the hell up." Mr. Roberts no longer looks merely irritated. He is furious. I also detect a bit of apprehension. And so much for my good opinion of him. Something is definitely awry.

"I'll shut up. When I'm ready. You owe me. You owe me a hell of a lot more than you know. But, see, the problem for you is I don't trust you. Roland did. Quinn did. I don't. You need to know that I don't. And, you need to know I've taken out some insurance just in case something happens to me."

"Somebody got overzealous with Roland Walker, I'll admit, but I don't know what the hell you're talking about with Rivers." And there's the confession. At least one. I will admit to being stunned and a bit sickened. This is the father figure I so recently admired?

"Don't you?" Dawson's voice is quiet and menacing. "I did what I had to do but I blame you. Never forget that."

Clearly the underling believes himself to have the upper hand. And perhaps he does, as even my villain pales at his blatant admission of murder.

"You need to get out of here and if you're smart, you'll disappear for a good long time."

"No can do." *Dawson's expression is almost taunting.* "I'm leading the circuit right now. Lot of money riding on that – more than what you've paid me the past six months – and I ain't walking away from it. I'm here to let you know that it's best you make sure I come out of all this safe and sound. It won't go well for you – or your son – if I don't."

Uh-oh, Frank Roberts' complexion has gone flushed rather than ashen. He looks much closer to stroke-city as the younger set of humans might say. "Shut your damn mouth about Luke. He has nothing to do with any of this."

"Well, the way I have it set up in my insurance policy, it sure looks like he does. Remember, if I die or go to jail, you go down, and him with you."

Dawson pushes away from his comfortable prop against the tailgate of the truck but he has one last thing to say. "And that girl Luke's so sweet on?" *I tense at the words. What has this to do with our Joss?* "The one that caught Roland's attention? He wasn't fooling around and let it get out of hand. He said there was something familiar about her, something that made him nervous. He wanted a better look at her. Didn't that last load of girls get away from your drivers at the Lake Charles rodeo? I happen to know that Malone Summers was running that weekend."

Frank is now as taut as I. He stares at Dawson's retreating back as if he'd like to place a sharp blade between those shoulders. I suspect he would if he had a weapon in hand and if he were not now frightened of whatever Dawson has put in place as insurance for his own safety.

But I care nothing for the fate of Frank Roberts at the hands of Dawson. I must protect those in my care. My mind is racing as to how I can impart this momentous new knowledge to Mr. Silver Eyes in order to enlist his aid. I rise slowly and stretch as nonchalantly as I am able in my highly alarmed frame of mind. Frank has turned and is staring toward the trailer where his son rests, his expression a mix of fear and frustration. I am feeling something of the same.

His steps are heavy as he goes inside and I am free to leap down and hurry along the railing of the bed of the truck. As I prepare to leap again, to the pavement below, something catches my attention. There, in the bed of the truck, a spur, unbuckled and discarded. A single spur with an inlay of black filigree. And there I have it. The means with which to persuade Mr. Silver Eyes that a man he has likely known for half a lifetime is not worthy of his high regard. Such losses are regrettable but unavoidable. I have no time to waste on lamenting the fact. Joss, and Ms. Rodeo by association, are now in great danger.

I turn to go and am startled by the realization that Tyge has reappeared. He's in the shadows but clearly visible due to my superior vision. He is certainly within hearing distance of the exchange between Frank and Dawson. Alas I cannot wait to see what he may or may not do with his knowledge. I leave him staring at the door of the Roberts' trailer in my haste to find Mr. Silver Eyes.

CHAPTER NINETEEN

Malone was more than pleased with her run and Joss was almost vibrating with excitement when she met her in the paddock outside of the arena.

"Oh my gosh, that was awesome. You were flying!"

Malone grinned as she leaned against the gelding's neck, breathing in the warm clean scent of horse and victory. "Frisco did his job and he did it well."

As they made their way back to the barn, Malone's mind slid from her success in the arena to the stress that lay ahead. She pondered how to broach the subject with Joss who, as usual, gave her an easy opening.

"What's wrong? You quit smiling."

"Honestly, nothing, but we do need to talk."

Joss gave a snort of laughter. "I've heard that's the kiss of death to a relationship."

Malone smiled. "Only in the movies or romantic novels. Ours is solid. I've got your back, Joss, I promise." Despite the fact that Joss had expressed a desire to protect other girls from her foster home experience, Malone was worried. Would she panic at the thought of talking with an officer of the law? Decide to run? The mere possibility sent a crushing weight through Malone.

"Now you're really worrying me."

"You worry me all the time." Malone gave her a hug and was pleased when Joss didn't stiffen on her. "You said you wanted to do something about your foster parents. Do you still?"

"Almost more than anything," Joss said fiercely.

Later, Malone thought. Later I'll ask what she wants more than anything without the 'almost'. "Cade has arranged for a U.S. Marshal to talk with you. He can help." She hesitated. "But, Joss, if you want to call it off all you have to do is say so. This is your choice." Her eyes stung. When had this young stowaway become such a vital part of her life?

Joss' steps slowed until she turned to face Malone who stilled the horse she led with a silent command. "I'm not going to call it off. I can guess what was going to happen to me if I hadn't gotten away. But, Malone, I would have died first. I promise you. I would have killed or died or maybe both. Some girls aren't that strong. I think about those two younger girls and I want to cry for them. I don't know where they are. If they even survived getting away. It makes me want to hurt someone."

Malone caught her up and held her close. "I know, Joss. Me, too. But you're what's most important to me now. Don't disappear on me. No matter what. Promise me."

"I promise."

Joss' voice was steady and Malone drew a deep breath of relief. "Let's get this done, then."

They made quick work of unsaddling and brushing Frisco and making sure everyone had hay and a clean bucket of fresh water.

Cade and Ryder stepped from the shadows as she and Joss approached their trailer. When Malone would have made introductions, Cade shook his head and gestured toward the trailer door. Malone made quick work of unlocking it. Her fingers were trembling slightly and she hoped Joss didn't notice. That would do nothing to reassure the girl that all would be well.

Once inside, Malone felt chilled. Ryder accepted her offer to make coffee. Cade simply watched with a steady gaze as she readied the coffee pot.

She was glad when Ryder took the initiative, holding out his hand to Joss, waiting quietly until she shook hands with him.

"You're the U.S. Marshal."

"My name is James. James Ryder. I'm here to listen to your story. I can't fix what happened to you but maybe I can prevent it from happening to someone else. Even one someone else. That's how I know I've made a difference."

At his words, Joss seemed to relax. Malone hoped the reason was at least partly because her trust was that strong in Cade and Malone, herself.

Without rushing or wasting time, Ryder opened the subject of Joss' abduction and escape.

"I want you to tell me everything you can remember, Joss, but I want you to start further back from when you woke up in that semi. I want you to start with the day you walked into your last foster home."

Malone tensed but where once the girl would have dropped her chin to allow her hair to hide her features and her emotions, Joss lifted her chin. She started talking, telling her story in a low but strong voice. Malone hated hearing it again but, for Joss' sake, she kept her expression neutral, glad to busy herself with the coffeepot even for a little while.

"So, you don't recall your foster parents having visitors."

Joss looked surprised but only for a moment. "Sorry, I didn't mean to make you think that. They did but always late, after I was in my room. At least he did. He had card games a couple of times a week. I know there was drinking and I could smell cigars and cigarettes, but I never saw anyone."

"What about voices? Did you hear anyone."

"I could hear that they were talking but not what they were saying. I'm sorry."

"No apology needed." Ryder's expression turned grim. "Except to you."

He deftly walked Joss through waking up in the false bottom of a trailer, of her escape, and her worries for the other girls, her hopes that Ryder could find them.

Ryder accepted a second cup of coffee from Malone. She offered one to Cade but he shook his head. Instead, he tugged her down to sit beside him on the sleeper sofa Joss used. "She's doing fine."

"I know," she whispered, "but I'm not."

Cade pulled her in close and she sighed as she allowed him that liberty. "Keena looks good," she murmured.

"Yes, she does but not as good as you." Cade said easily. He seemed to understand that Malone needed to tune out the sound of the conversation going on beside them. She needed to not think about what so easily could have been the fate of a young girl who'd come to mean so much to her. "And she still talks too fast and too damn much."

Malone laughed softly against his chest and felt more than heard his hum of pleasure at the sound. Malone liked the unexpected feeling that had her breath catching her in her throat. The timing sucked but timing usually did.

"The good thing I got from all that chatter was that we aren't likely to lose our contract for use of the facility, despite two deaths in two days."

"You were afraid of that?"

"Everything about that deal has scared me. It was a risk moving from a place we've done business with for years, with a team who knows how to set up – not just for a rodeo – but for something as big as this. I had no idea what to expect in spite of all the assurances. But it's been good for the association and Keena says it's been good for the city. Apparently, she dogged out the local PD over their failure to keep everyone associated with us safe. This modernization means a lot to her."

His admission surprised her. It also reassured her as nothing else could have. He was no longer the autocratic, always right, young adult he'd been. He wasn't afraid to let her see his insecurities. That was real strength in a man.

A change in Ryder's tone pulled Malone back into the moment. "I need you to tell me about the truck, the trailer. Describe it to me as best you can."

Joss hesitated. "I'll try ... but it was dark and my head wasn't clear. And I was so scared. It wasn't like a horse trailer."

"Maybe a stock trailer? I've seen some here at the back of the arena."

"Not quite like those. It was a big truck kind of trailer. It was a long way down when I jumped onto the guy with the gun. But the sides were slatted, not solid. I've seen them on the highways, hauling little calves or crates of chickens. I haven't seen any here."

"Any kind of logo or name on the cab of the truck?"

"I didn't look. I just got up off the ground and ran." She sounded disappointed in herself.

"You did exactly what you needed to do. You saved yourself. To have hesitated, even one split second to look around, could have cost you your life. Joss, I'll be honest. Chances are I'll never hear anything about the girls who were with you. I'll also tell you that could as easily be a good thing as a bad thing."

Ryder got to his feet and Malone studied Joss anxiously before giving a sigh of relief. The girl looked less tense than at any point since the day she and a stowaway had faced each other down.

CADE DIDN'T WANT to leave Malone but he had no real reason to linger. It was late and she and Joss looked exhausted.

He touched her cheek in a silent message and exited the trailer with Ryder. They walked a short distance and paused to talk quietly. "Did that help?" Cade knew it had been traumatic for Joss to share her story with a stranger. He didn't want it to have been in vain.

"Everything helps. I just don't always know how at the time," Ryder admitted. "I gather slivers of information however I can get them and put them together when I can. I'll find these bastards. I can promise you that much."

"And the foster parents?"

Ryder's smile was somehow grim while genuine. "Now see, that's the best part. I get to nail those bastards for sure. And, with any luck, they'll spill their guts to lighten their sentences."

"I don't want their sentence lighter." Cade's hands were clenched into fists and he knew what he wanted was a chance to pound the couple, both of them, into the ground.

"I'll do my dead level best to make sure it isn't – even if they come out feeling like it is at the time. And this could lead back to a real bust, something a hell of a lot bigger than this one couple. If it does, you getting Joss to talk to me could mean a lot of people in jail right along with them."

Cade shook his head. "I won't take any credit. Joss wanted to talk to you, didn't want other foster kids put in that home. She's one brave girl."

"She'll have to be brave again when she tells her story to the judge but I'll push for that to happen soon. She's a minor and a victim. I suspect we can get her testimony in a closed session so she never has to see the bastards who sold her again."

As Ryder walked away, Cade snapped his fingers to bring Townsend to heel. A streak of black nearly bowled the Aussie over but the dog gave only a slight yip of surprise and Cade recognized Trouble. He was almost anticipating the swipe of a sheathed paw against his leg and the head-butting that warned he was expected to follow. And to be fast about it.

With Townsend at his side, he shadowed the cat closely, praying he wasn't destined to find another murder victim. They moved in silence through the neat rows of now darkened trailers. The grounds were so quiet around them he could hear the click of Townsend's toenails on the pavement. There wasn't a sound from the black cat.

In less than ten minutes, the cat looked at him from the rail of a truck bed. Cade stepped closer. A security light cast enough glow for Cade to make note of a tire jack, a worn pair of boots and a spur. He stared, trying to make sense of what he saw, denying it even as he recognized the plain leather strap and the tracery of black inlay.

With a heavy heart, he turned to look at the trailer, forced himself to move, to knock on the trailer door. After a moment, he heard a stumbling inside and then Luke peered out at him sleepily and a bit anxiously.

"Mr. Cade? Is something wrong?"

"I need to speak to your dad."

Luke looked even more anxious. "He's not in here. I came in while he was talking with Dawson White. Is everything okay?"

"Probably. Just something on my mind. Tell him I came by."

"Sure. Should I call him?"

"No." Cade had to force himself not to respond with alarm at the suggestion. "It's not urgent. We can talk in the morning. Get some rest."

By the look on the boy's face, Cade didn't think that was likely to happen. He hoped the kid stayed inside and safe until Cade figured out what was going on. As much as he disliked the sight of that spur in Frank's truck, recognizing it as a match to the one he'd given Ryder, he disliked the thought of Frank in conversation with Dawson White even less. Things were about to get ugly.

His most urgent thought was to get back to Malone and Joss. There were now too many ugly connections. Joss' abduction. Ryder's investigation. The deaths of two men. No way was all of this coincidental. And somehow, Frank Roberts, a man he'd always considered a good role-model for kids learning to rope and ride, was caught up in all of it. Perhaps more than caught up, he might be front and center.

It seemed to Malone she had barely locked the door behind Cade and the marshal when she was opening it again to Tyge's voice and the pounding of his fist on her door.

"What the hell, Tyge!" She had a moment's thought that she didn't need to be cursing in front of Joss who sat on the edge of the sleeper couch, watching warily.

"You've got to get out of here, Malone. You and the girl! You're both in danger."

Joss stood abruptly and Malone glanced her way, seeing the fear in her eyes, the scattering of light freckles, suddenly emphasized by a face leached of color.

Malone's gaze swept the fading bruises on Tyge's face. "What's happened now?"

"There's no time for explanations. I've got to get you someplace safe."

"I don't know what's going on, but I'm not leaving, Tyge. I've got a gun and I'll fight, but I won't leave."

"Shit, Malone." Tyge grasped her arm and for a moment, she thought he might pull her from the trailer, then she heard a sickening thud and Tyge was falling forward into her arms. She stared in shock at his back, at the hole in his shirt, the blood that welled instantly.

In that instant, she froze, realizing her danger. Framed in the open doorway with Tyge heavy in her arms, she was exposed to whoever held the gun. She looked up, gazed without understanding into the eyes of Frank Roberts. She thought he said 'I'm sorry' before he lifted the gun again but the words were lost to Joss' scream and a shot fired wildly as Frank fell beneath Cade's weight.

. . .

Cade suspected that, for the rest of his life, he would never forget that heart-wrenching second of fear between seeing that gun aimed at Malone and finding the wits to launch himself at a man he would never have suspected of committing any crime, much less murder.

Even now, leaned against the trailer with Malone cradled against his chest, his arms wrapped around her as they waited for the ambulance and Ryder to arrive, he couldn't slow the hard thuds of his heart beat.

Lying just inside the trailer door, Tyge was alert and cursing with pain. Cade suspected the bullet had hit a rib but, thank God, not his heart. The slow welling of blood wasn't the gush of heart or artery. As little fondness as Cade had for the cowboy, he didn't wish him dead and he sure as hell didn't need another body on the grounds.

Frank sat with hands tied with hay string, staring at the gun in Cade's hand. Every now and then he glanced at Townsend who growled each time the man moved even though he wasn't trying to get away.

Joss stood close and quiet, holding Malone's hand.

When Ryder showed up, he looked from the gun in Cade's hand to Frank. "He might've made you shoot him."

"He might have," Cade said quietly and Ryder nodded. Cade added, "I didn't call Hendrix."

"Out of his league. He'll be mad as hell, but I'll take care of it. This one belongs to the feds." He paused. "I guess the cat helped you nail him."

Cade sighed. "I'm afraid so, and, no, I can't explain any better than that."

Ryder shook his head in amusement. "Any others to go along with him?"

"You'll want to look hard at Dawson White."

"I can help with that." It was the first time Frank had spoken since Cade had planted him on the pavement. One side of his face looked like he'd been dragged across asphalt. Cade took great pleasure in that but it was far less than he wanted to do to the man.

Cade felt Malone shift and reluctantly let her go. She walked over to Frank and looked down at him. "Why?" He heard the bewilderment in her voice. "You tried to kill Tyge. Then you aimed the gun at me and you were going to pull the trigger. And Joss next? Why?"

Frank shook his head and looked away. Joss crossed to her and looked down at Frank without expression before she turned her back on him and hugged Malone.

Cade wanted more than anything to stay with Malone but, now that she was safe, there was something else he had to do. And he dreaded it. "Someone has to tell Luke what's happened."

He'd spoken softly, but Frank heard him. "Cade. You take care of my boy. He doesn't know any of this. He's going to need someone."

"I guess you should have thought of him sooner."

Cade made the walk to the trailer where he knew Luke wasn't asleep. He knocked on the door and, once inside, told Frank's son what had just happened.

"I don't know the whole of it, Luke, but I know he was involved in some ugly stuff."

Tears leaked from Luke's eyes. "My dad's not a bad man. If he did bad things it's because of money. He thinks I don't know but we still get bill after bill from when mama was sick. There wasn't insurance and the year after she died the drought hit us hard. We lost crops and calves and couldn't pay that year's mortgage on the farm. We caught up some last year..." His voice trailed off and Cade suspected he realized the 'catching up' had come at someone else's expense.

"I'm sorry, son." As much as he would have liked to agree with

Luke that his dad wasn't a bad person, he couldn't say the reassuring words. "I've called your uncle. He's on his way to get you and take care of things here." Cade hadn't a clue if the man would try to post bond for Luke's dad. He didn't even know if a judge would set bail, considering the crimes committed. He doubted it. But that was for someone else to learn and share with Luke. Cade wouldn't speculate.

What Cade could do was comfort a frightened and grieving young man, and he pulled Luke against his chest and let him cry.

TWO MORNINGS LATER, Ryder made one more trip to the rodeo grounds, striding into Cade's office with an air of satisfaction. Cade laid aside the bills he was approving for payment and got to his feet.

As the men shook hands, he said, "The first time you came in here you were a man on a mission. Now you look like a man with mission accomplished."

"Not entirely," Ryder admitted, "but a satisfying part of it." At Cade's gesture, he took a chair opposite the desk. "The foster parents are nailed. Because of Joss, we got there just in time to stop a fifteen-year-old kid – boy this time – from being loaded on a truck to hell."

Cade was glad for that, gladder than he could say, but his thoughts went immediately to Joss. "So, she won't have to testify, right? You've got all you need?"

"All we need and more, but – the thing is – the boy wants to talk to Joss. He doesn't know her name, but he knows her story. That she had courage and character to come forward. And because she did, we were there and ready. And this kid, and who the hell knows how many others, are safe now."

"Joss will be happy at the outcome. Whether or not she'll talk with the boy is her choice and I don't know how she'll feel." Cade was adamant on that. It was Joss' decision.

"Fair enough. But I've got them on standby waiting for a call back. I need to know. I need you to ask."

Cade pulled up Malone's number, experienced the now-familiar rush of emotion in the moments it took her to answer. "Good morning, again." They'd shared coffee outside her trailer door, watched the sun rise together. Coffee and memories and possibilities. Joss had figured into that conversation. "Can you bring Joss to my office? No, nothing's wrong. Ryder's here with news. Good news."

He put the phone aside and nodded at Ryder. "It will take them a few minutes. They're at the barn."

While they waited, Ryder brought him up to speed on other aspects of the case. Frank would likely spend the rest of his life in prison. The charges against him were staggering. Ryder hoped he could use some of those charges to convince Frank to talk, to help him locate the head of a crime organization of monumental proportions. The man had eluded capture for far too long. Ryder needed this to be the case that brought him and others to justice.

Both men stood when the door opened. Malone glanced quickly at Cade. Whatever she saw must have reassured her because she found a faint smile for the deputy marshal. Joss looked just as tense but she also looked determined to see this through, just like she had everything else that had come her way.

Before Cade could close the door, Trouble slipped by him and made the leap over Townsend to the windowsill.

When they were all seated, Cade nodded at Ryder who started talking. By the time he was done describing the eleventh-hour rescue of another teen, silent tears streamed slowly down Joss' cheeks.

"You did it," she said huskily. "You really did it."

Ryder shook his head. "No, Joss. *You* did it. And the boy you saved wants to thank you for that. He's waiting for us to call him, if you're willing."

Joss swiped at the tears and lifted her chin. "I'd like that."

Ryder pulled up a number and slid the volume up on his cell so they all could hear. His agent answered promptly and Ryder said, "Joss is here. Put him on."

There was a faint rustling at the other end, then, "Joss? My name's Kevin and I just – I just wanted to thank you. I can't believe what happened. What almost happened to me." His voice was low and breaking in places as a boy's voice often did in early teens. And, perhaps, as much from the horror of the past hours as his youth.

"But you're safe now." Joss' voice was firm. "Everything's going to be okay."

"I wouldn't be safe if you hadn't been brave, if you hadn't stepped forward and made someone listen."

Cade saw the glance Joss gave Malone, the soft smile. "It didn't take much 'making'. All I had to do was open my mouth and say the words. There was someone here ready to listen all along."

CHAPTER TWENTY

I suppose this rodeo life is perfect for those who love it but it seems like much hard work to me. I ascribe to the theory 'work smarter not harder' and there doesn't seem to be much leeway with this sport. But it is exciting, I'll grant you that. Especially now, on this final day. I've ascertained that Malone is neck and neck in money earnings with two other contestants. It all comes down to this final day, this final 'run for the money'.

Malone is 'up' as they say on the big mare she calls Jaz. I recall the day Malone came to Summer Valley Ranch to pick her up. There was an immediate rapport between the two. And now I hear the announcer extolling the virtues of both.

"Ladies and Gentlemen, our next rider is Malone Summers, a long-time professional in the sport of rodeo. Her fellow competitors know that Ms. Summers lost her beloved Jupiter to a tragic accident two years ago. Then just a few months ago, just as he was clocking some of the best times on the circuit, her good horse, Mylo, was sidelined with an injury. Some barrel racers only get one true champion barrel horse in a life time. Ms. Summers has had - or should I say created - many more than that. And now I'd like to introduce you to JJ's Red Jasmine, a rescue horse that has been rescued indeed. Ms. Summers calls her Jaz and most of us believe Malone has saved the best for last with her hopes riding high on the big red mare's ability."

Quite unexpectedly, my own heart is pounding with excitement. There must be something supremely exhilarating about riding an agile equine through an intricate pattern of incredible speed, brief slow-downs and what look to be sling-shot turns. There is also that twinge of fear for my temporary human who looks so small and fragile above the massive creature.

As they fly back toward the alleyway, the announcer, always so professional and in control, unexpectedly shouts with excitement as he calls out the time. Apparently, my human has set a new record for the week. I am pleased, to say the least. Life has not been easy for her but I don't think she expects it to be nor grieves that it is not. She takes each day with a sense of joy as does my Tammy Lynn whom I have begun to miss enormously. It is always so at the end of a case and I am no longer caught up in the urgencies of saving lives and solving crimes. Time for me to return home and I will be glad to do so.

MALONE SLOWED Jaz as they hit the alleyway. Her heart was so full she wondered that it could contain her happiness in that moment. Jaz was everything she'd hoped and needed her to be. Never a replacement for Jupiter. Never a replacement for Mylo, if it had come to that. But a treasure and a joy in her own right. Malone knew she was blessed to be able to make her living in just this way and she never, ever took that or the animals that enabled her to do it for granted.

Midway down the alley, a cowboy stepped away from the fence panel and placed a hand on Jaz's rein. Malone looked into Cade's eyes and it felt like coming home. For a moment, she was twelve to his seventeen, at the beginning of a crush that had turned into so much more and lasted a lifetime. For both of them.

EPILOGUE

I ride shotgun, looking out Cade's truck window. I switched vehicles at the last truck stop ... quite a bit of girl talk going on in the other rig which is all well and good if you're a female. I'll admit new beginnings are exciting. Malone is moving herself, Joss, and her horses back home to LaGrange, Georgia which is satisfyingly close to Mr. Silver Eyes' family abode. No coincidence in all that I suspect. It is also in nice proximity to my home with Tammy Lynn in Wetumpka so they'll make a wee stop there to ensure my long over-due arrival.

Although, in my estimation, it would have been fitting for our Joss to witness the arrest of the couple who had so sorely betrayed her, I suppose Ms. Rodeo has the right of it. Joss should be spared any further sight of them. Would that she could be spared the thought of them as well, but Ms. Rodeo is of the firm belief that time and love will heal all wounds.

Otherwise, the wrap up of our case was entirely satisfying to me. I enjoyed watching as the villains were arrested, even the gentleman with the starburst scar whose part in this drama I've yet to discern. I think I would have enjoyed, even more, seeing the moment when the nefarious foster parents were handcuffed and forced from their homes but it must suffice that Joss was assured it was so. Never again will innocent victims be at their mercy.

There was a bittersweet moment for Ms. Rodeo when the Tyge was carried away on a stretcher in handcuffs. He saved her life, after all, and they were once much to each other. We've since learned that Tyge has a chance at probation or at least a lighter sentence. Although guilty of transporting drugs, he didn't knowingly transport guns or humans and has wisely expressed a willingness to share information with the law.

I've a concession that must be made. The sight of the Aussie standing guard over our villain was unexpected and must be acknowledged. I suppose it now behooves me to leave off the scathing abbreviation of his given name. He has earned the right to his dignity. Townie is no more. Townsend, it is.

There's another touch of sadness mixed in with the happy. It seems the renowned veterinarian, Dr. Tucker, has determined that Mylo will live to a comfortable and ripe old age, but his career days are over. Ms. Rodeo has a nice pasture in mind for him to graze and play to his heart's contentment right where she can take good care of him.

She and Joss will be busy for a while turning the old homestead into a thriving training facility for young equestrians who have a goal of becoming as great a competitor as Ms. Rodeo. Not that she's planning to retire from her own competitive endeavors. She assures Joss there's plenty of opportunity for both, as long as she's not competing in two circuits.

Yes, they will be busy indeed with lots of hard work, but I think Mr. Silver Eyes will bring much to that endeavor in terms of willingness, energy, and muscle. I suspect I hear wedding bells tinkling in their future. I do hope they recall that I am quite fond of wedding delectables.

Now if Townsend will quit trying to climb up beside me on this seat, I believe I can take a much-needed nap.

ACKNOWLEDGMENTS

Thank you to FB Launch Party contest winners, Susan Eiland Hayes and Katylynn Thomas Wright. Susan submitted the name Townsend and Katylynn suggested the breed of Australian Shepherd. I hope you love reading about him as much I loved writing him into my story.

Continued thanks to my sister, Janice Jones for stick horses and prayers.

And, ever, to my daughter, Stephanie Chisholm, who supports me mentally and physically in all the things I love to do.

And, always, to my son, Jeremy Rogers, who does for me all the things that need to be done so I can focus on doing all those things I love to do.

ABOUT THE AUTHOR

Although Susan Y. Tanner is best known for her historical romance novels, she is finding her niche in a new genre – contemporary romantic mystery. In *Trouble in Summer Valley*, her first book in the Familiar Legacy series, she introduced readers to the rescue horses of Summer Valley Ranch. In *Turning for Trouble*, she combines her passion for barrel racing with her passion for rescue horses in a rodeo setting. Tanner continues to barrel race and write with equal enthusiasm.

www.susanytanner.com

facebook.com/susan.tanner.376

amazon.com/author/susantanner

TROUBLE'S WEDDING CAPER

Familiar Legacy #8

TROUBLE'S WEDDING CAPER

Chapter 1

"*A*re you ready, Trouble?"

My new human mate, Annabel Wilder, scoops me up, mind you a little too eagerly, and scratches the top of my head.

With a sophisticated purr that only the most refined cats can conjure, I let her know that I approve of the delicious scratches. I tilt my head, so she can properly get behind my ears.

"This is going to be the one. I can feel it." Her excitement over visiting the Public Storage facility piques my natural curiosity. I've never heard of anyone purchasing the contents of an abandoned storage unit filled with someone else's belongings. While I find it highly unlikely that humans in England do such things, I believe that the remarkable Sherlock Holmes would find it an utterly fascinating opportunity to study human nature.

Annabel's racing heart beats against my body as she glances between the elevator and me. She taps her foot, too, as if that will make the doors open more quickly. At least her touch on my fur is still gentle. I find I rather like this energetic young woman.

I've quite enjoyed my stay thus far in Jupiter, Florida. It's a quiet place, not like other parts of Southern Florida. Once you cross the bridge over the Intracoastal, the sea of cars clogging the roads magically disappear, and the sense of urgency to be in the right place at the right time slips away. My owner, Tammy Lynn, told me I'd have a nice, relaxing, drama-free time with her friend's niece while Tammy Lynn boarded a yacht for a remote island to examine a few rare books with a dear friend.

I'm rather glad she didn't take me. I doubt I'd appreciate the boat, surrounded by a salty ocean, no matter how good the fish might be.

The second the doors ding open, Annabel dashes through the modest lobby and races across the parking lot to her bright-red, hardtop Jeep. I'm thankful that, so far, she's only taken the very back part of the top off. Unlike a dog, I do not like to stick my head out the window with my tongue lolling out.

Such an unrefined species!

Annabel settles me on the pink, plaid cat bed she bought the morning she agreed to take me in for a few days. The bed is comfortable, and it was very sweet of her to procure it, but pink is no color for a male cat of my stature. Here in the US, pink may be the new masculine color, but I prefer more dignified tones.

After kneading the appalling bed for a few moments, I settle in for the ride. Annabel hops into the driver's seat, amped up as though she's drunk an entire pot of coffee, even though I know she hasn't touched a drop. As she pulls out onto the road, her fingers tap constantly on the steering wheel, and she fidgets in her seat.

Her restlessness is bad enough, but her attire is even more distressing. I have no problem with a woman wearing denim shorts, but hers are frayed and full of holes, as though they've been chomped on by wild creatures. And her tight, red-sleeved T-shirt bears the words SALTY CREW. Whatever can that mean? In other circumstances, the origins of the phrase SALTY CREW might be worth investigating. But right now, I'm on vacation.

However, I shall make it my mission to help her wean herself away from wearing her rather grubby baseball cap backward on her head. With her sapphire eyes, high cheekbones, and flawless skin, she could be a fashion model. She has a devastating smile that can turn even the cloudiest mood to a sunny one. The cap makes her look like a troubled teenage delinquent.

Ding, ding, ding.

Ahead, the Intracoastal drawbridge on Indiantown Road that allows tall boats to ease through the waterway signals that it's about to lift. Annabel slows the Jeep to a stop.

"Crap. I can't be late. I can't be late," she mutters.

I press my paws against the dashboard to get a look at the rising bridge. My earlier experience with the bridge tells me that it will take ten minutes to cross. Because we're one of the first few vehicles in line, we'll be on our way quickly enough. I recall her saying the facility is ten minutes away, and she has to be there by 9:30. I remember because I have a superior memory. It's only 9:05. We shall make it.

When we finally reach the other side of the bridge, Annabel, her fingers still drumming, soon pulls the Jeep into an establishment containing acres of metal buildings and a rough gravel parking lot. We park in a spot near where a crowd of people have gathered.

"Want to come with me?" Annabel gets out, leaving her door open. She smiles at me.

No way am I going to sit in this heat and wait for her. She might do something foolish. She'll need my help and advice.

I raise my paw and reach out, tilting my head. I've seen many a cat pander to humans in this manner. After all, Annabel doesn't know I'm a superior cat with intelligence and wit. Not yet, anyway.

She lifts me from the car seat, and I settle myself in her arms. I could walk, but why? This pavement is cracked, and twenty-two people stand right outside the office door, waiting impatiently, tapping their feet. I have no desire to be anywhere near that.

Being as smart as I am, with more than impressive detective skills, it's hard for me not to take a look-see around. There is a four-door sedan parked in front of the gate at the entry to the storage facility. I note an outstretched arm fiddling with a keypad before a fist bangs against the door of the vehicle. A man, wearing a short-sleeved white dress shirt, pink shorts, and a baseball cap steps from the car.

A young boy, no more than twenty, based on his complexion, races from the main building toward the unhappy man.

My human scratches my head, reminding me I am indeed on vacation and being aware of every detail around me is not necessary, though, out of the corner of my eye, I continue to watch the heated discussion.

An older woman with graying hair steps from the office, greeting the crowd with a welcoming smile, but it's obvious, she too is slightly interested in whatever is happening between her employee and another customer.

It isn't until the customer disappears into the office that I focus my attention back to the older lady as she explains the rules with such enthusiasm that even I feel a tinge of excitement. Okay, I'm more indifferent, but I'm listening, and one thing strikes me as odd. If a person can't afford to pay their storage fee, how can anything of value be left behind?

Well, I'm about to find out as the woman cuts the lock off the first unit. Now, the humans are not allowed to enter the box. They have to make their bids based what they see from the outside. This one happens to be filled with unopened boxes, but maybe, deep in the back, there is something of value.

I press my paws against my human, and she kindly sets me on the ground. I pop inside, making my way around, nudging a few boxes along the way. The musty scent tickles my nose, so no sniffing around. I know Annabel has limited funds, so I want to help her get the most for her money, and this one isn't it.

A man, not much older than Annabel, wins the bid for a thousand dollars. I sincerely hope the contents are worth it.

I follow the crowd to the next unit. This one too has a lot of boxes, but the tops are open and one in particular catches my interest. A white wedding veil cascades over the cardboard.

I shudder. Even months later, the world is still abuzz about the Royal wedding. I watched days of coverage on the telly from the comfort of Tammy Lynn's lap, but really, even my love of all things British was taxed by the gossipy and sometimes tawdry American perspective.

Careful not to draw too much attention to myself, I enter the storage unit. I'm an expert at blending in, and it's one of the reasons I'm the best detective.

And I know Sherlock Holmes would agree.

I weave my way through a maze of boxes filled with more veils, dried flowers, and now I'm standing in front of a mannequin, dressed in a beautiful, lacy, white gown. Not as eloquent as Meghan Markle's, but it has potential, had it not had a big tear down the side of the train.

As much as I want nothing to do with weddings, this is the unit for Annabel, and I need to find a way to tell her without cueing the rest of the group that the contents are indeed worth a pretty penny. I hear a male voice start the bidding at one thousand dollars. Lucky for Annabel, I'm quick on my feet and a great cat-to-human communicator.

I rub my side against her leg, then take a few steps toward the storage unit. I repeat this a few times, making sure I look directly at Annabel before turning my head.

"What is it, Trouble?" she whispers, kneeling.

Someone in the back of the crowd raises their hand and yells, "Fifteen hundred."

I raise my paw, glancing over at the woman asking for another bid.

"You think this is a good one?"

Bingo. Not that I would ever say bingo, but Annabel is turning out to be smarter than the average human.

"Two thousand." Annabel lifts me once again. I could get used to being carried around wherever I go. The view up here isn't too bad either.

"Twenty-two hundred," the competing voice shouts.

I raise my paw, giving Annabel a look that says keep going until you can't go anymore. Not all humans would understand this look, but I have faith in this one.

"Twenty-five hundred," she says.

"Twenty-seven hundred," another voice insists.

I hold my paw high and tap her shoulder. My amusement in storage wars fades as the temperature in sunny Florida rises and the humidity sticks to my elegant coat. I really want to get back to the windowsill in the master bedroom. I love the way the sun beats down this time of the morning while the fan above pushes a cool air-conditioned breeze in my direction, making it a perfect place to relax and take a nap.

"Twenty-nine hundred," Annabel bids.

"Sold to the lady with the cat."

Finally. We can go back to the condo.

"Let's go see what we've got," *Annabel's tone is electric.*

I yawn and climb up on one of the boxes where a tad of sunlight brightens the dingy storage area and curl up, licking my paw.

My work here is done.

ANNABEL STOOD in front of a lacy wedding dress with a high neckline, much like she would have picked for herself maybe five years ago. Just above the breast line, woven into the mesh fabric was a pattern that looked as if it were the sign for female.

Annabel took a step back, admiring the classic dress with a frown, noticing the tear in the back, but being handy with a needle, she knew she could easily stitch it since it appeared to be on the seam.

The sleek, satin fabric of the bodice glided across her fingertips like velvet. The same silky material flowed down the sleeves to the wrist where an elastic band coiled around the hard, cool mannequin finger with a broken gold band.

"That's odd, don't you think?" She ran her finger over the bent ring, wondering how that had happened. It wasn't like gold metal was easily damaged.

She circled the dress, holding up the traditional train pooled at the floor, showing off a rose petal-like pattern, making sure she could indeed fix the tear.

She eyed the detail of the beads woven into the dress. They glowed a soft-pink color when the sunrays caught them just right.

It reminded her of her great aunt's gown that her cousin had altered in an attempt to modernize it without stripping it of its elegant history. A clash of present day style and timeless beauty.

Another beautiful wedding where Annabel had been a bridesmaid. Another event that reminded her of the eight years she'd wasted waiting for a man to commit to the long-term part of their relationship.

But the only thing Devin could ever devote his life to was his bank account and countless one-night stands that she had refused to acknowledge until her best friend's wedding.

What a wretched night that had been.

Another gown peeked out of a bag hanging on a rolling rack. This one was lined with ruffles, all big and fluffy. It had a princess neckline and was sleeveless, although, the material wasn't nearly as soft as the one displayed so eloquently.

She glanced back at the decapitated mannequin and shivered. It needed a head with a painted face, fake hair, and a veil. Otherwise it looked like it should be in some horror movie where the bride wandered the dark halls of an old church or the headless horseman raced down the street.

Pushing aside the feathery gown, she came across a pink bridesmaid dress. And not just any pink, but Pepto-Bismol pink. She cringed at the thought of having to wear it with its large shoulder pads and plunging neckline that ended in a point right above where she suspected her belly button would be. She'd been lucky, most of the dresses her friends and family had put her in were tasteful, and some she'd even been able to wear to other special events.

Not that she had anything special these days to go to, but it was nice to know she had a few options if her prince ever rolled in.

Next to pukey-pink was a yellow taffeta dress with a massive bow resting in the back, spanning the distance across the waistline, and two matching smaller ones on each shoulder.

Whatever bride made their maid of honor wear that hideous thing should be shoved into a mud puddle right after saying 'I do.' Talk about bad taste.

Annabel adjusted her baseball cap. Who was she to talk? Ever since her breakup with Devin, she'd been sporting rags. Her mother had been so mortified the last time she'd dropped by that she sent Annabel a gift card to the mall.

"I think I'll open that box first." Annabel folded open the chair she'd found and sat in front of the open door, letting the sun hit her face.

The black cat circled the mannequin a couple of times, climbing up on hind legs as if to take a better look at the wedding band.

Curious kitten.

"What do you think?" Annabel asked.

Trouble slinked back in her direction, leapt up on a box, and curled his tail and licked his front paw with meticulous care. She'd never had a pet before, but she could get used to having a cat around.

Especially one as easygoing as Trouble.

She flipped open the top of the box and pulled out a tiara. Running her fingers over the top, she wondered if any of the jewels that dotted the silver material could be real. They certainly sparkled like a rainbow after a warm summer's rain. She set it down next to Trouble, who shifted to the edge of the box, eyeing her suspiciously. "Aww, come on. Let's see how it looks." Before Trouble could scramble away, she managed to wrest the veil over the cat's head.

He meowed and hissed as he twisted and subsequently toppled off the box, tangling himself in the veil.

"You should have held still, you silly cat." Annabel carefully helped Trouble out of the wedding accessory.

He found a box a little farther away to curl up on.

She pulled out a small, white teardrop hat. A veil about two feet in length with white beads lining the bottom had been glued to the back of it. She tugged off her cap and rested the hat on her head and pulled half the veil over her face. "How about this one?" She cocked her head and put on her best sarcastic grin.

Trouble held up one of his front paws and lowered his head, as if to say, 'hell no.'

"I don't like it much either. Not my style and I doubt I'll do the white dress thing now, anyway. I'm more of a sundress on the beach kind of girl." It wasn't that long ago that she and Devin had been discussing the possibility of getting married. Well, she discussed it, and he always had a reason for waiting a few more years. At first, she was just fine with that. She never wanted to marry young and figured walking down the aisle sometime near her thirtieth birthday would be the perfect time.

She'd be thirty in a month and had not a single prospect.

She pushed the thoughts of Devin out of her mind. You couldn't make someone love you, and he loved someone else.

Himself.

Digging through the box, she found a velvet pouch. She dumped the contents into her hands and gasped. "Oh my, look at this," Annabel whispered, holding a large diamond ring in front of the cat, who blinked once, only mildly impressed by the shiny rock.

It sparkled as it caught the sunlight shimmering through the open bay door. The only question now: was it real?

"What do you think, Trouble?"

The sleek, black cat perked his head up for a moment, his tail swishing with a sophisticated swagger. Smart cat. She might not have held out for this particular unit had it not been for her furry new friend. Ever since the cat had shown up, her luck seemed to be changing, and after the year she'd had, she welcomed a little positive shift in the cosmos.

Whoever said black cats weren't lucky hadn't come across Trouble.

Darn, she hoped she hadn't just jinxed herself. She made a mental note to make sure a ladder never entered the same space as the cat.

"The stone is real, right?" The only way to find out would be to have it appraised, but she'd need to do some research first and take an inventory of everything in the unit. She didn't have to rush this, like she did so many things in her life. When she moved too quickly, she screwed things up.

A frustrated male voice caught her attention. She glanced toward the main building where a tall man wearing a short-sleeved, white dress shirt, pink shorts, and a baseball cap pointed in the direction of the storage units. She squinted, but the blazing sun made it impossible to get a good look at who it was, much less what he was saying. He delivered the words with fury and anger-fueled waving of his arms.

"Wonder what that's all about?" she asked, shaking her head, realizing she was conversing with a cat.

Trouble left his post and stood as if on high alert at the edge of the storage unit.

Curiously odd cat, but good company.

She grinned and focused on the rings. There had to be a story behind these items. Perhaps they belonged to a couple who'd been happily married for fifty years.

Or, they could belong to a divorced couple.

She took one of the rings and held it up in the sunlight as a Jupiter police car made the turn into the parking lot.

That couldn't be good.

Like a doe in headlights, she stared at the vehicle. Deep down she hoped the cop behind the wheel would be Ethan Ferris. She'd been in Jupiter for three weeks now, and she had yet to run into him. Not even when she'd had coffee with his sister, Rosie, and their mother, at his childhood home in the Bluffs. Not that she wanted to see him for any particular reason, she told herself. She was four years younger than him, and they traveled in different circles, but he was her best friend's brother, and by default, her friend.

The last time she'd seen Ethan had been at Rosie's wedding. Talk about awkward. Nothing like having your childhood crush walk you down the aisle as the maid of honor while his girlfriend flirted with your boyfriend.

And her behavior afterward. Her cheeks burned, remembering that scene in the hotel bar. Why she'd dared him to do a shot out of her belly button was a question she had no answer for.

That encounter successfully ended her relationship with Devin and destroyed Ethan's pending nuptials, though both had been about to end anyway.

A man stepped from the patrol car, but the angle of the sun blinded her. She stood, pulling her ball cap over her eyes and got a better view.

Officer Ethan William Ferris stuffed his sunglasses into the upper right pocket of his uniform.

He styled his brown hair in a high fade crew cut, which showed off his defined facial features. He hadn't changed much over the years. If anything, he'd gotten better-looking.

She squinted, trying to get a good look, remembering his amazing green eyes. In her nearly thirty years, she'd never seen eyes the color of an emerald before. When she'd been in high school and she'd spend the night at Rosie's house, her cheeks would run hot every time she caught his gaze.

Trouble tilted his head, one paw folded over the other, indifferent to the man in uniform.

"Nice specimen of a man, isn't he?" she asked the cat.

Trouble cocked his head and blinked.

"Come on, he's hot," Annabel mused as she sat down, kicking her leg back and forth restlessly. Ethan had been captain of the football and baseball teams and every girl's dream prom date. But Ethan only saw her as his kid sister's sidekick. "I'm tripping down memory lane talking to a cat. I'm turning into an old spinster." She shook her head and checked her watch. "Let's go, Trouble. We'll come back tomorrow and take inventory." Her heartbeat kicked up a notch as she rushed so she could at least say hello. No reason to avoid him.

After she boxed everything up, she locked her storage unit and made her way toward the gate where Ethan stood, thumbs looped into his belt, nodding his head at the storage facility manager's comments. The irritated customer was nowhere to be found.

She scratched the top of Trouble's head. Her pulse accelerated like it had when she'd been fourteen and Ethan had once driven her home from school.

Without Rosie.

Ethan had pulled into her parents' driveway in a well-hidden, gated neighborhood a few blocks from the Bluffs. When she pushed open the car door, turning her head to say good-bye, Ethan winked.

At her.

Hitting the button on the key fob to her Jeep, she reminded herself she was no adolescent, and she sure as hell didn't need a man. What she needed was to get her real estate license, since her New York one did nothing for her in the state of Florida.

Ethan snagged his sunglasses and just as he slid them up his nose, he turned his head and did a double take. "Well, I'll be damned. My sister told me you were back in town. She said something about buying a condo in Ocean Way?"

"Moved in three weeks ago and I love it," she said, reaching for the passenger side door and pulling it open.

He sauntered over, closing the gap between his patrol vehicle and her car. "You look great." He leaned in, dipping her cap, and kissed her cheek. A normal greeting for old friends.

"You don't look so bad yourself, Officer."

He laughed. "Who's your friend?" He scratched behind Trouble's ear.

She watched his fingers dig and twirl in the cat's fur. "This is Trouble. I'm cat-sitting for a week."

"Interesting name for a cat." Ethan, with his square jaw and high cheekbones, had the kind of smile that mesmerized anyone who dared to look.

She dared way too often. No matter how old she'd gotten, or who she'd been dating, Ethan always managed to make her heart beat just a little faster.

"Easiest cat I've ever met. And the smartest, too." When she set Trouble on the cat bed, he stood there for a long moment and stared at her with his head tilted. It was as if he were amused by her interaction with Ethan.

"I never did get to apologize for what happened the night of Rosie's wedding," Ethan said, leaning against her car and folding his arms across his chest.

"Nothing happened," she said, trying not to let the memories flood her mind.

"Your boyfriend caught us in a slightly compromising position, and I'm sorry if that caused you more problems with Devin."

"We did nothing wrong."

"I was sucking alcohol off your stomach." Ethan grinned.

"Adolescent, poor decision-making, sure. Alcohol fueled, you bet. But he was screwing someone else anyway." She closed the passenger door and made her way to the driver's side, slipped in and started the car, making sure the air-conditioning kicked in.

Ethan leaned against the hood of the car. "What a pair we are. I mean, my fiancé was doing the nasty with what's-his-name right under my nose."

"You mean—"

Ethan held his hand up. "They're getting married next weekend, and I just prefer not to hear his name. It's worse than fingers on a chalkboard."

"Rosie told me. That was really fast." She opened the driver's window and closed the door. It would take a few minutes for the cool air to fill the car.

Ethan shrugged, but he turned his gaze away. "Well, not really when you consider she was cheating on me for six months with what's-his-name."

Brett. That was his name, and he owned a restaurant down in West Palm Beach. And he'd been at the wedding too. Lots of sex happening the night of Rosie's wedding, but not for Annabel.

Or for Ethan.

Nope. All they got were a couple of broken hearts and a pair of hangovers that, in her case, lasted for two days.

"Better to find out before you got married." Or spent eight years of your life waiting for a man to decide that he 'just wasn't marriage material.'

"I would have rather known before we got engaged. Why she said yes is beyond me. What's really funny is the ring I gave her, she conveniently lost two weeks after we broke up."

"Now that really sucks."

"I'm honestly over it—and her—but she invited me to the wedding." He raked a hand across the top of his head.

"That's weird."

"It is and I'm not going, but it just brings it all to the surface, and seeing you again, well..." he laughed, shaking his head, "in spite of it all, I had a really good time with you that night."

"I did too," she admitted.

"I have to say I'm really surprised you came back. I remember when you were a kid, you couldn't wait to get out of God's Waiting Room."

That had been her nickname for Florida because so many old people came there to live out their senior years. "I got out, and the grass isn't greener on the other side."

"Is there grass in the Big Apple?" Ethan graced her with a big smile and that damned wink.

Trouble meowed as he settled into the seat, his front paws crossed, and his eyes locked on her. If she didn't know better, she'd swear the darn cat just winked too.

"You're a funny man, Ethan."

"I have my moments."

"So, what brings you by? Should I be worried about my things stored here?" she asked. "I saw a man upset with the office manager just as you pulled in."

"I'm not sure what that was about," Ethan said, glancing around. "No one said anything to me. I used to have a unit here, and I just stopped by to pick up my lock that I left." He pushed away from the hood of the car. "I better get back to work, but I'd like to meet for a drink sometime, maybe tonight?"

"I could do tonight," she said, biting the inside of her cheek. "Rosie has my number. I'm working part time for Coastal Realty until I get my license, but I'll be off at six."

"Perfect." He pushed his silver-rimmed, dark sunglasses up his nose. "I'll see you tonight. I'll bring the Jameson."

She laughed. "I gave up shots and letting men near my belly button."

"I'm not just any man." He gave her a lopsided grin. "Have a great day, Annabel."

"You do the same." She buckled herself in.

Ethan took a few steps back and waved.

She drew a deep breath, letting it out slowly as she backed out of the parking spot, and pulled out onto Military Trail, constantly looking in her rearview mirror.

Did she just agree to a date with Ethan?

∼

End of excerpt from *Trouble's Wedding Caper*
by Jen Talty
Familiar Legacy #8

TROUBLE'S DOUBLE CONTEST WINNER
Sable

My daughter Piper is holding Sable in this photograph. Sable is a lovable, loyal cat who lives with her tabby brother Gus, two pups, and two human siblings. She was the runt of her litter which her nickname, Piglet, comes from because she is about the size of a baby pig. We adopted her into our family in 2009 from a local animal shelter to keep Gus company. She spends her time snoozing with Gus and catching rays in the window. She loves to be snuggled and enjoys a good game of fetch with her catnip mouse. She is very patient with her human siblings who dote on her and Gus. We can't imagine our family without her!

— CORINNE MARKEY

FAMILIAR LEGACY

For more contests and news, please join our Familiar Legacy Fan Page and Trouble's Double Photo Contest on Facebook.

Familiar Trouble | Carolyn Haines

Trouble in Dixie | Rebecca Barrett

Trouble in Tallahassee | Claire Matturro

Trouble in Summer Valley | Susan Y. Tanner

Small Town Trouble | Laura Benedict

Trouble in Paradise | Rebecca Barrett

Turning for Trouble | Susan Y. Tanner

Trouble's Wedding Caper | Jen Talty

Bone-a-fied Trouble | Carolyn Haines

Trouble in Action | Susan Y. Tanner

CPSIA information can be obtained
at www.ICGtesting.com
Printed in the USA
FSHW010706250819
61398FS